Split

My skin prickled with goosebumps and he moved the chair to stand behind me, his body touching mine but barely. I gazed at the stuffed birds in the dome on the piano, knowing better than to turn and, without preamble, he lifted my long skirt and slid his hand down the front of my knickers. I caught my breath, a quiet sound that was loud to my ears because it was so full of truth. With a single probing finger, he split my lips apart and rubbed, finding me hot, swollen and milky. His other hand stole under my jumper and he rested his arm across my stomach, half-holding me to him, half-caressing, as his right hand explored. He had to bend his knees to reach me – most men do – and the ungainliness of that always turns me on.

'I want to find you,' he whispered, still rubbing at me.

I couldn't speak. My thighs were so heavy. His fingers were slithering through me, and my vulva was like soft, warm butter. The hand on my stomach undulated, squeezing the flesh it found. The fire spat once and, apart from our breath, the rain and my occasional moans, that was the only sound for a while.

By the same author:

Darker than Love
Asking for Trouble

Split
Kristina Lloyd

BLACK LACE

Black Lace books contain sexual fantasies.
In real life, always practise safe sex.

First published in 2007 by
Black Lace
Thames Wharf Studios
Rainville Rd
London W6 9HA

A catalogue record for this book is available from the British Library.

www.black-lace-books.com

http://lustbites.blogspot.com/

Typeset by SetSystems Ltd, Saffron Walden, Essex

Printed and bound in Great Britain by CPI Bookmarque,
Croydon, CR0 4TD

The paper used in this book is a natural, recyclable product made
from wood grown in sustainable forests. The manufacturing process
conforms to the regulations of the country of origin.

ISBN 978 0 352 34154 9

Distributed in the USA by Holtzbrinck Publishers, LLC, 175 Fifth Avenue,
New York, NY 10010, USA

1

My story starts last autumn. I want to set it down because I understand now that I'll never be able to leave this place. And I want you to remember me as a good person.

I'm in Heddlestone, living in the attic above the puppet museum. I know that must seem odd to you. It does to me at times but I'm getting used to oddness. Can you picture the museum? It looks like a building flung out by the village, a grey stone cottage, hunched and brooding at the bottom of a rutted track. Beyond it lie the moors, more desolate and beautiful than anything I've ever known.

In the glass porch there's a neon sign in looped pink lettering: Puppet Museum. We saw it from the top road, glowing in the dark. 'Incongruous,' you said, adding that it looked like some lonely whorehouse in the Midwest. And that's not what you expect to find in Yorkshire.

Some lonely whorehouse. You were fairly close to the mark with that.

These are the things I remember most from that holiday: rain, rain, rain. Diagonal rain stinging our faces like needles of ice. Initially, we toughed it out – it was, after all, a walking holiday – but by the end of the week we were beaten. 'Glory be to Heddlestone,' I said when we discovered that the telly in our room had porn. And that was us sorted. No more thick socks, compasses or maps in plastic bags. Instead, in an en suite decked out by Mrs Tiggywinkle, we watched fake blondes fake orgasm, implants jiggling, while Pennine rain crackled against chintz-curtained windows.

'Maybe we read the brochure wrong,' you said,

sprawled across the sheets, your hand between my thighs. 'Maybe it said "ideal base for wanking holidays".'

We laughed, fucked, made love, slept, got crumbs in the bed, and talked about nothing in particular. It was a strange kind of bliss but it was bliss all right. I remember you saying how much filthier porn was from the perspective of a Laura Ashley duvet, corn-dollies pinned above the polished pine drawers. 'It's like doing it in your mum's bed,' you said. And it *was* different. It felt so blank and suburban, a thrill not to be sniffed at when normality's a one-bedroom in London.

'Fuck me, fuck me,' I said. It was unnecessary because that's what you were doing anyway. But I felt some urge to shock the chintz, and the wind, whipping leaves from the trees and throwing rain at the glass, made me feel daring and abandoned. We'd stopped doing stuff like that: talking dirty, playing naughty. We knew each other too well.

Other things stick in my memory: the purple curtain in the puppet museum and what we saw that night on the edge of the moors.

'Would you like to make a Gift Aid donation?' asked the woman at the museum.

Well, why not? So I merrily filled out a form, ticking a box stating I'd be happy to receive newsletters. It'll be like a souvenir in my inbox, I thought, and then I forgot all about it.

The puppet museum was weird. After the monochrome moors, it was a Technicolor blaze, cartoonish and hyper-real. In glass cases lining the walls were strange beautiful displays of glove puppets, marionettes, vent dolls and rod puppets, hands raised, heads tilted, paralysed mid-action. Vacant eyes gazed out of polished faces, and I imagined them stilling their little puppet-lungs, trying not to breathe. Later, when the clocks struck midnight, they'd blink, shake out their stiffness, and laugh at how they'd duped us.

'I'll have nightmares tonight,' I said. But there was

more to come. By a doorway hung with purple drapes, all swagged and tasselled in bronze, was a sign warning 'Over 18s only'. There were no other visitors but us. We'd been talking in whispers as we walked around and now, slipping past the heavy curtain, our voices grew quieter and our footsteps softer.

In a small dark room, in lit glass cases, were numerous puppets engaged in lewd behaviour, a freeze-frame of obscenities. There was Mr Punch in his belled hat, a monstrous prick jutting from his red velvet breeches. Two semi-naked marionettes were locked together, doggy-style. Pinocchio's nose was, on closer inspection, carved like a phallus. A severe doll in black PVC, body as narrow as an insect's thorax, raised a multi-tailed whip, one thigh-high boot plonked on a kneeling male. We put 50p in a slot and watched a clockwork girl's head bobbing in the lap of a rosy-cheeked vicar, his grinning head swivel-ling left and right. Projected high on a wall, silhouettes of satyrs, mythical beasts and long-limbed people copulated in profile, 2-D cocks sliding like pistons.

All around us was the sound of breathing, so gentle it was barely audible. It came through the speakers, the slow, steady breath of someone sleeping. Without that, I might have just smiled at the exhibits, found them kinky and amusing, nothing more. But the breathing was sopo-rific and the room so warm. It pulled you to a deeper place, drew you into dreaminess. I felt drowsy, as if I were being immersed in lulling, sexual waters. The room was painted chocolate brown, the lights so low. My perception felt fuzzy. I remember thinking: I'm not quite with it at the moment. I'm not entirely here.

I can only ask you to try to understand, to forgive. Because you see, I think this is where it started, where something inside me changed. In that place, I felt touched by an eerie sensuality. That's the only way I can describe it. I wasn't exactly aroused but I was affected. Oh, I was definitely affected.

'Kate,' you whispered. 'Puppet show in five. Look. Through here.'

In an adjoining room, spotlit in the gloom, stood a striped canvas booth with a high curtained stage, three rows of wooden chairs in front of it. We stumbled for a seat, feeling like trespassers. Surely they wouldn't do a show for two, would they?

'We forgot the popcorn,' I said as we waited.

Beneath a sign saying 'Next Performance at' was a toy clock, its red plastic hands set to three.

You wondered aloud if it had stopped.

'Maybe they mean three in the morning,' I said.

'That's OK,' you murmured. 'We can wait. No rush.'

You switched off your mobile, reminding me to switch off mine. It was already off. It'd been off for days. Even then, I was getting used to isolation.

Jake, of course, was hidden in the booth, listening to our every word. Jake is the puppeteer and curator of the museum. He's the man I'm having a relationship with. Well, he's one of them and 'relationship' is probably the wrong word. God knows what the correct one is.

He was standing there, his puppets hanging like kippers beneath the stage. He could hear us quite clearly. In my mind's eye, his head is bowed, dark curls falling over his pale cheekbones, his mouth agape. It's the expression he wears when he's absorbed in concentration, carving his dolls, bent over the sewing-machine or bent over me. But who knows? He might have been grinning wryly. Either way, he was there. Ridiculous that it didn't occur to us.

It was a traditionally violent Punch and Judy complete with sausages, crocodile, policeman and noose, and lots of things met a sticky end. Judy, for the main, was a skull-faced ghost in a mob-cap, scaring Punch who was lusting after Polly. Punch, however, had his way with Judy before she shuffled off this mortal coil. She didn't seem too happy. 'He's behind you,' you hissed as the glove of Punch thrust against the glove of Judy, his shiny wooden shoe clattering against the booth. Judy looked ashamed, her head hidden in her stubby little arms.

'That's the way to do it!' cawed Punch. 'Up the bum! Up the bum!'

I laughed in shock and you snorted with delight.

Judy shook her head, and said, 'No! No! I don't want it there!'

'Oh yes, you do,' argued Punch, pumping away at her. Jake uses a swazzle to make that high, squeaky Punch voice. I've learned a lot since I've been here – not all of it about puppets, mind you.

'Oh no, I don't,' said Judy.

'Oh yes, you do!' That was you, chiming in with Punchinello. Embarrassed, I thumped you on the thigh in rebuke. Jake must have been thrilled with that, a hint of our fracturing.

Later, on the track heading back to the village, I said, 'Correct me if I'm wrong, but didn't Punch just anally rape Judy?'

A mist hung in layers over the fells, smudging out the distances, and ahead of us was the village, veiled and spectral, the church tower visible through half-bare trees. Drystone walls dipped up and down over the vast landscape, disappearing into blankness, and the fog was cold and clammy. A car with yellow headlights drove slowly along the top road.

'They're only puppets,' you replied. 'It's just a laugh.'

'No, it's not,' I said. 'Puppets represent. It's not just a laugh.'

'Lighten up,' you said. 'Nobody died.'

Our breath puffed out in cloudlets as we walked, and my skin felt moist. I looked over my shoulder. Behind us, the museum seemed to be melting into the air, just an electric pink cloud now, glowing through the mist. We could have had an argument then but we obviously didn't want one.

'A madhouse,' you said, conciliatory.

'Nuts,' I agreed.

We were still talking about it that evening in The Griffin.

'Maybe the show was just for us,' you suggested. 'Maybe they'd clocked we were a couple and thought we'd find it funny.'

'Yeah, it's a bit off though, isn't it?'

You probably don't remember these details, although I'm certain you'll remember what happened when we left the pub, probably for the rest of your life.

'Hang on, I need a piss,' you said, turning off the main drag.

You headed down the slope of a dark cobbled lane while I loitered on the flagstones, waiting. There was no one else around. The lights from The Griffin glinted on a couple of parked cars, and the old market square was still and serene, at its centre the slim grey spike of a war memorial. I remember now you took a picture of it one afternoon, saying you liked this place because it was good and honest rather than pretty-pretty. Good and honest is debatable but you were right: it has none of the gentleness that pretty requires. It's a huddle of stone, wonky rooftops and suspicious little windows, a place hardened against the elements. It's fierce and austere, and I can't say I blame it. The weather here can be pitiless. Some days, it's like the wind has teeth and, according to Jake, there have been times when they've been snowed in for days, no one able to leave because the top road was impassable, all the village having to act as one.

In some ways, the village is always like that.

But it was mild that night, and the air was so fresh and clear. I remember thinking I wish I could take some of this back to London, pure unpolluted air tasting of sweet wild grass.

Then you called me. You came up the cobbled slope, and when you passed a streetlamp, your face looked

6

gargoylish in its light, full of worry and shadows. 'Something's wrong,' you said. 'But I'm not sure.'

I followed you downhill past a small row of terraces, their doors opening straight onto the pavement. We walked as quietly as we could. The village has a noise of its own, sounds echoing off all that hard, grey stone. The ring of hobnailed boots didn't feel so many years behind. We crossed a side road to a corner building, a square, no-nonsense affair and the last in the street. 'Heddlestone Working Men's Club' said a sign above the door.

'What?' I kept asking. 'What?'

But all you could say was, 'I don't know. I'm not sure.'

I was scared of the dark and of the distant hills, humped and silent beneath a sky full of cloud, moon-pale and blue-grey. From far away came the scream of foxes mating, a sound to chill anyone's blood. At the side of the building, I could make out some allotments, ragged with bean wigwams, their corrugated sheds silvery in the night. A path of loose stone and grass led to an empty car park behind the clubhouse but before that, you drew me beneath a fire escape, nodding towards a grimy little window.

Beyond the glass, the room was starkly lit and there was only one thing to see: a woman, alone and motionless, wearing a shabby ballerina costume, ivory froth spilling from a red sash around her waist. Her arms, thin and milk-white, were raised above her head, her wrists tethered to a length of rope hanging from the ceiling. Her head lolled forward, scruffy blonde hair falling over her face, hiding her features. It looked as if a dancer from *Swan Lake* had got knotted up in fisherman's wire.

'Oh shit,' I breathed.

'What do we do?' you asked.

My pulse began to rush. I wished I'd gone on that first-aid course at work. 'I don't know. Phone someone.'

'We should help her,' you said. 'Break a window. She might still be ...'

The room was bleak and bare, its linoleum floor reflecting the glare of a strip light. The walls were nicotine-yellow, tulip-shaped wall lamps bracketed between windows where thin red curtains gaped from their rails. I could see a bar at one end, closed over with a wooden shutter, several stools in front of it. Edging the room were rows of red vinyl benches and small tables, chairs upturned on them. It had the air of sad sociability and masculine neglect. I wondered how long she'd been there.

'We could run back to the pub.'

'Her feet are on the ground,' you said.

They were planted there quite firmly. She was wearing beige Ugg boots and, despite all the panic, I remember wondering what she was thinking when she'd got dressed that morning. Or an earlier morning.

'But why isn't she moving?' I asked.

'Maybe an ambulance,' you said, rummaging for your phone.

'But they'll take ages to –' I didn't finish because the woman flung back her head. Her straw-coloured hair frizzed witchily around a face so shocking I almost screamed. Her skin was caked in white make-up, her eyes lost in kohl-black depths, her cheeks rouged with two spots of red. Full of defiance, she scowled at us, looking like one of the undead or some ghastly oversized doll.

'Fuck-a-duck,' you said quietly.

My heart was in my mouth. 'Christ Almighty.'

I was ready to run but you tugged me closer, an arm around my waist. 'Wait. Keep still. I don't think she can see us.'

The way she looked made me think she could see into the depths of our souls. But we were outdoors in the pitch black and on reflection I think she was, well, probably looking at her reflection.

'Do you think she needs help?' I whispered. 'Someone to untie her?'

You didn't need to reply because, right then, a figure

crossed in front of the window, a balding burly man with a threatening swagger. You squeezed me through my layers of clothing, either for your own comfort or to reassure me, I'm not sure. Perhaps both.

Hardly daring to breathe, we watched him approach, hands in his jeans as he circled her, his mouth tilting in mild amusement. His hair, pale and receding, was closely shorn and he had a round, confident face, handsome and well-proportioned. He was one of those guys who'd look good in a suit, mildly intimidating like a friendly gangster or nightclub bouncer. For now though, he was wearing a T-shirt, the broad slab of his chest evident through the fabric, his forearms thick with easy muscle, a tattooed Celtic band peeping below a sleeve. He might have been made of millstone grit though he carried his strength lightly. Next to him, the woman was a fragile creature he might snap in two.

As he stalked her, she followed his movements as best she could, her head twisting and straining. When he stopped, he spoke close to her ear and waited, smiling. Eventually, she muttered a response and he nodded, apparently satisfied. Dirty rain stains coated the window and no sounds reached us, making the scene seem far-away and mysterious, a weird apparition or a glimpse into another realm.

The woman's clothes were so odd, a thin cotton boob-tube studded with diamanté, her white skirts falling in tatty layers, scraps of net hanging below the hem, all cinched at the waist by a brilliant red sash. I scanned the room, looking for equipment, a camera or camcorder that might explain the situation, but saw nothing.

Again, the man spoke. This time the woman didn't reply: she just stared ahead, a white-faced ghoul gazing into infinity. Then, carefully, the man folded down her top, exposing her breasts. She had good tits, full and high, though perhaps over-large on such a petite frame. She didn't even flinch.

We were gripped, not daring to speak in case we broke the spell. Behind us, the moors swept away for miles, silent and indifferent. We were just a few animals engaged in our nocturnal business, no better or worse than all the bats, badgers and weevils out there. Nature doesn't judge.

With detached and fussy attention, the man smoothed out the wrinkles in the woman's top, taking care not to touch her breasts. He spoke again, lips moving in silence, and again he bared that smug, predatory smile. Still she ignored him. Then the man turned, laughing, his manner suddenly changed. He continued speaking and, with a jolt of arousal, I realised he was addressing someone else in the room, or perhaps several someone elses.

'Can you see?' I whispered.

You shook your head and your hand slipped down to fondle my arse.

My heart was thumping. I watched the man trace fingertips over the woman's skin, moving from her neck, over her shoulders and across the swell of her breasts. She gave a stubborn toss of her head, her mouth set firm. The thought someone else was watching had me horny as hell. I could hardly blink for fear of missing something. Idly, the man grazed a stubby thumb over one tight nipple, brushing it back and forth, tick-tock fashion.

The woman was like stone, unyielding and emotion-less. Like stone, that is, until the man cupped her flesh, massaging with his big, thick hand, and then she was lost and soft, and oh so human. She closed her eyes, her body slumping as she gave way to pleasure. Gently, she tugged against her restraints, hips starting to roll.

She seemed so lovely and vulnerable at that moment, lit up like a crazy angel as she melted into her own desire, resisting nothing. I was melting too, wondering how it might feel to have someone do that to me before an audience. I wasn't sure I'd be able to let go so easily. I wasn't sure I'd even want to try.

I never told you how turned on I was by that scene. Oh sure, you knew I liked it but you would never have guessed how much. When the second man stepped into view, I swear, my legs nearly buckled. He reminded me of an Elizabethan courtier, slightly built with a clipped brown beard, and I could picture him wearing a doublet and hose rather than the jeans. The two men exchanged a few words and laughed, their deeper bass tones reaching us through the window.

Then the brawny guy stepped back, gesturing at the woman. All yours, I thought his lips said.

The bearded guy stood in front of her and bent to suck her breasts, holding her by the waist, thumbs rubbing the red sash. The other man watched, smiling, his hands in his pockets where his erection bulged.

Your hand on my arse grew more insistent, sliding down to push my skirt between my thighs. I stood wider and pushed back, wanting you. I was wearing a long cord skirt and beneath it, thin woollen tights. I felt big and clumsy, so awkwardly physical compared to that strung-up sylph, hanging there for the men like some weird, tragic bauble. But I was super-sensitised, feeling all your fingers as they probed through my layers.

I wanted to be that woman. I was scared for her and yet I ached to be in her place, two strong horny men prowling around me. Her powerlessness was horribly appealing. She was entirely in their hands and they were randy and reckless. God, what luxury.

'Do you think she's OK?' you asked.

A small moth fluttered at the window before settling there, its cottony wings mottled with silver-grey, camouflaged against the dirty glass.

'I'd say so, yeah,' I replied, and I cupped a hand to your crotch, thrilled to find you hard within your jeans.

The bearded courtier walked away, out of view again, and the first guy, the bruiser, took up his position, standing before the woman. He fluffed up her skirts in a gauzy snowstorm, reaching beneath them. With his feet apart, his arm hidden beneath her nets, he began to work her, just a slight movement of his elbow to betray what he was doing, his tattooed band flexing on his beefy arm. Only when one of them moved could we see her face. For a while she was expressionless, just a black-eyed, rosy-cheeked mask of madness, then her mouth was open, her neck taut, her breasts jutting. We watched her panting silently, her body writhing, her arms tugging on the rope.

She seemed to climax in a frenzy of pulling and gasping and immediately the man untied her. His mean expression faded and he kneaded her upper arms, the two of them talking normally as she rolled her shoulders and rubbed her wrists. The courtier came into view again, and he was dragging across the lino an old gymnast's vaulting bar, the suede of its padded beam worn and patchy.

I hadn't seen one since school days and the mere sight of it was enough to make my stomach churn in anxiety. I associated it with public humiliation. I hated games, especially gymnastics. I was always too chunky, too soft and fleshy to go hurtling about as if my body were light as a feather.

Together, the men moved the vault into the centre. Without a word, the woman leant over it, her upper body lying along its length, her sheepskin boots just touching the ground. She wriggled for comfort as the bruiser untied her red sash and wound it around her body and the beam, knotting it so she was bound to the apparatus.

The woman was calm, lying there with her cheek pressed to the bar, her panda eyes two holes in her panstick face. The man walked around, appraising her from different angles. My heart was thumping. He had such a cool arrogant manner, such a swagger in his attitude. His face was impassive and he showed no emotion either when, with a couple of sharp tugs, he pulled down the woman's skirts, tossing them aside. Her pale buttocks were bared, and he looked at them as he fiddled with his zip.

His jeans crumpled around his knees and he shuffled closer, penetrating her with a quick jab. He fucked her with a light, casual manner, one hand pressing on her back as he gazed blankly ahead. It was like seeing an animal fuck, his pumping so regular and functional. Every now and then, he glanced down, perhaps to check if she was still breathing. She seemed so unimportant to him he might have been masturbating alone.

I couldn't take my eyes off his thighs. They were immense and glorious, full of curves and muscle, sheathed in fine hair.

Next to me, you said, 'Ah, c'mon, fuck.' In a hurry, I began undoing your fly and you undid your belt, moving into position behind me, stones scuffing up around us. We might have looked over our shoulders to check we were alone. I don't recall. In London, we'd have been scanning for CCTV, wondering if grainy footage of us was going to end up in some murky corner of the internet. But not in Heddlestone. There's nothing like that here. There's no need. Everybody watches everybody else.

Do you think we were alone that night? I doubt it. Someone, somewhere, would have been watching, night-vision binoculars trained on us, two unknown figures fucking in a ghostly, green-tinged world.

You lifted up my skirt and I shimmied down my tights. The air on my skin was cool and thrilling, and the exposure made me loosen. I felt earthy and lewd, and I could picture my buttocks, plump pale moons surrounded by dark rumpled fabric. Urgent and hard, you drove into my wetness, clasping me around the waist as you thrust. My arse cheeks jiggled as your hips bumped up against their flesh. The stone crunched beneath our feet.

Flakes of paint, I noticed, had chipped off the window frame and the corners were furred with black mould. Beyond the glass, the bearded guy was grinning at the woman, thrusting out his pelvis and rubbing his crotch with comic lewdness. Then he unbuttoned, and wanked close to her face before he stripped completely. In one swift movement, he straddled the vault, edging forward until his erection was by her head.

The woman raised her mouth for him, her body jolting from the impact of the hulk pumping her at the other end. Eagerly, she swallowed his cock and I could see the bulge in her cheek as she sucked up and down. He wound her blonde hair around a fist, exchanging a few words with the other guy who was still ramming her with detached regularity, his arse cheeks hollowing above those giant thighs.

You and I weren't so cool. Your finger was on my clit, tapping as we fucked. Where I braced myself, the stone was cold and rough beneath my palms. We got into a good rhythm, me slamming back as you shoved high and hard. The air snagged in my throat as I panted, 'I'm coming, I'm coming. Just keep me there. Just...' I could feel that soft, gorgeous easiness in my hips and thighs, waves of it carrying me closer. And at the same time, voices from the village road. 'There, yes,' I urged, desperate to come and not be interrupted. 'There, there.'

You nuzzled past my hair, your breath warm on the back of my neck, teeth scraping, half-kissing, half-biting as you fucked and frigged me to climax. Indoors, the bearded guy closed his eyes, head tipped back, mouth parting slackly. He might have been coming, I don't know. But his small moment of surrender nudged me past my limit and I hit orgasm, gasping quietly. There was no time for you.

Subdued male voices had turned into our road, foot-steps clattering on the flagstones.

'Come on!' you hissed, slipping out of me. We moved off, buttoning and straightening our clothes as we hurried to the back of the club. A security light clicked on. We were in a makeshift car park edged by barbed wire, a couple of wheelie bins and a lean-to. That was it. We were gone. We struggled over the barbed wire, ripping clothes and scratching skin as a man called out, 'Who's there?'

The voice was full of that broad Yorkshire slowness. Ooooo's thurrrr? The beam of a torchlight trailed over the allotments. We scrambled across a field, supporting each other. I stumbled once but you hoiked me up before I even hit the ground.

'Are they following?' I gasped.

I glanced back. The torchlight was bouncing here and there, its thin yellow beam swooping over the field. I could make out two or three figures in the security light's blaze.

'I think we're OK,' you wheezed, slowing. We trotted at a gentler pace. 'Doubt they're interested in us, anyway.'

We made it back to the village, unscathed and unseen. The next day, we laughed about it. Bizarre, we said. Kinky. But, hey, whatever gets you through the night. After all, there wasn't much to do in Heddlestone, and it's got to beat Morris dancing. At least we didn't get caught.

Back in London, the memories wouldn't leave me alone. I kept reliving that strange threesome, imagining myself as that strung-up woman, a man stalking me, cool and menacing. Or I would fantasise about being caught in a pair of thick arms, me and two guys fucking in an eerie wonderland. At night, I'd wake in a cold sweat, plagued by dreams of life-size puppets boarding the bus or sitting on the tube. I sat in the cinema and when my mobile went off, all the rows in front of me turned around to glare, and they had lacquered faces and sightless eyes.

I got a couple of email newsletters from the puppet museum. They didn't say much: a history of the place, some forthcoming winter events, a new show using puppets created by Jake Duxbury. But it fuelled my strange hunger. No, it became more than hunger. The usual post-holiday yearnings didn't fade, and the urge to return became so acute it was almost a physical tug.

I've been infatuated with people plenty of times, but never with a place. I kept dwelling on that muzzy half-aroused state I'd experienced in the museum, wondering what it was. Again and again, I looked at my Yorkshire photos, wishing I was there, out roaming the blustery moors, not stuck on the enquiry desk, traipsing round a supermarket or having sex with you.

You didn't do anything wrong. I'm not blaming you. But you must have noticed how things had started to sour. We were getting stale and lazy, contentment sliding into lethargy. And I was miserable at work, bored with the same old same. Privately, I was reassessing, wondering where the my life was going. The answer looked like 'nowhere'. I wanted a change but couldn't think of one. I was restless and full of longing, pulled by some shadowy compulsion into fantasies of Heddlestone, of that woman and those men. That's how I escaped; I let my mind take me elsewhere, to a world more extraordinary, richer in emotion, darker in sensuality.

It might have stayed at that level, a spot of daydreaming to get me through a bad patch, but reality intervened – if reality's the right word – when I got a mailing from the puppet museum. They were looking for a general assistant, a six-month temporary post involving admin and a chance to learn about museum management and the art of puppetry.

I considered it seriously for about five minutes then realised it was impossible. The place was miles away; my life was in Hackney, London. I had a good steady job in a library with – oh, it's embarrassing – an excellent pension plan. But the thought gripped me. I could take extended leave, I told myself. The library was set for a major refurb so they might be amenable. And then I could return to my London life, refreshed and energised. 'Get real,' said my more sensible side. 'You'd be bored stiff in the countryside.'

But I didn't believe it. I wouldn't be bored. I reckoned a

lot went on in Heddlestone. I might not have done anything about it if we hadn't had an almighty great row about ... God knows. The usual: nothing. You stormed out of my flat while I opened a bottle of wine, got creative with my CV, and emailed j.duxbury to express my enthusiasm for admin work. Oh, and puppets, yes. I've always wanted to know more about puppets. *Pinocchio* was the first film I ever saw. I cried buckets when he got swallowed by the whale. I love puppets, I really do. Almost as much as I love admin work.

He replied the same evening. 'Have you ever visited us at the museum?'

Something about the tone of the question made me send just one word in reply: yes.

It was the easiest job interview I've ever had.

2

My motto used to be: scare yourself every day.

I didn't mean the living daylights out of. I meant take a risk, try something new, otherwise you'll end up dead before your time, sleepwalking through your days. Those words haunted me as my train streaked through England, the suburbs and soft southern fields already like memories of home. The scenery grew craggier, the ashy dusk closing in on the hills and on those stern Victorian towns made of stone and brick, mill chimneys and misery. With every passing minute, I felt more alone and adrift.

What am I doing? I thought. I'm trying to run from my problems and we all know that's a mug's game. Is it too late to have a change of heart?

Be brave, I told myself. Everyone in London dreams of escaping to the countryside; only a fool would turn down such a chance. All the same, I was shaking as I gathered my luggage. I felt like a fugitive, fleeing broken love, and as I stepped onto the busy platform I half-expected to be surrounded by a bunch of slow, smooth-talking police-men, jostling me into submission.

'There, there, Katie,' they'd say, snapping on a pair of cuffs. 'Everything's going to be all right. No need to make a fuss. Your boyfriend's been worried about you. You're a danger to yourself, he said. He's been looking for you. He wants you to come home. Now, now, Katie, calm down. You're with friends. Trust us.'

And I'd be protesting: It's Kate! Kate! No one calls me Katie. You've got the wrong woman. Let go of me!

I should have told you I was leaving and I'm sorry for that. I'm sorry for hurting you. I was a coward. I couldn't face you. And I was scared you'd try to talk me out of it. I ought to have been suspicious of landing a job so easily and, knowing what I do now, I realise I was naive not to question it. You always said I was suggestible.

But I longed for Heddlestone. I longed for its clean air, the space, the sight of those stark, blasted moors with their folds and secrets, and a sense of something lingering. I still feel it now I'm living here. I go out walking, climbing up and down, the wind roaring in my ears, and it feels as if there's something out there in the enormity, waiting for me.

That was the pull. And I might have resisted if it hadn't been for the push as well. The push? It's difficult to pinpoint. I'd started to believe the grass was greener. I couldn't see anything wrong in our relationship that could be put right, so I ended up thinking its entire existence was wrong. Change seemed to be the only solution. I could take a risk on that or stagnate. I felt so trapped it hardly seemed like a choice. The move looked perfect.

The library have been supportive, agreeing to six months' leave (for personal/professional development), and I'm subletting my flat to a friend of Sally's. Sally's been in on it all along. She agreed to send more of my possessions up if it looked like working out. Don't judge her. She wasn't happy being dishonest but perhaps she's a nicer person than me. Because the awful truth is I kept it from you for weeks, making plans behind your back and, this might seem cruel, I swear I hadn't felt so alive in years. At last, I had something completely my own, a secret to nurture and cherish. I was starting to feel like me again, whole and autonomous. Me. Not me and you, you and me. Just me.

Alive, yes. I felt brave, brilliant and alive.

I am Kate Carter, five foot nothing, freckled and fair, pear-shaped but sprightly, a librarian on the run. And I am alive.

Alive but not so bold, however, as I got off the train.

My mouth was dry and my limbs quivery. It was rush hour, although the rush is slight, and the platform glowed with an ugly light, greenish and pale like the colour of old celery. Between the stone walls and canopied roof, the sky was a blue-black stripe, and already I could sense how vast that sky was compared to ours.

'How will I recognise you?' I'd asked Jake on the phone.

'I'll be wearing a safari hat,' he said.

I laughed. 'And what else? A giraffe on a leash?'

'No, straight up,' he replied. 'Look out for the hat.'

I didn't know what a safari hat was until I saw him, a fey Indiana Jones at the top of the platform, lithe and lanky in a skinny-fit suit, walking boots and that incongruous hat.

I know what you're thinking: that Jake is going to be one of the guys we saw in the clubhouse. I'd been wondering that too, sometimes hoping for it, but mainly fearing it. But no. I'd never set eyes on him. We'd emailed a lot and had spoken on the phone a few times, mainly about practicalities, the job, Heddlestone, so-and-so's granny flat I could rent for next to nothing. He had a lovely voice, quiet and softly accented, and his laughter was warm and easy. I knew I was going to like him but I wasn't prepared for how much.

As I struggled with my bags, he walked towards me, a dishevelled eccentric and such a misfit among all the drab dressers returning home from work. He was too tall for his suit so he was all wrists and ankles, a man almost as gangly as his puppets. For some reason, I always look at men's feet. His walking boots were big and sturdy, caked in dried mud, and the hems of his trousers were muddied too.

He was smiling, eyes locked on mine, and I smiled back, feeling immense waves of relief wash over me. I've made it, I thought. I'm here, on time, at the right place and now I can relax. This man is kind and he's going to look after me. I am safe.

with this man was starting to make me edgy, yet the heat of the car and the surrounding blackness soothed.

My situation felt unreal, muzzy. I thought back to the museum, remembering the kinky puppets in that brown-walled chamber, someone's breath floating from the speakers, making me feel half-hypnotised and lost. Perhaps it was the country air. I was becoming disconnected again although it wasn't unpleasant. I swayed with the jolts of the road, feeling vaguely sedated and having a sense that if only I could concentrate, I might recognise I was in trouble and do something sharpish.

I tried to think of danger. Supposing he were to pull over, switch off the engine and coolly say, 'Open your legs for me.' What would I do? Would I run? Would my body even work? I was scared of everything beyond the car, of rabbits, sheep and werewolves; of stumbling over unseen ground, running blindly because there was nothing to run to, only something to run from. If he chased me, he'd have me in no time, knocked to the ground and pinned beneath him, taking whatever he had to give. I thought of his face above me, half-laughing, half-panting as he raped me, as bestial as a creature of the wilds.

Open your legs for me.

The car would have central-locking. I would fumble with the door while he, cool as ice, would sit there, waiting for me to realise I was trapped, not by the lock but by the terrible emptiness out there, the vast, unfeeling blankness of the moors.

Open your legs for me.

Well, I would open them. It was too cold outside, anyway. So I would open them in the car, for him and for me, skirt up and knickers down, making myself suddenly and shockingly white-thighed and pubic. I would tip the seat back and he would place his slender hands on my flesh, caressing my inner thighs before he leant over to plunge his hot wet tongue into my hot wet folds. The hat would come off. I'd wrap my fingers in his curls, holding him there as I pushed forward, hips tilting to meet his mouth, the windows misting around us, a huddle of puppet-faces peering in, tapping at the window, hands bouncing and their wrists on strings.

'It can get lonely out here,' said Jake. 'The moors play with your mind. It doesn't suit everybody.'

My heart stuttered and I snapped back to reality. Nervously, I shifted in my seat, a small slick of wetness seeping from me. Had he seen into my head?

'You look worried,' he added, by way of explanation. 'Are you?'

'A little,' I admitted. 'Sleepy too.' And horny, I thought, although I'm disturbing myself with where my mind's going: rape fantasies and living dolls. Get a grip, Kate.

For a while he didn't reply. He just gazed ahead, a bony hand loose on the steering wheel as we glided along the road at a steady, cautious pace. His wrists are lovely, sort of flat and oblong, delicate and hazy with hair. When he's working with his hands – carving, cooking, tying me up or making love – his wrists bend at such strong, perfect angles.

A couple of insects flickered in the headlight beam, and I wondered if he'd ever squashed any rabbits, hedgehogs or worse. It was bound to happen. He slowed as we took a bend, the headlights swooping over a tumbled stone wall.

'I'm looking forward to it though,' I said, sounding falsely bright. 'I could do with a change.'

He gave an abrupt laugh. 'It'll be that all right,' he said. 'London, isn't it?'

Now it was my turn to laugh. I half expected him to add, 'They say as that's where t' King lives.'

'Hackney,' I said. I was slightly perturbed that he hadn't remembered my details. It suggested he didn't appreciate what a big step I was taking. But I didn't let it concern me too much – it was my business, not his – and soon we were chatting about ordinary things, although the image of his head was still in my lap and my clit still twitched at the thought of his tongue. He pointed out Heddlestone, a cluster of lights like distant stars, disappearing sometimes as the road turned, obscured by dark shapes.

'There's been a bit of bother with the granny-flat,' he said. 'Their boiler's on the blink. No one's lived there since Ada Hesketh died and they hadn't thought to check. I thought it best you stay with us till it's mended.'

'Us?'

'Me and the dogs.'

'Oh,' I said. 'You mean at your house?'

'I've an attic room,' he said.

'Oh. I see. But ... for how long? Sorry, I don't mean to be ungracious. An attic? It's very good of you. In fact, it's great. Thanks. It's just that –'

'It's a proper enough place,' he continued. 'Nicely furnished. Own bathroom. It's big, one big room, more or less. Used to be a nursery. I had it converted for guests. Not that I get many. So now it has a bathroom. Double bed and a cot. But we can soon shift the cot if it's getting in your way.'

'Oh. A shame about the granny flat. I don't want to put you out.' I couldn't help feeling disgruntled. I knew his house adjoined the puppet museum and just the thought of staying with him made me claustrophobic. I wanted to ask if it was self-contained or if I'd have to traipse through his territory to reach it. And what about cooking facilities? Would I have to share his kitchen after spending a day in the museum with him?

But it seemed mean of me to question the finer details so instead I stared dumbly ahead, trying to adjust to the fact that all of a sudden, I had no space to call my own. This man was kindly accommodating me, so I would be his guest, beholden to him in some way. I didn't like it, no matter how much I fancied him.

'It's just to tide you over till someone has a look at the boiler,' he said. 'I've put a kettle up there, toaster, micro-wave. And there's a coolbox for milk and that.'

'Thanks, it's very good of you,' I said and I left an interval of several seconds before casually asking, 'So when might the boiler be fixed?'

'*Mañana*,' he said, and I laughed because it was the most unlikely pronunciation of '*mañana*' I'd ever heard.

'Eee by gum,' I said, trying to mimic a Yorkshire accent. 'Mun-yarna, eh?'

He laughed and turned to me, amused and curious. 'I'm glad you came,' he said. 'I reckon we're going to get along fine. Just fine.'

Jake's house is crazy. No, the whole village is crazy. Most days, I think I'm the sanest person here. Other days I question that and think maybe I'm as nuts as they are. When you're living here, the weirdness becomes normali-sed. You start to accept. Who knows? It could be that I've become as la-la as the rest of them and I can't see it. It would certainly explain a lot.

The house is L-shaped, part eighteenth century, part 1970s, with the museum and workshop in the new-build. I know it's not polite to walk into a person's living room and go, 'Jesus Christ' but that's what I did. It's a surreal and freakish bedlam, a cross between a macabre Victorian parlour and a student dive, ferns and foliage sprouting among a junkshop of antiques, toys, musical instruments, trunks, boxes, books, LPs and God knows what else.

The room is long, divided more or less into living and dining areas, huge kilims and carpets covering scuffed wooden floorboards. At the furthest end, tatty sofas and armchairs are gathered around a log fire, and above is a glass chandelier, shimmering with pendants. I moved tentatively, scared of knocking something over.

A carousel-style rocking horse stood in one corner, tucked away behind an upright piano on top of which was a glass dome, a taxidermy confection of small vivid birds perched on a sprig of branches. There were two guitars, a Hornby train set, a dressmaker's dummy, a polystyrene head in a bowler hat, a keyboard, accordion and all manner of dolls, clockwork toys and dismembered puppets dotted high and low, a leg here, a head there. Marionettes hung from stands, limp on their strings, their painted smiles suggesting they'd something to hide.

Astonishingly, Jake has two greyhounds, skinny loping creatures who somehow move without upsetting anything. They spend a lot of time sprawled in front of the fire, as muscled and spare as anatomical drawings. They sniffed around me, friendly and curious, gazing up with big docile eyes, tails wagging. They might have been objects in the room that had briefly come alive.

'You don't mind dogs, do you?' asked Jake.

'No, dogs are fine,' I said, thinking, It's everything else that's insane.

I felt I'd entered a grotesque and sinister cavern. The walls were wine-coloured, covered with photographs and dark, fantastical prints – Goya, Dalí, Brueghel, Bosch – not to mention a pair of stag antlers, art posters, play bills, tambourines, masks, postcards, newspaper cuttings, a high mirror above the fireplace draped in fairy lights, and a case of dead moths, wings pinned apart.

Feng shui obviously hadn't reached Yorkshire.

The white-walled attic, by contrast, is a cool, airy sanctuary, and I was more than relieved to set down my bags. This is fine for the meantime, I thought. It's not ideal, and I'd rather have my own place but for now, I can cope. Several weeks later, and I'm still coping – just. The lack of light can get me down but that's the least of my worries.

The windows are an odd mix. There are a couple of veluxes set in the angled ceiling and four original tiny windows at floor level, down there between the skirting boards and the sloping wall. They're wooden framed and just a couple of feet high, meaning you have to lie on your belly to see the moors. I later came to think of them as windows for the puppets to look out of, but initially that didn't occur to me.

It's pristine and dust-free, not what you'd expect of an attic, and with its strange slanting walls and peculiar corners, I feel as if I'm inside a piece of origami, though perhaps not so Zen.

For the first few days, it rained almost solidly. It was a disorienting time. I hardly went out. Jake and I muddled towards a way of being together. I felt I was neither one thing nor the other, a hybrid of guest, lodger and employee, and I didn't quite know, for example, where the politest place was to make a cup of tea.

I loved his company and was eager to talk to him but felt it appropriate to maintain a professional distance. Unprofessionally, I was thrilled and excited by him. I couldn't help wanting to look at him, couldn't help dreaming of him naked while I rubbed my clit at night.

Work didn't exactly start or stop. It just merged into the days. Jake showed me some of his marionettes, and I sat sideways in an armchair in that outlandish living room, watching him bring them to life. They were large, thigh-high creatures, and it was as if we'd been joined by a party of little people. I was transfixed, falling quickly into Jake's world of miniature make-believe, staring at the puppets as they performed for me, heads tilting, knees lifting, their bodies seeming forever on the verge of collapse.

Jake transfixed me too, standing tall in his shabby suit, dark curls spilling forwards as he gazed down at his dolls, pulling strings, face rapt. His fingers have a flexibility I found disturbing at first, almost repulsive because it's not quite human. He can spread his hands in all sorts of positions, the joints in his fingers bending this way and that, knuckles all knobbly.

I find it sexy now, deeply sexy, because those fingers have touched me in so many places. Like his body, his hands are graceful and supple. I've looked at them a lot, at his long strong fingers, his broad flat nails and the dark hairs thinning out from slender wrists.

He'd put on some terrible music, an industrial soundscape of hacksaws, helicopters and smashed pianos. 'Stockhausen,' he said, and the living room became a theatre of bad dreams as he animated a folkloric girl in clogs, a hippyish white witch named Nikki, a Mexican with a preposterous moustache, a wizened and cowled monk. It was like a series of small, strange ballets.

'Do you give them voices?' I asked.

'No, I think it's wrong to impose on them. It's in the movement, their bodies. I only do voices for shows, Punch and Judy, museum things. I don't do it for my own work.'

'I saw a Punch and Judy when I was here on holiday,' I said. 'It was rude, a bit silly.'

Jake laughed, making the white-gowned Nikki-witch raise her hands, pleading to the heavens as water droplets plinked in the music, filling the room with huge aural tears. 'I don't remember you, sorry,' he said. 'I get bored in the museum sometimes, start messing around if I think I can get away with it. Here, have a go.'

I stood beside him as he showed me how to work a simple marionette, a gangster with black and white shoes, suspended from a T-bar frame. 'It's called an aeroplane controller,' Jake explained but I proved a poor pilot at first.

I laughed and cursed as he moved around me, splaying his fingers for me to copy, instructing me to lift that, pull this, lower that. I was aware of how tall he was and how easily he moved his limbs around my dumpy five foot nothing, reaching behind and beneath to nudge my elbow, lift my arm, tilt my wrist. He was like a big leggy spider invisibly enshrouding me as I struggled with the strings, or perhaps I was a pupa being cocooned in spun silks.

He smelt nice. He always does, having a subtle scent of ... of Jake, of himself, his skin, the closeness of him.

Maybe it's pheromonal, but it seems to me in life you meet some people, catch a hint of how they smell, and it's so attractive and known to you it feels as if you've been sleeping with them for months. I inhaled him secretly, imagining I might already have nuzzled into his groin, wrapped my lips around his cock, kissed his neck, chest and lips a thousand glorious times.

When I finally got my mobster walking neatly we were equally thrilled, and I tipped Al Capone in a nifty little bow. It was like play time, cooped up in a weird old house, making our own entertainment as the rain rattled against the diamond-paned windows.

Beyond the glass stretched the bare moorland, the wind and the wet eddying among its dips and crags, greasy little sheep pinned to the slopes. 'Does it ever stop raining here?' I asked.

'Not much,' replied Jake. 'Fancy a walk?'

I thought he was joking but when I realised he wasn't I was up in the attic, donning woollies and waterproofs, as excitable as someone dressing for a date. Oh, I liked him such a lot, had done from the start, and a racket of alarm bells was ringing in my head: he's your boss, the only person you know here, the man who's offered you lodgings. It can only end in disaster.

As we were leaving the house, lacing our boots in the utility room by the kitchen, I asked an awkward question about my job. 'I'm not really sure of my hours,' I said. 'Or quite when I start.'

'We'll formalise it next week,' he said. 'It'll be easier when you've got your own place. To be honest, I'm not that organised yet. I'll pay you for this week, thirty-seven hours like we agreed, then we'll play it by ear.'

He whistled and the greyhounds, Twiglet and Noah, came trotting in from the house. The utility room smelt of dogginess and blankets, and rain fell loudly on its rippled plastic roof. The dogs looked distinctly doubtful as Jake fastened jackets onto their bony frames.

'So technically speaking, I'm at work now, am I?' I said. 'Because if I am, it's about the best job I've ever had.'

Jake laughed, his grey eyes silvery and amused. 'Make the most of it,' he warned. 'Because next week you'll be slaving away on your hands and knees.'

I blushed, lust-addled fool that I was. I didn't know where to look or what to say. My mind said, 'Say something funny' but I couldn't think of a single word. Instead I laughed and fiddled with a Velcro pocket, unable to shake from my head the image of me on all fours, Jake fucking me. When I did glance up, I saw that he was blushing too, though not as idiotically as me. I blushed all the more. I'm always blushing. It's the curse of pale skin and shyness, and it was nice that he shared a hint of it too.

'Come on,' he said laughing, and he put a hand on my back, ushering me out of the door.

I was horny. I could hardly believe myself. That little exchange had turned me on enormously, making me as ditsy as a fourteen year old. I ought to have been stipulating job conditions and expressing misgivings about work and leisure sliding dangerously into one. But as we walked out into the driving rain, all I could think was 'on my hands and knees' and 'he touched my back'.

It was cold and brutal outdoors, the heavy skies pressing in on the moors, the distant fells a faraway haze. The grass was coarse and slippery, and bulky clothing made it difficult to walk. The wind whipped our waterproofs and pummelled our faces, and my nose grew numb, water sliding down my face. The dogs, one brown brindle, the other jet black, ran and ran, graceful skeletal creatures streaking through rainfall, as we lumbered behind, struggling over stiles and stumbling on tiny paths.

If I hadn't been new to the area, and if we hadn't been quite so keen on each other, the walk might not have lasted two minutes. The dogs were ready to return long before we were. But we were eager and slightly high, made giddy by the fact we were walking in the rain, braving the weather with the devil-may-care foolishness of lovers who think the world is theirs, and theirs alone.

Jake pointed things out, shouting above the wind: 'That's the old West Riding.' 'Bradford's that direction.' 'That ruin over there? A shepherd's cottage.' 'Used to be a tree swing here, I lived on it as a kid.' He was showing me the landscape he'd grown up in, and I felt so honoured. Usually, you have to know a person a while before you see such intimacy.

He led me to a small wood, half-hidden in a dip, extending a gloved hand for me as I edged down its tricky terrain. The trees were black and bare, the ground thick with muddy rotting leaves. We were sheltered from the wind, and I heard water gushing. My heart leapt when I saw it, a swollen brook cascading downslope, frothing and spuming over a tumble of mossy boulders. It was crystal clear and bursting with energy, and I thought, Oh, it was worth leaving London for this alone.

'Heddlestone Brook,' said Jake. 'We don't like to be too original with names.'

The weather seemed to have calmed by the time we'd clambered back up. We strode along saying nothing, our breath fast and misty, and I was exhilarated with fresh air and infatuation. At the top of a field, we stopped by a gate to gaze out over the rough empty miles. Green moss glistened on the jagged stacks of a drystone wall, and the ground at our feet was mud. The dogs, cold and tired, sniffed around the base of a contorted hawthorn. I pointed out some sheep being rounded up, tiny white blobs swarming in the distance, forgetting he saw this all the time.

He turned with a grin. 'Sheep,' he said. 'They make wool. Go "baa" a lot.'

I reached out to give him a playful swipe but he was fast, catching my wrist in a surprisingly strong grip. He smiled down, holding my arm back, his gloved hand on the layers of my sleeves. His eyes were so sparkly with mischief it looked as if raindrops had found their way inside.

'City girl,' he teased. A silvery rain-droplet shimmered on his nose before it dripped off, another one soon following.

'Bumpkin,' I replied.

We edged closer, waterproofs hissing as we touched, rain pattering on our hoods. He released my wrist, sliding a hand down my side as he did so.

'You have to do this every day,' he said. 'Walk the dogs, come rain or shine. It's in your contract of employment.'

I laughed. 'I don't think so.' The wind snatched our words away.

'Small print,' he said. 'Always read the small print.'

'Lucky for me I haven't signed anything yet.'

We gazed at each other, the hesitation before a kiss, and I thought about how stupid I was being and how beautiful he was, even when his pale, delicate face, still unshaven, was framed by a woolly hat and khaki drawstring hood. I imagined he saw me as an apple-faced, peasant woman, albeit one swathed in electric-blue Gortex rather than floral scarves, but I truly didn't care. I was getting the sense he liked me, no matter my appearance, and I felt fresh, liberated and healthy. I wasn't even wearing mascara. In Hackney, God help me, I wear mascara to put the bins out.

He smiled. It was as if the elements had removed a layer from his face making his bones sharper than usual, his cheeks hollower. His skin looked raw and scorched, lips drained of their usual colour, and I could see the tiny lines in his thirty-something face. I like the lines, especially the crinkles around his eyes. I like the life they suggest. Without them, he might look too pretty but as it was, at that moment on the moors, he reminded me of a

33

weathered, degenerate shepherd boy. 'You signed something last night,' he said. 'In your sleep. I crept into your room and forced you.'

I smiled back. This man knew exactly how to push my buttons. A beat flickered between my thighs and the wind licked a curl of hair across his jaw, plastering it to his damp skin. When he moved it with a gloved hand, a fibre of wool caught on his stubble, clinging there a moment before being washed away.

And then he was bending towards me, nose going dripdrip, and our lips touched, ice to ice and tasting of rain, our faces slippery and wet. We embraced, awkward and fat in our clothes, synthetics rustling. His warm tongue coaxed my mouth open, his chin prickled, and he tasted faintly of strong, black coffee. In our blustery sodden isolation, our mouths made a pocket of humidity, soft and shapeless, our tongues gently teasing. I must have closed my eyes because I felt a new wetness sliding on my eyelids, and then my brain was melting as fast as my groin, leaving me with just one thought: that nothing matters but this moment in time, this here and now of lust.

And that was it. I was gone. With that one windswept kiss, he had me and I knew it meant trouble. With a hand to his chest I stilled him, drawing back. 'We can't do this,' I said. 'It's such a bad idea.'

He gazed down at me, lips wet, eyes all dreamy as if he hadn't heard a word. His black eyelashes were spiked with wetness and his mouth was slack for more kisses. When he leant towards me again, my mouth was the same. He turned us together, and the gate clanged as he pressed me against it, kissing harder.

'Stop,' I mumbled, making a gesture of holding him at bay. 'Please. I'm not ready for this. I don't want to be in a relationship.' I could feel the warmth of his lips lingering on mine, and I wanted it again. 'I've just split up with someone,' I continued. 'I need time to . . . to . . .'

'OK,' he said gently. 'OK.'

I like to think at that point it could have gone either way. We might have stepped back, end of story, or we might have carried on. But at that moment, despite what I'd said, I was ready and willing to be kissed into oblivion. When our lips touched again we didn't stop till I was so horny I could barely stand, and the dogs had nearly caught their death.

3

At times in this place I've felt a sense of something in the house, an otherness or a presence. I felt it that night in the attic because, believe it or not, I didn't sleep with Jake after that kiss. I was close though. My God, was I close.

I tried to explain as we walked back, shouting as the wind tore the words from my mouth. 'I like you,' I said. 'But I don't think we want to get into this, do we? I've only just arrived. I've a boyfriend in London. Well, I guess I haven't any more but . . .'

'It's OK, I won't rush you,' Jake replied, and I liked him all the more for that.

In the evening, however, he seemed to change his mind and I suppose I did too. He cooked a Thai curry, fragrant and sexy, and we ate at a big oak table at the top of the living room, surrounded by the clutter of that bizarre Aladdin's cave. There was a vintage doll I hadn't noticed before, a slender-bodied antique on a small chair, staring glassily into the middle-distance. She had a china face, straw-blonde hair and wide startled eyes, an anxious half-smile displaying little ratty teeth. It was a creepy thing, not least because it was wearing layers of creamy-white, a red sash around its waist.

I thought back to the woman from the working men's club, her panda eyes, over-rouged cheeks, messy blonde hair and a costume in similar colours. It was as if she'd been shrunk and mummified, translated into a plaything from an era long dead. That scene seemed so long ago. I wondered, not for the first time, if that was part of the pull that had drawn me back. Was I here because of the tattooed thug who'd fucked the painted ballerina over a gymnast's vault? I didn't think so, or maybe I preferred not to think so.

'Who's your lady friend?' I asked Jake of the doll.

'Meredith,' he said. 'She's a lucky mascot. I like having her around.'

I didn't think that much of it: white dress, red ribbon. After all, it had a fairly common symbolism: the virgin purity of white splashed with the red of a woman's shame, her menstrual blood and defloration. And there were so many oddities about the place, the doll didn't seem that peculiar. Coincidence, I thought, nothing more, although like many of Jake's treasures, I wished it didn't have eyes. I feel so watched here. And I am watched. I know I am. But I didn't know that then.

We sat at opposite ends of the table, drinking wine, not even close enough to touch. Rainfall lashed the curtained windows and a log fire blazed, Noah and Twiglet on the hearth rug, feet twitching as they chased their dreamy rabbits. A few feet away from us, the fairground-bright rocking horse brayed into space, a bit between its teeth, its wide eyes black and apocalyptic.

Despite my surroundings, I felt so relaxed and at home, and when our conversation dipped, it didn't matter. It was OK just to listen to the rain. I was starting to see an easiness in Jake that was a far cry from the suited skittish woodland creature who'd met me at the station.

He smiled at me, swirling his glass of red, and said, 'Why've you come here?'

The way he says 'come' is so sexy, so outdoorsy and dirty, but it was the phrasing of the question that struck me. He was speaking as if I'd intruded.

'You offered me a job,' I replied.

'No,' he said, gentle and coaxing. 'Why have you come here? They have jobs in London.'

I looked at him, wondering how to reply. Why have I come here? He deserves a good answer, I thought. He's taken a risk with me just as I have with him. Unfortunately, I didn't know what that good answer was.

'I needed a change,' I began. 'The man I told you about. I needed to get away. But it's more than that. This place . . . I don't know.'

He watched me from across the table, arms resting on the surface, slim fingers on the stem of his glass, that elegant face patient and attentive. There was nothing on the table now except our wine, cups and a pot of coffee, still untouched. Jake's curls are the deep rich brown of conkers, and firelight gave an orange tint to the frizzed edges. He has a couple of moles on one cheekbone, one high, one low, and I thought how like a Pierrot doll he was with two dark tears gone awry.

'I needed changes,' I said lamely. 'My relationship. My life.'

He gave me a steady look, grey eyes soft and serious. 'So why here? It's a bit of a trek.'

'I don't know,' I said. 'I visited once before. I told you that. I like it . . . No, I'm not sure that's true. Like's not the word. It's . . . there's something about this place.'

He smiled, nodding. 'Yes, yes there is.' He gave me a long, calm look. 'You feel it as well, don't you.'

I was relieved yet unnerved. He seemed to understand what I could barely articulate.

'Yes,' I said. 'But I don't know what it is.'

'No,' he said quietly. 'We don't either.'

At that, he stood and walked towards me, tall and brisk. I thought he was about to leave the room but instead he stood behind my chair, bunched my hair in a fist and tipped my head forward. My forehead pressed against the cool wood of the table and my heart raced. What was he doing? I sat perfectly still, seeing my hands on my knees, and below that, my feet on the carpet. I felt his breath on the back of my neck and then the wetness of his tongue. Slowly, he licked a strong line across my neck, moving from left to right, his tongue tip flattening the downy hair on my nape, and leaving a trail of dampness on my skin.

I swallowed, feeling my throat muscles thicken. No man had ever touched me like that. My desire for him was so sudden and all-consuming I was frightened for myself. I stayed as he held me with my head to the table, meek and still, waiting for him to do what he wished. His saliva dried on my skin and I felt vulnerable, neck exposed as if here was my execution. He did nothing and, because I could sense how intently he was looking at me, I began to tremble.

For the first time in my life, I thought, I am known. This man sees in me something he can reach, and I will never escape him.

I am Kate Carter, five foot nothing, freckled and fair, pear-shaped but sprightly, a librarian on the run. And from now on, I thought, I will always be on the run, always fleeing the Jakes of this world because they have the power to devour me. I'm enthralled as much as I'm scared by that. I will always run from them and yet I will always seek them out.

I was beginning to understand what had brought me to this place.

'Stand up,' murmured Jake.

My skin prickled with goosebumps as he moved the chair to stand behind me, his body touching mine but barely. I gazed at the stuffed birds in the dome on the piano, knowing better than to turn and, without preamble, he lifted my long skirt and slid his hand down the front of my knickers. I caught my breath, a quiet sound that was loud to my ears because it was so full of truth. With a single probing finger, he split my lips apart and rubbed, finding me hot, swollen and milky. His other hand stole under my jumper and he rested his arm across my stomach, half-holding me to him, half-caressing, as his right hand explored. He had to bend his knees to reach me – most men do – and the ungainliness of that always turns me on.

'I want to find you,' he whispered, still rubbing at me.

I couldn't speak. My thighs were so heavy. His fingers were slithering through me, and my vulva was like soft warm butter. The hand on my stomach undulated, squeezing the flesh it found. The fire spat once and, apart from our breath, the rain and my occasional moans, that was the only sound for a while.

'Will you come?' he said. 'If I keep on doing this, will you come?'

I was already close. His fingers were magical. 'Please,' I whimpered. 'Please stop.' I wanted him to resist for me because I was incapable myself. I wanted to come, I wanted to fuck, I wanted him in my arms, naked and hard. And yet to come would be to surrender and show him how I was when I was beyond myself, defenceless and ecstatic.

I couldn't do it. Emotionally, I was too raw. 'Stop,' I repeated, and this time I moved, pushing away his hand. It was agony.

He let me go, staying near. He put his fingers in his mouth, tasting me. 'Come to bed,' he said.

'I can't,' I said. 'Please, give me some time.' I really meant it. I was feeling pretty wrecked. I hadn't been in Heddlestone two days. You didn't even know I'd left London. 'I'll call you in a few days,' were the last words I'd said to you. 'I need some space right now.' You respected that, didn't try to phone. I feel terrible now because I exploited your decency, making my escape while you were accepting my request. I wasn't thinking straight is my only excuse. It might seem as if I was being a cool operator, packing half my flat away, booking train tickets, arranging the sub-let but I was on auto-pilot, focusing on practical stuff to blot out the pain.

'I have to go to bed,' I said to Jake. 'Alone. I'm sorry. This is much too fast.'

Gently, he clutched a handful of my curls, turning me to face him. My groin was pulsing, and I just wanted to come and forget everything.

'Will you masturbate?' he asked. 'In the attic?'

I laughed shyly. 'You're not watching.'

He grinned. 'Go on, let me.'

'I have to go,' I said, my voice a throaty whisper. 'I can't sleep with you.'

'I want you,' he said. 'I want you now, tonight. I'm so hard for you. My dick –'

I gave him a steady look. 'And I'm so wet,' I breathed. 'But that's not –'

'I know you are,' he said. 'I felt you. I want you. I want to –'

'But that's not the point, is it?' I continued. 'Hard, wet. It's not the point.' I don't know how I managed to say those words, I really don't, because when it's hard and it's wet, it seems that's the only point in the world, the only reason for breathing.

Somehow, I managed to say goodnight. Alone in the attic, I made myself come, once quickly, twice slowly, liquid silk sliding on my thighs and hands. I thought of him on the sofa or in bed, I wasn't sure which, fist on his cock, faster and faster, his mind spinning as he pictured me, my knees wide, fingers flying. How frustrating for us to be in the same house, rooms apart, doing to ourselves what we'd rather do to each other.

I slept fitfully, waking and drifting off, my head jumping from one dream to the next. At some point, I woke in a panic. My father in his lemon-yellow sweater was standing in his Kentish conservatory, pouring over an OS map of West Yorks, the moorland contours crunched and dense. He was frowning, baffled because while everything else was correct – the roads, the landmarks, the nearby towns and villages – Heddlestone wasn't there. It was just contours and emptiness.

I lay in bed, trying to shake off the scene. It was so vivid. Only a dream, I told myself. Just my unconscious responding to my new seclusion. And yet there was definitely something odd about this place.

'You feel it too,' Jake had said, and I did, yes, although I didn't know what it was. I'm still not sure. Sometimes I think I've been drawn here by some dark sensual compulsion. Sometimes, I think that's nothing but a cheap excuse to justify my jumping ship.

Jake had implied there was more to Heddlestone than met the eye but maybe he was just talking about the inevitable attraction to a place so wildly beautiful. Either way, I was close to getting out of bed to check my own map, to see if Heddlestone still existed, and I might have done if I hadn't nodded off again.

I don't recall any more dreams that night. When I next woke, my mind was blank with terror. Someone was on the other side of the door. Someone or something. Don't ask me how I knew. I just did. A sixth sense.

My first thought was Jake. He's come to get me. I'd been a prick-tease, turning him on then backing off, and now he was now a man possessed. He was standing out there with a weapon, maybe a gag, trying not to breathe, a hand on the doorknob then tiptoeing in with his cock stiff and greedy. Despite my fear, the thought of him pinning me to the bed, a scarf tight between my lips as he fucked me got my pulses drumming to a new beat.

I strained to listen, wishing I'd locked the door. The darkness was so thick it seemed tangible, like a veil I might sweep from my eyes. Except I couldn't. I waited for my eyes to adjust but it doesn't happen here unless there's moonlight. Even my hand, held inches in front of my face, was invisible to me.

It was so dark there might have been someone in the room and I wouldn't have known. I heard nothing more.

Maybe I'd imagined it. Maybe a dream had seeped into reality. I'd had a heavy few days. I was traumatised and miles from home. No wonder I was twitchy.

There's no one here, I told myself. So get up, girl, and lock the door. Switch the light on, cross the room, turn the key.

Perversely, I was now afraid of the light. I was scared of what might confront me if I switched it on. I just sat there in the midst of what felt like eternal darkness, trying not to breathe. I listened. Nothing, not even the hoot of an owl or the scratching of a mouse. Nothing, that is, until a floorboard creaked outside my door.

I was bolt upright, scrabbling for the lamp. Light blazed. My glass of water hit the ground, a clunk and a glug. Wet carpet. I squinted in the brightness, blood rushing in my ears as I scanned the room.

Sloping white walls. Wardrobe. Chest of drawers times three. Cot with my previous day's clothes draped over it. A stiff-backed armchair. En suite bathroom.

Nothing except what I knew to be there. And yet still I had such a keen sense of not being alone. I wondered if one of the dogs was sniffing around on the attic landing or if Jake, my intruder, was now creeping down to his own room. The door is painted avocado green, thick with gloss, and the knob is Bakelite. I considered getting up to lock it but all I did was stare at that knob, half-expecting it to turn.

Of course, it didn't turn. But then it wouldn't, would it? Because it's never what you're looking at directly. It's what's glimpsed in the corner of your eye.

The feeling faded but I was spooked enough to turn on my phone. It was comforting to see the screen light up. Everything felt safer and more prosaic with that. After a few seconds, the phone beeped, a text message from Jake.

'Wish you were here. My bed. Next floor down.'

He'd sent it a couple of hours earlier.

I didn't reply until the morning. 'Go to sleep,' I wrote.

He texted back at once: 'Breakfast in half an hour.'

You see what he did there? He didn't even add a question mark. It was an instruction rather than an invitation. It's in all the subtle ways Jake gets to me. With that missing piece of punctuation, he'd reeled me in a tiny bit further.

The museum was closed for winter, so our work was mainly backstage. As well as running the museum, Jake makes puppets on a commercial basis, mainly hand-carved marionettes in handmade costumes which he sells to individuals and outlets all over the world.

Some of his work is breathtaking. There are elaborate marionettes costing hundreds of pounds, and I don't know how he can bear to part with them. He describes himself as 'old school', eschewing modern options of plastics and chemicals for traditional woodcarving, casting and papier-mâché. He enters festivals and competitions where he shows quirkier experimental puppets made from metal and junk.

There are two rooms on the floor where his bedroom is, both higgledy-piggledy with dolls, puppets, boxes, stage sets, costumes and drawings. Part of my job was to bring order to this, to make an inventory of the hundreds of creations he's lost track of over the years, to take and upload photographs, add descriptions, create categories, and generally bring my cataloguing skills to a whole new realm.

But first I needed to sort out his office because his paperwork and admin systems were a mess. It was easier said than done. I was constantly having to question him. 'Do you really need invoices from 2001?' 'Which of these magazines do you want?' 'What about a filing system for catalogues?' 'Why don't we try and separate out museum-stuff, business-stuff and your own art?'

'You're such a librarian,' he teased.

'Hey, librarians aren't what they used to be,' I replied.

'We surf the information super highway, you know.' I did a surfer move, riding a wave. 'Some of us don't even bother with books these days. We're hip, we're cutting edge, we're cool.'

Jake glanced deliberately about the room. 'Not any more, you're not.'

The workshop was a nightmarish explosion of puppetry with strange objects dangling from the ceiling. Painted marionettes, limbless trunks, dyed fabrics and puppets wrapped in bags all hung there like a scene of magnified undergrowth, a weird layer of bright insects and distorted nectar globules.

Beneath this was a woodburning stove, tables, workbenches and rickety shelves crammed with tins, pots, tubs and bottles. Sketches and scaled designs were pinned to the walls. Huddled under table legs were buckets of plasters and bewildering concoctions, plus piles of newspaper threatening to topple. Blocks of wood, foam and polystyrene squatted in corners, and scarred, paint-spattered surfaces were strewn with tiny body parts and joints, eyeballs on brackets, heads in vices, torsos without genitals and all manner of tools, wires, glues and knives.

Jake worked steadily in the midst of it all, the eye at the centre of the storm, a giant god peopling his world with creatures of his own imagining.

Adjoining the workshop was the office, meaning I could call out to him as and when. He was reluctant to let me throw stuff away but gave the nod to most of my suggestions for reorganisation. And then I did it! Oh, what a thrill. I'd grown used to working in libraries where the smallest idea would have to pass through various subgroups to be discussed and minuted ten times over before finally being implemented. Jake and I simply did things. It was incredibly energising, as was having Jake in the next room, sometimes in view, sometimes not. Scents from the workroom drifted in to the office, sawdust spiked with fumes of paint, turps, coffee, hot glue and sometimes a mildewy waft from wet papier-mâché, all undercut with cold, peaty air spilling in from the moors.

I once complained about the open windows. Jake told me about an artist he used to know, Toxic Tony, who'd poisoned his system by working in badly aired conditions. Environmental illness, he called it. Can't touch chemicals now, can't breathe them, processed food is off, can't use shampoo, can't paint. It's like being allergic to the world because the world is full of crap. Poor guy practically lives in a bubble. Used to sleep sitting up because lying down gave him tremors and bad dreams.

I kept thinking about Toxic Tony, sitting up somewhere, asleep and alone. I didn't complain again.

I don't know how I functioned the day after our unfinished night before. I was 90 per cent lust, 10 per cent brain, and that's probably making myself out to be clever. Whenever Jake came near or I approached him, my insides danced. There were times when I barely heard a word he spoke because I was so focused on whether or not we'd touch.

When he came into the office to answer a query, I secretly leered at how neat and narrow his hips were, and at the springiness his thighs seemed to contain. Once, caught on the dark fuzzy hair of his forearm was the golden curl of a wood shaving, resting there so delicately it might have been floating. Our hands brushed as we both reached for a stapler, and the wood-curl fell off to lie gleaming on the dusty desk. My groin sparked up. It had been sparking up all day.

'Catch!' he said another time as I walked into the workshop. I cupped my hands as a little puppet head rose in a parabola across the room, grinning as it spun. It had a mop of red woollen hair and a rosy-cheeked face reminiscent of a cartoon character on old-style saucy postcards.

'Hamish,' said Jake as I examined it. 'He wears a kilt. Some tourist shop in the Cairngorms makes a mint on these.'

'Very original,' I said dryly, handing back the head. Our fingertips touched and again my groin sparked, ready for more. I wanted to stroke his hands, to fumble over his lips, to kiss his stubbly neck and nibble on his ear lobes. In the clear light of day, I'd begun to think I'd imagined the creepiness of the night before. I didn't think him likely to be loitering outside my bedroom door. He had better things to do, like sleep and masturbate. All the same, shadows shifted in the back of my mind, dark blurry emotions I couldn't pin down. In some eerie way, I still felt I'd been called there although I couldn't isolate what or who was calling. Was it Jake? The moors? The village? Maybe it was the puppets or the ghoulish ballerina from the club.

I'm not cuckoo. I'm not credulous. Generally speaking, I err on the side of scepticism and going to yoga is about as whacky as I've ever got. In my working life, I'm an information professional. Or I was. I deal in facts and knowledge, not flights of fancy. Yes, I know I can be idealistic, foolhardy and ridiculous but at heart I'm a pragmatist. That I'd even given credit to the notion of being drawn to Heddlestone was fairly out there for me.

But I'd gone further than that: I'd actually upped sticks and followed the compulsion. The pull had left me struggling with a sombre semi-erotic longing, enough to override my world view, to crush my doubts and dismissals, and drive me to appease it. All the same, I couldn't quite fathom it. Even calling it a 'pull' or a 'draw' seemed too much of a definition for the obscure hunger I felt. I didn't feel I had a mystery to solve but I knew I needed to understand Heddlestone better before it would leave me alone.

'I want to find you,' Jake had said the night before. I didn't know if I wanted to be found. It'll all be so much better, I thought, when I've got a place of my own.

But I'm still here, still in Jake's attic. I think that was probably the plan all along. I don't think he even tried to find me a place of my own. The story about the Heskeths getting the boiler fixed was bullshit. I still don't know what the grand plan is, or even if there is one. I just know that, on the whole, Jake likes to know where I am and what I'm doing. If he could fix strings to my limbs and make me walk as he wished, I'm sure he'd do that too.

And he'd do it, of course, in that inimitably clever way of his. When you can't see you're being manipulated, you don't know you have a master.

4

'Get in the box!' said Jake.

I thought he was talking to the dogs,

Barking and frantic, they'd run along the hall at the sound of knocking, claws clicking on bare boards. The noise had scared me half out of my wits. Just someone at the door but it was so unexpected. Jake pulled the curtain aside, squinting through the window to see who was out there in the cold evening. In the diamond-panes of glass, the reflected chandelier fractured like a colourless kaleidoscope.

Jake turned to the room, scanning nervously.

'It's Eddie, my brother,' he said. He strode over to a large wicker chest, lifted the lid and looked at me. 'And his wife. Get in.'

'No way,' I hissed.

'Please,' he said sternly. 'Just get in.'

'I'll go upstairs.'

'No time,' he said. 'Do it, Kate. I'll explain later. Please.'

The knocking came again and a voice called out, 'Let us in, you bugger. I know you're there.'

The basket was heaped with clothes and fabric of various textures and colour. It creaked as I got in, smelling of tangy wicker, musty textiles and camphor. Hurriedly, I curled into a loose foetal position, shoving tweed from my face as I arranged a nest around me, a seam of silver buttons by my arm. The basket was partially lined with linen, much of it ripped. Through the exposed weave, I could see the centre of the room. I worried if I moved I'd be spotted.

'Keep still. No one'll know,' said Jake, reading my mind.

He dropped the lid shut, placing something on top – books or a paper – to create a rectangle of black on my lattice roof.

I listened to him walk down the hall, wondering what the hell I was doing.

'You should have phoned first,' complained Jake as voices greeted him. 'Twig! Noah! Oi! Inside!'

There were two other voices, a man and a woman's. The woman spoke with an East European accent, buoyant and excitable.

'Jesus, these fucking dogs!' she said. 'Hey! You miss me, boys? Jake, we buy you present. A big bottle wodka. And you know, this time I don't drink it first.' She laughed, an amused, infectious cackle. 'You see? Every drop for you. I make you drink it with gherkin like before, hey? Good Russian tradition!'

Again, her laughter rattled out, punctuated with squeals as the dogs barked and yapped. 'Down! Down!' Jake kept calling.

Into the room came three pairs of human legs and eight long paws. I got the impression visitors were a rare treat for the dogs. Most of the time, the dogs are asleep. They're ex-racers from a rescue centre, lazy, gentle creatures with forlorn slender faces and big doe eyes. They're more like cats than dogs in their attitude.

A man's voice said, 'Hello, mate. You caught that leccy rabbit yet?'

Then to my horror, my view of all those legs was partially obscured by one of the dogs, Twiglet, the brindle, taking a sudden interest in the basket. Its long, sharp muzzle nosed along the weave, snuffling eagerly, its melancholy eyes fringed with dark lashes. I heard a faint whimper in its throat and as it sniffed close to my head, a blast of meaty breath reached me through the wicker.

How come those dumb mutts could ignore me for most of the day, then I get bundled into a box and suddenly I'm interesting? I held my breath, praying my scent would be masked by all the grotty rags. In the background, I could see Noah leaping up at the woman as she laughed and shrieked.

'Noah! Down!' yelled Jake, paying attention to the wrong dog. Close to my head, Twiglet scraped a claw down the basketwork, its hooked tail wagging, a whimper rumbling to a growl. I caught a glint from one of its big black eyes and I closed my lids, fearing it might be able to see the whites of my own, shining in the gloom. Again a claw scraped at the wicker, then again and again, a whine in its throat as it began pawing at the box. Just when I thought the game was surely up, Jake intervened.

'Kitchen!' he barked, and the dog barked back as he pushed or perhaps kicked it away. 'Kitchen, go on! Scram!'

The dogs retreated and I exhaled slowly, trying not to move a muscle in case the basket creaked or I disturbed a flock of moths. What I was doing? Why couldn't I meet these people?

Peering through the wicker, I could see the woman, young and bright, standing in front of the fire's mesh guard, fizzing with energy. She had shortish hair, perhaps an elfin crop that had grown to scruffiness, auburn dye and brown roots giving her a spiky two-tone effect. But what struck me immediately was her bizarre outfit: a snow-washed denim ra-ra skirt over green lycra leggings, speckled hiking socks just visible above flowery welling-ton boots. Over that lot was a lilac puffa jacket which she slipped off to reveal a snow-washed dungaree bib over a multi-coloured angora jumper, sequins on one shoulder. A denim ra-ra skirt with a dungaree flap? I wondered who on earth had designed such a garment, and whether they'd been shot yet.

Standing with her back to the fire, the woman tilted forwards, lifting up her layered skirt to wiggle her but-tocks at the warmth.

'Oooo, Yelena, you have such hot bott!' she said with another rattle of dirty laughter.

Whoever this woman was, I liked her already. From what I could tell, there was more life in that laugh than in the whole of Heddlestone put together.

Eddie said, 'Put kettle on then.'

'You're not stopping,' warned Jake.

'Wouldn't want to,' replied Eddie. Then he added, 'Yeah, nice holiday, bruv. Great. Thanks for asking. You get our postcard?'

'No,' said Jake. 'Can't say as I did.'

'Ah, well. Don't hold your breath. You know how it is. Out of sight, out of mind.'

'What mind?' muttered Jake, leaving the room.

As he left, a pair of sandy-brown Timberlands passed by the basket, then in my view rose a pair of legs, a strong pair of legs with thick, muscular thighs in denim jeans. I'd seen those thighs before and my heart skipped a beat as my clit twitched at the memory. Mentally, I stripped him, and I saw him pounding the ballerina, his expression dead and blank, thighs flexing as he fucked with light indifference.

It was him, the man from the clubhouse last autumn. He'd been in my imagination a long time, memories of him screwing the woman over the vault, fantasies of him doing likewise to me. It was odd to see him now, so solid and real, so very present and ordinary. He approached Yelena, and I was left in no doubt it was him, recognising that shorn head and the jaunty arrogance in his face.

How on earth could he and Jake be brothers? It was hard to imagine them having *anything* in common, let alone a mother. Jake, in body and mind, had such sensitivity and grace. Eddie, however, looked such a lunk. Acted like it too. I watched him reach for Yelena's arse, a palm cupping each cheek, rubbing her with a vigorous playful jiggle. 'That'll warm you up, lass,' he said.

I'd found it easy to dislike him from the off, yet there was some warped part of me that found him enticing and darkly thrilling.

'And now you are also hot,' said Yelena, turning to cup Eddie's groin. Then she snatched her hand away, stifling a giggle as she feigned guilt, saying something like, 'Orbsa-daisy!'

Jake had obviously returned. 'Dogs are playing up,' he said. 'I'll have to take 'em out. Kettle's on. Help yourself.'

'How long are you going to be?' asked Eddie.

'Twenty minutes,' said Jake. 'Not much more.'

You bastard, I thought. You complete and utter bastard! Don't you dare leave me here. Don't you dare!

But he dared. I heard the back doors go, the dogs' barks fading away. Twenty minutes in this festering, stinking heap of dead person's clothes. And then I thought: Hang on, mister. What makes you think I'm going to stay here? I could fling back the lid, spring up like an oversized jack-in-a-box. I considered it for a few moments but I didn't really fancy the attention and besides, I was curious to watch.

'What's on telly?' said Eddie. He plonked himself on the sofa, a hand crawling along the cushions, searching instinctively for the remote. 'Yelena, turn the telly on.'

'Ah, man, I love this TV,' said Yelena, obliging. 'It's so cute! Your brother's fucking weird, you know that? Jesus, this room. All these puppets, these toys. He's like kid. But man, this TV . . .'

I love Jake's TV too. Anyone would. It's an old portable housed within a mini theatre-booth, its curved screen framed with tiny crimson drapes tied with tasselled gold rope, a scalloped pelmet above it. It's adorable and I would happily swap ten huge plasma screens for a TV as sweet and crazy as that.

Some soap opera conversation started up and Yelena removed her wellies before joining Eddie on the sofa, lying on her back, head in his lap, feet on the arm-cushion.

'It does my head in,' said Eddie. 'It's not a telly, it's a fucking toy. Look at it. Too small. No remote. I'm not watching fucking *Emmerdale*. Change it, Yel.' He jerked his pelvis to make her move.

Yelena laughed. 'Change it yourself, you lazy bastard.' She made it sound as if it were all one word – lezzibastard.

Eddie didn't budge. Instead, eyes on the TV, he slipped a hand beneath her denim bib to give one of her angora-clad breasts a gentle squeeze, an idle affectionate gesture of jokey-sexiness. They stayed like that, watching *Emmerdale* while engaged in a distracted grope, and it occurred to me that maybe this was the woman from the clubhouse.

She was probably the right shape, being on the top-heavy side, although it was hard to gauge if that was genuine or a consequence of her terrible clothes. Good tits and odd clothes. How many people like that were there in Heddlestone? Even as I asked the question, I thought this village is probably nuts enough for there to be several, a bunch of identical Russian octuplets who'd married into a family of poor but honest inbreds.

Jake had recently explained the history of the house. It used to be an orphanage set up by a charitable Victorian, Elizabeth Rotherham. The kids would run amok on the moors, lost little savages from towns crammed with dark satanic mills, earning themselves the nickname of Betty's Bastards.

'You can laugh,' said Jake, 'but probably half this village is descended from Betty's Bastards.'

Heddlestone certainly has that feel to it.

On the sofa, Eddie removed his hand from his wife's breast and, eyes still on the TV, he lifted the ruffles of her denim skirt, sliding his hand down the front of her green leggings.

'Ah, you're so dirty,' said Yelena approvingly. She opened her legs wider, dropping one foot to the floor while the knuckled hump of Eddie's hand moved beneath the lycra, a sight that made my groin flush hotly.

'Mmmm,' she said after a while. 'Why you don't do this to me at home?'

'Telly's better,' he replied, and they both laughed, amusement quickly fading as desire mellowed them again.

Before long, Yelena was groaning softly and Eddie shifted his position, chest barrelling as he fiddled with his fly. His cock sprang out, a stout column of flesh, and he wrapped his fingers around it, jerking slowly, his glans bulging like a big ripe fruit.

'Suck me off,' he said gently.

'What about Jake?' murmured Yelena.

'Nah, I don't fancy him.'

Yelena laughed, turning to lie on her stomach. She licked and kissed his tip then pushed away his hand, swallowing him in a greedy gulp. Eddie looked down at her, smiling with zonked pleasure as her head bobbed in his lap, her fist at his root. 'Dirty bitch,' he said affection-ately. He caressed the back of her neck, ruffling her softly spiked hair.

After a while, in a quiet, level voice, he said, 'Tell me you want Jake.'

Yelena gave him a couple more slow, luxurious lengths then raised her head. 'I want Jake,' she said flatly. 'Let me go on your dick.'

She stood astride his feet, lifting her skirt and shoving down her green leggings. Eddie perched on the sofa edge as she bared her arse, his hands ready to hold her. There was something crude and defiling in the way Yelena pushed down her leggings, as functional as a peasant woman squatting to relieve herself. That sudden lack of prettiness, that blunt exposure made my groin clench on itself in a fist of arousal. There wasn't an atom of shame or daintiness in her appetite. She wanted his cock and she was having it. Her leggings, rumpled below her knees, hampered her freedom and she tried to stamp herself free, managing only to turn the fabric inside out over a bunched-up sock.

Through the thin bars of my cage, I watched her reverse herself onto Eddie, her white arse jutting as she poised mid-squat while Eddie levelled his cock at her entrance. Then she sank onto his lap, groaning long and low as she took him deep.

'Ahhhh,' she said, tipping forwards and pushing back, filling herself in a flurry of shallow bounces.

Something about the way they worked together, about their breezy, offhand communication, again reminded me of the scene in the club. It seemed increasingly likely this was the same woman, and if so, then this was the second time I'd watched them going at it. Bizarrely, I found their ordinary domestic fuck almost as hot and horny as the kinky games I'd witnessed the first time. This was sweaty grunting sex, unplucked and unperfumed, for no one's benefit but their own. It was deliciously private and unshowy. And hiding in the dressing-up box made me feel even more the voyeur, the girl with the sordid secret, the woman who liked to watch.

But this was more than watching. I felt involved. I could hear them, the sound of their breath and voices, their bodies bumping, feet on the carpet, the odd squeak of sofa springs. *Emmerdale* mumbled in the background, the fire crackled, and Yelena gasped and panted, jolting up and down on Eddie who clasped her around the waist, sometimes fondling her breasts through her thick fluffy jumper.

'Say it,' he whispered darkly. 'Tell me you want him.'

Yelena gave a whimper of reluctance.

'Tell me,' urged Eddie.

'I want him,' she said through snatched breaths. 'I want Jake. I want to fuck him.'

Eddie groaned appreciatively. 'More,' he said.

'I want to fuck him,' she gasped. 'Fuck him and you

watch ... make porn film with your brother. I suck his dick, we fuck hard ...'

Eddie muttered something, making her moan. I strained to listen, catching some of his words. 'Yeah,' he breathed. 'She's a hot little whore, aren't you? His cock in her cunt, that's what she wants ...'

Yelena bucked harder, a hand on Eddie's knee, the other on her clit, her face fixed in concentration. She panted rapidly then emitted a volley of sounds that left me half-terrified. I didn't understand a word. It was a burble of guttural nonsense I took to be Russian. She fucked and frigged, speaking in tongues.

'Ah, I'm coming,' she gasped, reverting to English. 'Come, come.'

She sounded gorgeous, her voice high and breathy, a sound twisting closer to pain as she neared her peak. Hurry up, come, I thought, worrying Jake might return any minute. Eddie's face was a flushed grimace, and he clasped Yelena's hips, shunting into her rhythm. My cunt was plump and wet, opening up for nothing, and their urgency had me aching to be filled. Yelena's every bounce was torment and I strained for her to climax, imagining I'd find my own release in hers. She seemed to be poised for an eternity then, to my relief, she came with a long, low groan. Moments later, Eddie must have shot his load, his heavy breathing culminating in a couple of grunts.

Then they stayed there, Yelena gently rocking, Eddie rubbing her back as they recovered in a post-coital daze. My own hand, I realised, was wedged between my thighs, fingers pushing through my skirt. I'd indulge myself later.

'See that doll?' said Eddie. 'It's got a cloth cunt.'

'What do you mean?' asked Yelena.

'It's his Laura doll,' replied Eddie. 'It's got a big pussy-hole.'

I couldn't see what they were looking at but I assumed

they were talking about the vintage doll Jake called Meredith. Jake seemed strangely attached to that doll. It would appear in different parts of the room, staring out of its wide blue eyes, baring its little pin-teeth.

Yelena laughed. 'You are taking the piss. I don't believe.'

'Not a word of a lie,' said Eddie. 'Jake takes it to bed every night and he fucks it.'

Yelena snorted gleefully. 'You liar.'

'I'm not!' exclaimed Eddie, laughing. 'Have a look if you don't believe me. It's true. He sits it on his dick and –'

The back door banged just as Yelena was pulling up her leggings, half-way across to the doll.

'Sheet!' she hissed. She jerked her clothes into place, hurling herself full-length onto the floor. 'My God, this *Emmerdale* it is so interesting,' she said, pretending to watch TV.

Eddie chuckled, fastening himself quickly. 'Nice walk?' he called as Jake came into the room. Eddie and Yelena both looked excited and flushed, faces slack and puffy with pleasure.

'You forgot to bring dogs home,' said Yelena. She finger-combed her fringe, smoothing down the mahogany stripes. 'Where are they?'

'Muddy,' said Jake. 'They're not coming in.'

Eddie rubbed a big hand over his face. 'Put kettle on,' he said. 'I'm still waiting for my brew.'

'Lazy bastard,' said Jake, a note of scorn rather than humour in his voice.

'Yeah.' Yelena laughed, sprawling across the floor to give Eddie a playful kick. 'Lezzibastard.' Then she stood, brushing her stiffly flounced skirt. 'I help you, Jake. My husband is pig. He don't deserve tea.'

Bright with charm, she followed Jake out of the room and I couldn't help but feel a twinge of jealousy at the two of them being elsewhere and alone. I lay in the box, breathing in mothballs, hoping Jake didn't have visitors very often.

The granny flat smelt of rabbit and straw, not surprisingly since there was an occupied rabbit hutch on the work surface of the kitchenette.

'It's just while weather's bad,' said my potential landlord, nodding at Flopsy. 'We'll stick 'im in t' garage if you're taking it.'

The man's name was Badger. Probably in his late fifties and his nickname, I guessed, was derived from the streak of silver-grey in his otherwise black hair. He stood watching me, hands deep in his pockets, and gave a brisk smile that failed to reach his eyes.

Jake must be barking mad if he thought I could live here. Outside, thin snowflakes tumbled on the breeze, and the flat, at the bottom of an unkempt, twiggy garden, was probably as cold as a garage. Its walls were flock, the carpet a bilious swirl of turquoise and blues, and the armchair a chintz flowerbed so flouncy it was on the verge of stalking off. The bed, in the same room, was single, its thin mattress covered in a pink nylon sheet that looked crackly with static. Dusty Venetian blinds hung over the large window, green velour curtains to accompany them, and the kitchen sink was clouded with limescale, its plughole dank and brown. Shell-pink wall lights were positioned above a sideboard and chest of drawers, meaning there were no sources of illumination where you might reasonably want some. How would I read? How would I watch TV? The whole place was so dingy it would take the removal of an entire wall to let some light in.

And yet I looked at it, thinking, If I moved here, I could sleep with Jake.

I needed to get away from him. He was too much, way too much. 'I like to keep myself to myself,' he'd said, trying to justify the way he'd ordered me into the wicker trunk. 'Folk are nosy round here. Soon as one person knows you're staying, the whole village'll know.'

'I've got a life to lead as well,' I said. 'You can't expect me to –'

'I know, I know,' he countered. 'Out of order. I panicked. It's Eddie and Yelena. If they know you're here, they'll never be away from the place. I like it as it is. I like peace and quiet.'

Eddie, I'd learnt, was three years Jake's junior and the landlord of The Griffin, the village's only pub. Jake had bought him out of a joint-inheritance some years after the death of their father, Bill Duxbury. Their parents were divorced, ostensibly because of Dad's nine-year affair with a mobile hairdresser, Maggie Slack. 'Slack by name, slack by nature' their mother had railed, flinging some of Bill's most treasured puppets out of the front door.

The boys had wept and Bill had returned home to find the wreckage of all those tangled twisted dolls strewn across the grass, grinning in the rain. Pauline had sued for divorce and now lived in New Zealand with a retired pharmacist. The puppet collection and house had, for four generations, been passed from father to son but Eddie had no interest in it. He was a homebird, according to Jake, a man who'd never really left Heddlestone unlike Jake who'd attended art college then gone on to work with puppeteers and sculptors up and down the country.

'But I came back,' he said. 'Heddlestone's one of those places. It's hard to leave. People don't generally.'

None of this, however, justified his decision to walk the dogs and leave me stuck in that box. He buys clothes from charity shops to make into costumes for the puppets. That's what the trunk's for, kept in the living room because that's where he sews. It's weird to see him in the evenings, hunched over the sewing machine, its tiny spot of light illuminating his fingers as the needle flies.

'It seemed like a good idea,' he said. 'I wanted to know what they did, what they'd do if I left them alone.'

'You wanted me to spy on them?'

Jake shrugged. 'Only a bit. I was curious. You were in the box. It seemed too good a chance to miss.'

'Nothing happened,' I told him. 'They just watched telly and talked crap. And if you ever pull a stunt like that again, I'm out of here. Out of this village, your life. Everything.'

Even as I spoke, I didn't believe a word. I knew leaving wouldn't be easy. Weeks later, writing this, and I don't know if leaving is even possible. There's a cold intimacy to this place and the brothers have drawn me closer to its dark, disturbed heart. They had me from the start, Jake with his beauty and that clever careful mind, Eddie with his arrogance that gets me right in the groin. Even now, I don't know who I prefer. I'm split between them, relishing both but trusting neither. Lust has taken me to some strange places but none stranger than this.

I was so taken with Jake that it would need more than a minor humiliation to sway me. I felt as if he'd taken over my mind and I wanted him to take over my body. Add his brother to the equation, detached, dirty, clumsy and crude, and I didn't stand a chance.

The day after Eddie and Yelena's visit Jake went to Bradford and so I had my first weekend to myself. He'd invited me along but I declined, determined to explore Heddlestone alone. I wanted to establish myself there and find a way of existing that was separate from Jake. Identity. Autonomy. My need for independence. So many of the issues that had me running from you, were spilling over into the new set-up with Jake. The bad weather had kept us cooped up for much of the week and I needed time to myself.

It was a viciously cold morning, snow struggling to fall,

and I ate a late breakfast in the village's only option, the Punch and Judy Cafe, a peculiar hybrid of greasy spoon and twee pine. Cheap framed prints of puppets and, for some reason, storm-tossed battleships adorned the walls; plastic flowers in Perrier bottles stood on every table; and the placemats featured palm trees and tropical sunsets in lurid shades of orange.

I'd got Badger's details from a grandmotherly woman who'd brought me my scrambled eggs. I hadn't expected it to be so easy but it turned out she knew Badger's wife and soon I had a mobile phone number and an appointment to view.

'You staying up at the museum?' asked the woman, handing me the details. She had six fingers. The sixth was a small stump sprouting from the side of her hand.

I'd nodded, swallowing my food. 'Working there,' I said. 'Staying there for now. Could do with something else though.'

'Jake, is it?' she'd asked, and I thought I detected a note of sympathy in her voice.

I wasn't quite sure what she meant but I said yes, anyway.

'You're his type,' she'd said. 'Healthy appetite on you as well. Good girl.'

'It's a nice cafe,' I said, as if to justify my hunger. I felt as if I were in some grisly horror film, unwittingly being fattened up for the kill. Jake is spare and lean, the puppets all limbs and joints, the dogs all skin and bone. With my buttocks, thighs and breasts, I was the fleshiest creature in the house. Were they all eyeing me up, licking their lips in anticipation? It was almost enough to put me off my breakfast but not quite.

The woman had smiled, placing an over-fingered hand on mine. 'Watch yourself,' she said kindly, and she gave my fist a little shake, knocking eggs off my fork.

I smiled at Badger and heard myself say, 'Would you

mind if I changed things around a little? Maybe put up some different curtains? A few rugs?'

'Ay, I don't see why not,' said Badger. 'I'll ask t' wife if she's owt spare. Curtains and that.'

I kept smiling, stuck for a reply. Trying to accustom myself to the place, I wandered into the kitchenette and opened a few stale-smelling cupboards. 'Plenty of storage space,' I said merrily. Hanging by the fridge was a spiral-bound calendar turned to a photo of some soft-focus Westies. Beneath the picture, a week and a half of dates had been crossed off. The month was September 2006.

I remembered Jake's words when we'd first driven over the moors: 'No one's lived there since Ada Hesketh died.'

Had she died here? On that terrible bed? In September 2006? Oh Jesus.

So what if she had? asked my rational self. Dead people don't hurt, do they?

It didn't matter. The thought disturbed me, and I eyed the candy-pink bed, resisting an urge to remove my woolly hat as a sign of respect. Had they changed the mattress? Were they intending to?

'So what's the news on the boiler?' I asked. 'When's that likely to be fixed?'

Badger shrugged. 'We'll get Bob to have a look if you're taking it. No point fixing it otherwise. You met Bob?' He looked at me intently, flashing another of his empty smiles.

I shook my head.

'If you see a fella pushing an old pram about, that's Bob. Odd Job Bob. He does odd jobs and that.'

'Does he do boilers?' I asked.

Another shrug. 'Don't see why not.' The smile snapped again.

'Don't suppose he's Corgi-registered, is he?'

Badger chuckled. 'He's all right, is Bob. Knows what he's doing.'

But that's not what I asked, I thought.

The rabbit moved in its hutch, straw rustling. A drip fell from the tap, landing with a metallic plink. I turned the tap tighter but it still dripped.

'Bob can have a look at that as well,' said Badger.

I scanned the room again, trying to picture myself there. I could buy a couple of cream rugs, perhaps some voile to replace the blinds. If I unscrewed the wall lights, I could cover the damage with a big mirror and some pictures. Jake was bound to have a couple of spare table lamps and a throw to cover the frilled armchair. Jake and I would never, ever be able to have sex here but I could stay at the museum some nights and have this as my base.

'Can I let you know in a couple of days?'

'Course you can,' said Badger briskly. 'It's not going anywhere.'

We walked up the narrow side path, separated from the tatty lawn by a dismal concrete trim, circa 1970. Beneath a black bare shrub, on iron-hard soil, snowdrops shivered gently, and a chunky plastic tricycle, tipped over onto its side, was splodged with fast-melting snowflakes.

'Grandkiddies,' said Badger, noting my gaze. 'They don't come up so much.'

I wonder why, I thought.

Opening the side gate, I glanced at their kitchen windowsill, at its ceramic shepherdess, gleaming glass ashtray and jam jar holding a splayed and yellowing washing-up brush. The latch clinked and I tried to imagine hearing that sound every day, on leaving for work and returning, and I was struck by a bleakness so acute it's a wonder I was able to speak.

'Well, thanks again,' I managed. 'I'll let you know.'

And I walked up the hill into the village, footsteps echoing on grey stone, eyes watering in the bitter cold, face stinging. There's a beige-pink tinge in the flagstones, and I thought how like human skin it was. I could never sleep in that bed. The sky was full and furry. Snowflakes fell harder, twisting around the war memorial in the empty market square. I walked on, wishing with the hopelessness of loss, that I'd never left the delights of noisy, dirty, stressful Hackney.

5

I wasn't going to be defeated. I would find a way to make it work. I wasn't ready to go running back to London, tail between my legs, and anyway, I was captivated by the brothers, smitten with one, snagged by another. Ludicrous, I know, but I couldn't even consider leaving while I was in their grip.

The snow thinned so I went walking along a quiet road leading out of the village, keen to fall in love with the place. That day, it was an easy thing to do. The moors looked magical with their sugary dusting, and all the cracks and segments of the drystone walls were dark against the white. I could see the distortion of the trees, branches grown in the direction of that biting wind so they look like stunted half trees.

I might have kept walking a while. I was in the mood to stride out, even though it was cold, but when I was perhaps half a mile from the village, I felt the weirdness again. It stole over me, a dim tranquillity that slowed my footsteps. I'm tired, I thought, before it swelled to something else. I felt I was being pulled down and though there was a wooliness in my mind, my senses became super sharp, a sensation akin to horniness washing over me.

I had to go and stand by a stile because I felt very wobbly. I was detached and yet I was seeing so much more. The snowy world was overdefined. I held onto the stile, feeling bombed out and yet curiously lucid. Moss on the wall's stacked stones was a bright green spillage, snowflakes melting into its tufts. A leaf was veined with frost. A tuft of sheep's wool snagged on barbed wire was a cloud of spun silver. The moors were held in an elemental stillness, big shaggy flakes falling like goose down, feathering all the rocks and hollows.

I might have been trapped in a snowglobe, living in someone else's world. It was unreal, and yet too real. I wasn't quite there.

After a couple of minutes, the sensation began to fade and I set off on the return walk, feeling I ought to lie down. My steps grew lighter, my vision average. Tired, I told myself. Just tired and cold.

Jake's jeep was parked outside, home earlier than I'd expected. Unusually, the dogs didn't greet me when I walked in. I was still unsure about my place in the house, and I took off my coat and shoes, not knowing whether the done thing would be to go straight upstairs to the attic or say hello to Jake.

'Hi,' he called out from the living room, saving me the decision.

I was surprised to find he seemed to have turned part of the room into a photographer's studio. Arranged in front of the hearth was a pale screen backdrop, a camera on a tripod and a tall halogen lamp, the set fringed by boxes, chairs, bongo drums, ferns, puppets and all the other carnival freakery. Closer to the fire was a white reflector disc on a stand, facing the space like a dead sun.

He was kneeling, adjusting the lamp stand, and he looked over his shoulder, face flushed with excitement. 'I want to take your picture,' he said. 'I want lots of photographs. I want you to kneel here and take your top off and I want to take some photos of the puppets touching your breasts.'

Oh, Jesus.

There are some things in life you can never be prepared for, and this was one of them. I gawped at him, wondering whether I ought to move into the granny flat, pronto. He is such an unusual man. I don't think he sees it. He lives like a recluse and it seems there's no normality he measures himself against. I really don't think he appreciated how outrageous his request was.

'Mainly black and white ones,' he added.

'Oh well, that's all right then,' I replied. 'Where are the dogs?'

'Kitchen. I wanted them out of the way. Utility room's too cold. Where've you been?'

'Exploring.'

'Do you like it here?'

'Yes,' I said. 'But it's cold. And I went to look at the Hesketh flat and it's probably the horriblest accommodation I've ever been offered.'

Still on his knees, Jake crawled across the hearthrug and added a couple more logs to the fire. The flames crackled and spat. He was wearing his skinny trousers and a white shirt that was too small for him, looking as if he'd put his best stuff on to greet the world. He's completely impractical, wearing shirts and tatty suits at home, but he smartens up a fraction when he goes into 'town' as he calls any place that isn't Heddlestone. His shirt looked crisp and newly ironed. It was nice and it was untucked, his waist half on show revealing a section of pale hard back.

'Yeah, it's not good, sorry,' he said, using the poker on the fire. 'I'll work on it.' I could see the muscles of his shoulders shifting beneath his shirt, blades jutting, his back narrowing down to neat hips and a great little arse. His shoulders are quite large and angular for his frame, and I think maybe it's wrong to say he's skinny. It's more that he's flat and wide, leanly muscled and tall. He put the mesh guard in front of the fire and turned to me, still kneeling. He reminded me of an animal, crawling around down there, full of eager fleeting glances, his hair an explosion of brown woolly curls.

'You can stay here till it's sorted. I don't mind.'

'Thanks, it's good of you,' I said. 'But I don't want to impose and it's –'

'I like having you here,' he cut in. 'Do you want to do the photos? Will you be warm enough? I could make some tea if you want.'

Firelight flickered on his pale chiselled face, and he looked up at me, an appealing gaze that was scarily bright and deviant. I wished I had more of a handle on his mind. He was peculiar and arty, that much was obvious, but was he emotionally and sexually disturbed too? Did he need an intermediary to connect? Did he get his kicks from puppet porn?

'I don't want to do the photos,' I said. 'I can't believe you –'

'They'll look great.' He crawled back to the space the camera was trained on.

'It is off the scale,' I said. 'It's pervy. You want those puppets to touch –'

'They'll be gentle.' He grinned.

I shook my head. 'And I'm not taking my top off.'

'Only for a short while,' he said. 'I want to do a few different backdrops, maybe some props. I thought the accordion would –'

'Jake,' I chided. 'You must think I was born yesterday.'

'What do you mean?'

I gestured with my hand. 'Well, all this just so you can look at my tits.'

He laughed as he stood up. His dark curls looked extra crazy, and he reminded me of a lanky kid at play. He clasped his hands behind his neck, elbows high as he arched his back. His body bowed out, white shirt tight against his ribs, the creamy flesh of his torso peeping and offering a wisp of dark hair. He looks slightly effeminate sometimes, and in that position he had a sort of off-duty, glam-rock decadence that made me want to drop to my knees and blow him like a groupie. He seemed in an odd mood, a little wired compared to the more mellow behaviour I was used to.

'I think they'll look stunning,' he said. 'I thought of it

earlier. I like your hair. It's all curly and crinkly, and it's a lovely colour, flaxen. I want the light to catch it. You look old-fashioned sometimes. Do you know that? Well, timeless maybe is what I mean. I'd like to have a Victorian feel to the images, maybe something that's a bit goth-kitsch, a bit surreal. I could have you –'

'So it's artistic, is it?' I said.

He swung his arms down and hooked his thumbs in his pockets. With his head tilted, he observed me askance as if he wasn't sure of my humour. He has this way of looking that just melts me. It's almost girlish, an indirect gaze or a coquette's glance from the corner of his eye. It's strangely powerful, full of oblique, stalking cleverness.

'Well, yeah,' he said grandly. 'I am an artist.' He tried not to smile. 'Plus, I would actually like to see your tits.'

I laughed and for a long time we stood like that, several feet from each other, smiling coyly, stunned and nervous, two people rendered useless by lust. Then our smiles began to fade because desire, when it's like this, really isn't funny. His eyes were locked on mine, lids starting to droop in that way of wanting, lips parted a fraction.

I stared at him, knowing what I wanted but not knowing what to do. Take a risk on him or step back? I was aware of his chest rising and falling under his white shirt, his breath slow and controlled. I became conscious of my own breathing too, of my breasts lifting, those breasts he wanted to see. I knew damn well if we played a game of photographer and model, that it would be the start of something. And if he did have some dark perversion involving dolls, I guessed the only way to find out would be to go there. I could back off if it was too much.

How could I resist? He looked so hot, so sexily off-beat, wild and intense. My mind was dwindling to a horny mush as my body thumped out its message of want. I recalled how he'd played me with his hand the other night, fingers slipping through my juices and how he'd murmured, 'Will you come? If I keep doing this will you come?'

My legs weakened at the memory and they very nearly folded when Jake, with a stern tip of his chin, said, 'Take your top off, Kate.'

The room seemed to spin, a shifting jungle of memorabilia, dolls, masks, foliage and tat. I was wearing a thin, zip-up hoodie, beneath that a T-shirt over a long-sleeved top and beneath that a lace-trim vest, four sensible layers to keep me warm like my mother told me.

My heart raced. At the opposite side of the room, the curtains were open, the leaded windows overlooking the snow-powdered moors. If someone passed, they would see us. But no one ever passes here, I told myself. The road leads to the museum, and no further. There was a chance we might have visitors but, given Jake's apparent lack of sociability, it seemed unlikely.

Standing there, wondering what to do, one thought tipped me over: if I went ahead, you would no longer be the last person I slept with. Sex with Jake meant severance with you. I thought it was that easy.

So I took my last fully-clothed breath, held all four layers and pulled them over my head. I tossed them onto an armchair and stood there with my bra on show, brown and cream lace. Then I reached behind for the fastening, fingers trembling.

Jake didn't move. His arousal was obvious, the bar of his cock making an outline across his crotch. My cunt was pulpy with lust and I wanted that inside me, wanted him filling me with hard randy flesh.

When I let my bra fall, he looked at me for a few more seconds then stepped aside and, gesturing to the space before the camera, said, 'Come and kneel down.'

It was such a long walk. My knees seemed boneless and my groin felt as if it was my centre of gravity. No, make that the centre of my universe. I thought he might touch me as I passed but he didn't and instead, I went to kneel chastely where he directed me, nipples sharp and tingling. On the floor in front of the paper screen was a beige blanket in soft chenille and a fur throw. The throw was the colour of a brown bear, heaped like some crumpled beast, and the fire, though it was a few feet away, warmed me.

'You've got marks,' he said. 'From your bra.'

He crouched next to me, gently tipping me forwards with a hand to my head, and he rubbed my side, just behind one breast. He gave me three slow rubs as if trying to erase the mark. I could hardly breathe. Then he stood and said, 'Doesn't matter. I can get rid of it on Photoshop if it shows.'

He moved a wooden plantstand next to me, on top a fern spilling forest-green leaves. I felt like an oversized Alice Liddell. Then he switched on the halogen lamp, filling the arena with a cool clear light, and moved behind the tripod.

'Sit back,' he said, looking through the viewfinder. 'Push your tits out a bit.'

God, I love it when he tells me what to do. I hear it as a command but there's no bossiness in the tone, no clear assertion or force. It's almost as if he knows I'll obey and so he can say it so casually, so lightly, apparently oblivious that I've just become a puddle.

I leant back, hands to my ankles, breasts lifted, trying to keep it relaxed so I didn't look cheap. The murmuring fire spat a couple of times as Jake peered through the camera, adjusting the lens. I glanced around at equipment legs, human legs, puppets and clutter, feeling ridiculous, horny and gorgeous all at once. I guess that happens a lot in life, especially when life's good.

I was unnerved to see the vintage doll again, sitting in an armchair, arms and legs splaying out from a froth of lace, red ribbon around its waist. I didn't like its glass eyes or the little teeth in its rosebud lips. It seemed wrong for a doll to have teeth.

'What's the doll called?' I asked, remembering Eddie had referred to it as Laura.

'Meredith, I told you,' said Jake, peeking over the camera and back.

'Oh, yeah, I remember. And why's she lucky? What'll happen if we put her in another room? Because the way she stares is freaking me out a little.'

'You'll get used to it,' he replied. 'Your breasts are lovely. My great granddad started the collection. There's a family of similar dolls. I keep them in the spare room. My granddad was the puppet man. He was a carpenter, furniture-maker by trade, but he got into marionettes, buying them, making them. My grandmother was from the theatre, Manchester people, she made the costumes. They used to travel around with their own shows. Turn your head this way. Move your hair so I can see your neck.'

Watching me, hanging from metal stands resembling tiny gallows, was a small crowd of marionettes, some big, some small, all gazing fixedly ahead. There was the gangster I'd made walk, the white witch, a clown in a bow tie, a pirate with a cutlass, an old man in spectacles introduced as the Sandman, a grinning skeleton, a disembodied pair of legs, and a sparkling sultan turbaned in purple. They dangled limply, a freeze-frame of exotic and comic creepiness waiting to be animated.

'You don't mind, do you?' said Jake, and he took the turbaned puppet from its stand. It's one of his collectibles, and it's a work of true craft and beauty. Its varnished papier-mâché head gleamed with moustachioed menace, the facets of a yellow gem glinting in its turban. Glitter-encrusted slippers with bells on their toes curled below silken pantaloons and a waistcoat studded with sequins fitted snugly over a powder blue blouse, slashed to the navel to reveal a polished torso, dark as teak.

The puppet is nearly three foot tall, as high as Jake's thighs, meaning I was practically eye-to-eye with it. The way he brings them alive is so brilliant and appalling. You can't help but watch them, believing in their reality and forgetting their controller.

I was believing in the turbaned puppet then as it moved closer, its gait slightly bouncy, a tremor in its oversized head, shards of light glancing off the honey-coloured jewel.

'Are you doing black and white or colour?' I asked. I kept perfectly still, not taking my eyes off the doll's painted face and unseeing eyes.

'Shhh,' said Jake, and the sultan raised a limp-wristed hand, head tilting quizzically at me, body wobbling on its strings. 'Your breasts look nice like that.'

Jake had a remote cable release trailing from the camera, somehow holding it with the controllers, two for this doll because it was big and intricate. I was so transfixed by the puppet that when Jake pressed the trigger and the camera clicked, I jumped. The sultan jumped in response, belled slippers tinkling, and it looked at me, hands covering its mouth in shocked sympathy.

Oh, it was deeply creepy.

'Please,' I complained. 'Warn me when you're going to do that again.'

'Again,' said Jake, and the shutter clicked and clicked. 'Again and again.'

Can't we just have sex? I wanted to ask, but then I was holding my breath as the sultan took a pace forward. It reached out a small wooden hand to my breast. I watched its block of fine fingers, carved by Jake before I knew him, moving through the air, the joint of its wrist exposed, strings taut. The little hand rested high on my breast then stroked down the swoop of my flesh to toy with my nipple. Its touch was ticklish and frustratingly light. The tiny fingers moved on me, feeling the terrain of my nipple, my every bump and crinkle. And all the time, those emotionless eyes observed me until I was hard and pink and wanting, aroused by the caress of a puppet.

It felt as if Jake's hand was on me, and in a way it was. Jake's hands are all over the house and museum, there in the objects he makes, the stuff he touches, a sure, sensitive presence permeating my every day. Sometimes at night, he plays guitar, mellow music drifting through the house, and I think of his nimble fingers plucking more strings. His hands are big enough to trap mine in a fist; light enough to sculpt, carve and paint, to shrink the living, breathing world down to a tiny focused stasis.

His is such a delicate mastery. When I moved here, I really did put myself in his hands.

'You look good,' said Jake softly. He wasn't holding the cable release any more.

The sultan's other hand reached out for me, one on each breast, stroking and teasing, bringing my nipples to points and making my groin flood. Jake's feet were close, big and bare on the blanket. His toenails were like his fingernails, flat as spatulas. I felt a sudden rush of wanting my feet to be with his, my legs to be with his, the two of us lost in a blur of sweat and skin, grunting and fucking.

'Lift your skirt up,' said Jake.

He made me so nervous. I wriggled my long skirt from under my shins, and bunched it by my knees.

'Higher,' he said, adding a stern, 'Please.'

So I scrunched the fabric higher till I was offering a view of my plump parted thighs and a glimpse of underwear.

The sultan moved between my legs with a jingle of little bells. In a controlled collapse, he dropped to one knee, the jewel in his turban winking with light. He might have been worshipping at my altar, and I preferred to think of it that way. His cold little hand trailed along my thigh, stroking my flesh until he neared my groin. My heart was going nineteen to the dozen. It felt so wrong and yet so right, Jake and I in a bizarre idyll of erotic fireside puppetry while the world outside was silenced with snow.

I gasped as the hand touched the gusset of my underwear. I could sense Jake gazing down as the hand rubbed, an all too gentle touch moving over my lips and clit. I was wet, so wet, and I was glad he couldn't feel the dampness there.

'Move your knickers,' said Jake. 'Show me.'

My heart stuttered. 'Are we still taking photographs?' I'm not sure why, but I felt the need to stay perfectly rigid, as frozen as a mannequin. I was reluctant even to move my eyes, and found myself talking shyly to the puppet, not to Jake.

'No, I don't think so.'

'Then what are we doing?' I asked, voice a little strained.

'Just messing around,' he replied. 'A meet and greet. Is that what you'd call it?'

I gave an anxious laugh. 'So who am I meeting?'

The sultan rose so we were eye to eye and reached to stroke my face with a tender, horrible gesture. 'Me,' said Jake. 'Me and my friends.'

'You're nuts,' I whispered.

'Are you horny?' he asked. The sultan stroked my breasts then dropped to his knee again, a hand brushing my gusset.

'You know I am,' I said, still not looking at him. 'Are you?'

'Yes,' he replied. 'Really ... fuck ... I'm so horny. So, so horny. Always. I can't stop thinking about you. I wanted you with me in town today, wanted to show you things, drive you along the top road in daylight. Every night, every night since you got here, in bed, I think about you. Keep wishing you were with me, keep wishing I was fucking you and sucking you and ... Show me your cunt, Kate.'

The sultan moved away, knees lifting like he was on a backwards bicycle.

I swallowed hard, wondering what to do. Then I tucked two fingers into my gusset and pulled the fabric aside, exposing my plump vulva, dark-gold curls of hair and fleshy white thighs. I couldn't look at Jake or the puppet. I stared beyond, heart pumping fast. Then, seconds later, with a rattle of wooden limbs, the sultan fell forward onto his stomach. He sprawled between my knees and began nuzzling towards me like some hideous glittery man-snake.

I shrieked, shuffling back. 'Jake! For fuck's sake!'

I wanted to swipe at the creature but an irrational instinct stopped me: I didn't want to hurt it. But it didn't matter because suddenly, the sultan was an inanimate object being whisked away on its strings.

'Whoa, easy,' said Jake. He hooked the puppet onto the arm of a stand where it hung, limp and lifeless, swaying innocently. Jake turned off the halogen light, throwing us in subdued firelight and afternoon grey. 'Sorry.' He knelt on the rug and grabbed my wrists, holding my arms apart as if to stop me escaping. 'Hey, sorry.'

'It's just too fucking freaky,' I said. 'You're a weirdo. What is this? Are you scared to touch? Is that it? You need dolls, objects? What? Tell me?'

He looked stung but managed a smile nonetheless. 'No, I never thought of it like that. I'm not scared, no. Are you?'

I ignored the question. 'Do you get off on it?' I asked. 'The puppets? Do they turn you on?'

The light was fading outside and he looked down at me, his chestnut curls shot through with autumnal tints from the firelight.

'I don't see it like that,' he said. 'I don't see it as separate. The puppets are ... they're part of my world. A huge part. It's like saying, "Does breathing turn you on?"'

'You should get out more,' I said mildly.

'Maybe,' he replied, and his tone was perfectly indifferent.

He loosened his hold on my wrist, though he didn't let go, and sat back on his heels, grey eyes observing me. I've never seen eyes so grey. I've seen blue-grey and green-grey but these are grey-grey, quite without colour. It's almost as if they need to be so neutral to counteract the intensity of his colour-drenched puppet-world. For a while we stayed like that, paralysed, getting turned on by breathing. I could look at his face for ever, at that creamy pale skin roughened by shadows and stubble, his fine bones and those two moles like off-centre tears. He is beautiful and quite mad.

Then I drew a breath and said, 'Take your top off, Jake.'

He gave a small approving smirk. I wasn't sure if he'd respond to my attempt to assert power. I couldn't read his eyes and my heart was thumping. Then, with one hand, he hooked the shirt over his head, kneeling up straight as he tossed it aside. I caught a waft of male, intimate armpit scent, my desire swelling fast as I gazed at his nakedness. Reflected flame played on his tensed muscularity, his skin taking on a blood-orange hue. His shoulders were wide and square, and the scoop of his pecs was clouded with hair, moles dotted here and there. He seemed a living statue, arms made of alabaster. Before I could reach out to touch, he was unbuckling his belt, that clink of metal music to my ears.

His pushed his clothes to his knees, and his cock jerked up from a dark nest of curls, gloriously thick and hard. Veins cabled his shaft and his crown gleamed wetly, a bluish-tint beneath its crimson flare. It's such a handsome cock, a real beauty. He stared at me, mouth parted, lips shining with moisture, and tilted his pelvis forward a fraction as if to say, Suck on this.

And so I did, eagerly, greedily. I shuffled close, bowing to lick, kiss and slide my lips down his shaft. I gripped the root of him as I slurped, spinning with how much I wanted this, how hot I was to have him. I cradled his balls, loving their velvety skin and tucked-up tightness, my tongue sloshing wetly around his tip.

He clawed his fingers into my curls, gripping my head and using a touch of force to draw me onto him. His knob nudged at the back of my throat, making me edgy in case he went too far. But I loved the threat, loved the smell of him and the touch of his wiry hair, loved having my mouth full of his big virile cock.

Then I heard his voice above me, a slow, single, breath-light word, spoken as if it was steeped in decadent, wanton luxury: 'Slut.'

I swear, I thought my body was about to give way. It's such a dirty, debasing word and when he said it, it was as if he'd turned a key. Suddenly, I didn't need to be shy, cautious or anxious. He wanted me to revel in this, to be filthy and free, and that whispered word went straight to my cunt. I whimpered around his cock because I was done, I couldn't suck him any more. We needed to fuck.

I knelt up, breathless and frantic. 'Say it again,' I murmured. 'I didn't hear.'

His smile was slow and satisfied, and he gave me a long knowing look. He took one of my breasts in a wide pinch, sliding his grip down to pull on my nipple, twisting me to add a dart of pain.

He drew the word out, his voice soft and sibilant. 'Slut.'

I was gone. We both were. I lunged for him, my breasts crashing to his chest. We gasped and kissed, mouths on-target, off-target, hands moving in a flurry of stroking, squeezing and scratching. Jake fumbled with my zip, shoving down my skirt and underwear. Kicking off the last of our clothes, we half-crawled, half-fell towards the fire, Jake shifting equipment and dragging the brown-bear throw to spread over the hearthrug.

The fur slid against my skin, a caress like a billion and one filaments of silk. My hands were quivery but Jake's were calm, and he took a rubber from his discarded clothes, rolling it on while I lay there, thighs as wide as can be, all splayed and wet to him, thinking I couldn't wait another second. Then he grabbed an ankle, lifting one of my legs back, and pressed his cock at my entrance. I exhaled a long low groan as he drove in with wicked control, making me feel every sliding inch as he prised my wetness open. He held the deep stroke, keeping my leg high, and gazed down, that mass of gypsy curls framing his corrupted angel's face. 'Slut,' he breathed, and it sounded like adoration. 'Filthy little cockslut.'

Holding me in that half-rolled position, he began pounding deep and hard. I clutched the fur throw, my other leg hooked around his back as we slammed on and on, huffing and groaning. His curls bounced, his face grew red, his neck pulled taut with sinew and vein. We switched smoothly, Jake pulling me with him as he rolled onto his back. I sank down low, slathering him in juice as we ground to a new rhythm, slow and intense, our fuck so wet I thought my cunt was melting.

His precious word kept running though my head: slut. He placed a fist by our locked groins and, as I rode him, my clit knocked against his big, bony knuckles, urging me on. I became greedy and abandoned, bleating with nearness, our bodies a blur of fucking, our skin hot and sticky.

'I'm coming,' I gasped, right on the edge.

'Go on,' he said. 'Come on me. Come on my cock.'

I whimpered.

'Little slut,' he breathed. 'Come on me.'

And then, my God, was I ever doing. I cried out, clenching onto him, body racked, mind gone, convulsions shimmering until every last flutter of coming and every last grain of sense had ebbed away from me.

My arms were weak. I tipped forward onto my elbows, cheek on his chest, panting. He waited for me to recover, cock slowly pushing and stirring. I could hear his heart beating and I felt like he was the only person in the world.

It was dark in the room now, firelight gleaming on our skin, our surroundings fading into the shadows.

Jake's stronger than he looks: I'm not exactly a sylph but he moved me with such ease again, rolling me onto my back before I realised it was happening. He held himself high above me, cock buried deep, his pale athleticism sculpted by light and shadow. He gazed down, looking serious and lust-struck, inky curls stuck to his forehead.

'Come to bed,' he breathed, pushing deep. 'I want to fuck you.'

I raised my brows. 'I think you just did.'

With two long, deep thrusts, he replied, 'Again. And again.'

And that's what he did in his big sumptuous bed, again and again, our bodies humping in a tangle of bedclothes, our sweat glinting in the glow of a papery lamp. He dressed once to take the dogs out then came back, smelling of fresh air and the wily, windy moors, his skin cold enough to make me squeal. He brought a bottle of wine to bed, some bread, cheese, spiced meats and olives, and we ate, kissed and fucked some more.

At some point, we slept. I remember waking once in the middle of the night, wondering where I was: my place? yours? the attic? Ah, yes, Jake's bed.

Without streetlamps, it's so dark. I felt safe with Jake beside me, safer than I had done in the attic. I'd been unnerved by that room ever since I'd had that sense of a presence. But with Jake sprawled next to me, so physical and real, I was inclined to dismiss it as imagination. And that odd moment I'd had on the road? Those hazy times I'd felt myself slipping away? I didn't know. Maybe simple sleepiness, disorientation.

I didn't wake again till late. Jake was still asleep, twisted bedclothes and the brown-bear throw strewn across us. The room was shadowy, furniture of heavy wood veiled in the wintry dimness of morning, an iron-grey blade of light splitting the curtains, floorboards the colour of buttermilk.

Yes, I thought, I feel safe with Jake, protected from something I don't quite understand.

I trusted him. I thought he'd keep me from harm.

I think that was my biggest mistake. I should never have trusted him. Although I imagine, given the chance, I'd live it all over again.

6

Gran flat like death. Contains rabbit.

I set my phone down on the table, hoping to get a reply. I was in The Griffin, knowing Eddie was the landlord but not knowing quite why I was there. I was happy and sore, exhausted from Jake who'd gone into 'town', asking if I needed anything from the supermarket. I'd offered to help but 'No, it's fine,' he said. He had some errands to do anyway.

I was glad of another chance to explore alone and catch my breath. Everything was happening so quickly. It was crazy. I'd been there a week and I was practically shacked up with my new boss, asking if he could pick up Tampax and a banana smoothie from Tesco, agreeing to go halves on the food bill.

I really did need my own base. Earlier that day, I'd checked out a few postcards in the newsagent's window but, as I suspected, Heddlestone's not big on rental accommodation. Dog-walking services, cut log supplies, free manure, holiday lets in places I'd never heard of. I could have gone for a walk but the air was so cold it scorched my throat. I didn't want to rattle around the house alone, and a warm drink in the pub with the Sunday papers seemed like heaven.

A fire burned, and I sat among dark carved wood and crimson plush, drinking coffee and whisky. It's a small, cosy pub. Mid-week, it can feel oppressively local but at weekends you get a few people on country drives stopping in. The food's not up to much or you'd probably get more. I imagine it's deliberate. They don't take kindly to strangers here.

A couple of tables down from me sat an adulterous middle-aged couple, fingertips tangling across the beer-mats. I heard snatched references to work, to wishes they could get away. And once I heard the man, with sleazy bravado, say, 'I want to fuck your brains out, right here and now,' causing the woman to laugh delightedly.

Heddlestone's the sort of place where you can bring your secrets and lies, safe in the knowledge they'll stay here for ever, buried with all the others. The couple were so smitten with each other that I, reading the paper, was as good as invisible.

Eddie, however, had noticed me. He was bound to. I was a woman in a pub doing what men generally do, passing time alone, and that's still regarded as unusual no matter where you are. Every now and then, between chat and pulling pints, he glanced over. Twice, I caught his eye and both times I looked away, making nothing of the contact.

My phone bleeped, a text from Sally: *Glad u ok. Hack cold 2. Brave grl. O still angry. B strong. Spk soon. Hugs XXX*

O. You. Still angry. Well, of course you were and who could blame you. We'd spoken twice since my arrival, you raging down the phone, and I'd emailed briefly with some approximation of my reasons. I know they were feeble and unformulated, but I could barely explain it to myself. And I know, too, it was cruel of me to keep my whereabouts a secret but I was terrified you'd turn up.

Sometimes, when situations are muddled and grey, acting on black and white principles seems the only way out. I needed to get far away from you, from us, from confusion. I wanted to feel freedom again, to revel in change and let the wind whip my hair. I wanted to live and to taste that greener grass.

There are places other than Heddlestone I might have fled to, I know, but I felt I didn't have a choice. This pull, this draw. I don't know what it is, don't know how to explain it. After our holiday, it's almost as if I was besotted with the place, obsessed, wanting something that was here but not knowing what it was.

I thumbed a reply to Sally, keeping half an eye on Eddie. I kept searching for similarities between him and Jake but found none. Eddie was stocky and balding, jovial and bluff. Jake was tall and limber, his dark curls framing a finely boned face and, in contrast to Eddie's blokeishness, he had a mannered grace and quiet, dirty confidence.

Eddie confused me. Here, he seemed an amiable bloke at home in his pub but I could picture him in the clubhouse, all arrogance and disdain as he tormented the woman I suspected to be his wife. Ever since that night, some warped corner of me had been hungering for Eddie. I didn't like him. I didn't want to want him. But, like an alcoholic eyeing up the bottle, I couldn't stop glancing his way.

Phone u this eve? Cant talk now.

From the corner of my eye, I saw Eddie lift the flap of the wooden bar counter. When his arm flexed, it looked as if his bicep might burst out of its encircling tattoo. He started collecting glasses, sauntering in my direction. My heart quickened. He exchanged a couple of words with some people further down. I turned the pages of my newspaper, acting like a person reading.

'Cold enough for you?' he asked, picking up my coffee cup and saucer.

Full of nerves, I looked up at him. That was it. The eyes. Jake was there in those eyes almost as much as he was in his own: grey like the stone, the rainclouds and Heddlestone's bleak sunless dawns.

'Yes,' I said. 'It is a bit, isn't it?' I replied.

He smiled at me, open and pleasant. If I hadn't seen it for myself, I wouldn't have believed that merry glint could slide into a cruel disparaging leer.

I wondered what he saw in my face. Fear, perhaps.

He nodded towards the window. 'Probably too cold to snow now,' he said. 'Had it all yesterday.'

'Yes,' I replied. 'It looked lovely, so pretty.' He was moving away and, anxious not to lose him, I asked, 'Have you got the right time?'

He turned to the bar, reading the clock. 'Twenty to four. You're not local, are you? Not with that accent.'

I'd never thought of myself as having an accent. I'm from Kent. 'South,' I said. 'Kent. Well, originally. I'm, er, spending some time in the North now.'

'Holiday, is it? Come for the sunshine?'

I wasn't sure what to say. Considering how Jake had bundled me into the dressing-up box, I didn't want to reveal I was staying at the museum. Personally, I didn't mind Eddie knowing but it wasn't my house, he wasn't my brother.

'Sort of,' I said. 'Looking for somewhere to live, actually. Maybe round here.'

He laughed. 'What, in Heddlestone?'

'Maybe,' I said, feeling caught out. 'Just temporary.' Then, inspired by my newspaper, I said, 'It's a working holiday. I'm a journalist. Freelance. I'm doing a feature on...' The phrase that sprang to mind was inbred little villages but I managed to pull it out of the bag with, 'Um, rural economies.'

Even as I spoke the words, I regretted it. He'd find out who I was sooner or later although, knowing this place, he probably knew already.

He pursed his lips, suppressing a smile. 'Just you then, is it?'

'Yeah,' I said. 'My partner might join me later if –'

'Sort of place you after?' He set down his cluster of glasses, his broad fingers inside rims printed with lipstick and laced with beery foam.

I shrugged. 'Anything, really. A flat or a room in a house or –'

'We've got something,' he said. 'Above the pub. We live there, me and my wife, but there's a studio for the chef.

Empty if you're interested. Chef lives in Gimmerton so he drives over.'

'You're kidding?' I said, stupidly enthusiastic.

He grinned, a little smug. I wished I hadn't sounded quite so eager. I imagined a self-contained flat, Eddie as a distant landlord, my tenancy having no part to play in the Duxburys' sibling psychodrama.

'We just don't get on,' Jake had said when I'd asked about their relationship. 'There's no big story there. We tolerate each other and that's about the size of it.'

'Would you help if he needed you?' I had asked.

'Oh, ay,' he'd replied. 'Family's family.'

'You want to take a look?' asked Eddie.

'Well, yeah, I wouldn't mind.'

Even if the place was unsuitable, it'd be nice to know what was generally available. It gave me hope. Perhaps there were other rentals in Heddlestone.

'Give us twenty minutes,' he said. 'Couple of staff on their breaks but after that I can take you up. Unless you've plans.'

'No,' I said. 'No plans. Thanks. This is very good of you. I'm not putting you to any trouble, am –'

'No trouble,' he said, and the glasses clinked dully as he picked them up.

I stared at my paper, the words swimming meaninglessly in their columns. He'd spoken to me. He was going to take me upstairs to view an empty flat. We were going to be alone together, me and this crude boorish caveman. It excited me more than I liked to admit, a morbid excitement that echoed with all the fear and fascination I held for him. It baffled me too. Why, I wondered, is my desire is so dumb-brained and primitive? How come it wants to go grubbing around in the dirt, snuffling after some gorilla? Because it does, was my only answer. Because it does.

I'd thought about him that morning when I was with

Jake. I couldn't help it. The thought had come from nowhere. Jake's is a high, cast-iron bed and I was sprawled across it on my back, head hanging off the edge. Jake was standing by the bed, half-leaning over me, his cock in my mouth, a hand between my thighs. I was close to climax and an image came to me, a fantasy maybe, or even a wish: Eddie on the bed, naked, broad and tattooed, fucking me brutishly while his brother fucked my mouth.

He'd be sneering in that way that gets me hot, looking down at my tits, making them shake as he rammed me. I imagined him talking to Jake – you're right, she is a slut – and the thought had me hitting my limit. I came so hard, body arcing, gagging on Jake's cock, inner muscles clamping on his fingers . . .

'On the house,' a voice said.

I glanced up as a young lad from behind the bar placed a glass of whisky on my table, a double by the looks of it. The youth was away before I could respond but I clocked Eddie watching. He nodded and I mouthed my thanks, raising the glass in a muted toast, thinking of him fucking me.

I felt the whisky in my legs when, twenty minutes later, I walked up a flight of carpeted stairs beyond a door behind the bar area, Eddie leading. I'm just looking at a flat, I told myself. No big deal. I've no intention of moving in unless it's stupendous. We rounded the stairs onto an ordinary landing with four doors leading off. A tatty blue border of flowers ran around the walls at waist height. It reminded me of the blue stripe on hospital walls but chintzier.

At the top of the stairs was a huge poster-map of the world, stuck there with drawing pins. On another slice of wall was a framed photo of Yelena and a woman I took to be her mother, grinning in front of that mad gingerbread house in St Petersburg Square, both in fluffy hats. Elsewhere, postcards were fixed to the wall and the paper was stained with Blu-tack splodges. A heap of shoes, male and female, spilt out from under a phone table on which stood a basket of dried flowers, dusty and leached of colour. These people weren't houseproud, that's for sure.

''Scuse the mess,' said Eddie, kicking a shoe. 'We're going to decorate one day.'

I glanced past a door into a messy living room, again decked out like 90s suburbia. A window on the far wall gave onto a view of the village, a jumble of gaunt sloping streets, chimneys and that beautiful blue-tinged slate, all crisp with cold. The church spire jutted beyond black bare trees and the moors rolled away, faint lines and lilac humps sketched on the far horizon. The puppet museum was obscured by the churchyard but I was trying mentally to place it so I could get my bearings.

'You can't see it from here,' said Eddie. 'You have to go upstairs to our bedroom.'

I turned, confused, trying to look innocent. 'I'm sorry?' I said brightly.

'The museum. Where you're staying. You can't see it from here. We'd need to go upstairs.' He stood there, smirking like a bully. Fear made my neck feel strangely tight. 'Jake sent you, didn't he?' he said.

'No,' I said, reddening. 'I just came for a drink. And now I'd like to see the flat.'

He took a step towards me and I took a step back. He moved closer again.

He was broad-chested and muscular, and I'm short and dumpy but it hardly mattered. I was scared of him, irrespective of size, but I wasn't going to let it show. My heart was going pitter-patter, and I swallowed hard. 'You're invading my personal space,' I said in the most assertive voice I could muster.

I was backed against a section of wall between two door jambs and he placed his hands either side of me. He grinned down, cocky and gloating, his brawny arms inches from my head, his Celtic tattoo a blue-black chain of geometric links. He kept his body at a distance from mine and I could easily have ducked under his arms but this, I guessed, was a slower game of wits.

I had a bag over my shoulder. I let it fall then kept perfectly still, trying to block out the scent of his sweat, his masculine beeriness, and how grubbily excited I was to have him threatening me with his bulk. In front of me, that great block of a chest lifted gently with his breath, and I got to see the sprinkles of stubble on his jaw, the spidery blood vessels in his eyes, the hairs in his nostrils, the smallness of an ear lobe. With the sudden close focus of him after a couple of drinks, that's how his face seemed: not whole but a messed-up jigsaw of fragments, a pub-goer's Picasso.

'No,' he said coolly. 'You're invading *my* personal space.' I saw the crooked arrangement of his bottom teeth, and I pressed my head against the wall, not wanting him any closer and yet wishing he would try. I swallowed again, trying to get saliva into my dry mouth. Adrenalin sharpened my senses and I felt very sober, very alert.

'So what's the deal here?' he said without anger.

'I don't know what you mean,' I replied.

He looked at me, smiling faintly, and I had to turn away. 'What's your name, pretty lady,' he said. He knuckled a finger beneath my chin, tipping my head to make me face him.

I looked up, wondering what to tell him. His mocking tenderness intimidated me. I didn't trust him. And yet I thrilled to the set-up: me captive and meek, trapped by this smooth, smiling, unpredictable bully, the brother of the man I was falling for.

'Kate,' I replied thickly.

He nodded. 'Kate,' he repeated and, with gentle pressure, he trailed the knuckled finger down my neck, pressing lightly on my throat before resting it in the dip of my collar bones.

I felt weak at the knees so I closed my eyes, fighting my lust. I could feel sweat prickle under my arms, across the small of my back, and my eyelids felt thin enough for him to see through and peer into my brain. I could sense him looking and I could smell him, the pub on his clothes and the deodorant-tinged sweat. Closing my eyes probably wasn't a great idea. Instead of sight, I had a blank space in my head where imagination could thrive, knocking visual reality for six with its flood of dark possibilities.

'Tell me about Jake,' he said softly, and I heard his hand move to the wall again. 'Tell me what he does to you.'

I kept my eyes closed, thinking, Oh, God, what he does to me. Jake's lips, Jake's fingers, Jake's skinny little hipbones. Jake's tongue lapping between my thighs, the sweetest feeling swelling in my clit. His strong willowy frame, the way he walks across a room, his slim dexterous hands. Jake kissing me in the rain, water sliding down my eyelids. The flush in his cheeks when he gets hectic and aroused. The crackle-glaze of laughter lining the skin around his eyes. Oh Jake, fucking deep and moving inside me.

'Tell me,' cooed Eddie. My clit throbbed, as erect as any prick, and blood rushed in my ears. My face felt so hot. Did he want me? Or did he want me because Jake did? He'd ordered Yelena to make out she had the hots for Jake. Maybe Eddie got off on women who fancied his older brother. God, this village was weird.

'What do you two do together?' asked Eddie. 'Mmm? Does he let you play with his dollies?'

I opened my eyes and scowled.

He smiled down at me. 'Where did he find you, sweetheart?'

I turned aside, refusing to answer, and gazed at the hand by my head and his stout wrist.

'Tell Uncle Eddie,' he said. 'Go on. Talk to me, Kate. Did he get you on t'internet?'

'It's none of your business,' I murmured.

'Ah, so he did.'

'No,' I replied. 'How we met is nothing to do with you. I think I'd like to go now.'

'I'm just concerned for my brother,' said Eddie. 'He can be quite ... delicate.'

I glanced back. The playful arrogance had gone and he was looking serious.

'Don't fuck him about, Kate,' he warned. 'He bruises easily.'

'I've no intention –' I began, then stopped, realising that Jake and I were full-grown adults and I'd no need to justify myself to this brute. 'Leave us alone.'

He gave a mock-evil grin. 'Us,' he echoed. 'How nice.'

I didn't reply. I felt as surly and petulant as a teenager.

'So tell me,' he said again, the wheedling tone back in his voice. 'Does he fuck you nicely?'

'You're sick,' I muttered.

'I know.' He grinned in a rasp of mock-evil. 'That's what all the girls say.' He angled towards me, tattoo stretching as he did a few vertical press-ups against the wall. Again, I tried to escape, my head pushing back as if the wall might yield. 'Do you like it sick? Does Jake?'

'Why?' I asked. 'Do you get off on it?' As I spoke, I realised taking him on felt better than resistance. 'Do you? Does it turn you on to think of your brother fucking me?'

'Yes,' he said calmly. 'A lot.' He smiled, and traced two fingers over my lips, lingering there in an offering. So I parted my lips, not knowing if I would suck or bite. I licked and nibbled his fingertips, feeling the rough texture of labour in his skin. There was a malty, beery taste to them, and they were warm and thick, his fingernails smooth against the ridges of my teeth. My eyes were locked on his, staring into the steel grey shards of each iris, and I released his fingers briefly to say, 'He's always fucking me. We've hardly stopped since I got here.'

Eddie tried to keep his face impassive but I saw the faintest flutter in his nostrils as his breathing went a little wrong. 'How does he fuck you?' he asked. 'Hard and fast? Or good and slow? How do you like it, Kate?'

'I like it all ways,' I mumbled, and I made eyes at him as I drew his fingers deeper into my mouth, tongue lashing as I mock-fellated.

He stepped closer, body resting lightly against mine as he fed me more of his fingers. 'Do you like sucking cock?' he asked, and his body pressed harder.

The slab of his torso flattened my breasts, and his groin dug into my belly. I mumbled around his fingers and slowly he slid them out, awaiting my answer. 'Love it,' I breathed, and I gaped for his fingers again, sucking firmly when he returned them, tongue twirling, teeth scraping.

After a little more of this silliness, he said, 'Unzip me, Katie. Unbuckle my belt and unzip me.'

I wanted to so much it hurt. I didn't like him one iota. I'd had it in mind I might bite his fingers or laugh in his face if he tried taking it too far. And now he'd done precisely that, and I couldn't laugh because my fingers seemed to be on his belt, slowly undoing him, wondering whether I'd go through with this or pull back and scoff when he was exposed and vulnerable. His erection was pushing behind the denim and I cupped the bulge of him, reaching down to graze my nails over his balls where the fabric was faded and soft.

'Get my dick out,' he said, and seconds later I had his zip undone because I couldn't resist that instruction. He pushed jeans and underwear onto his hips, and his cock bounced out, thick and sturdy just as he was.

I melted, flesh turning to wet lust.

Jake's brother. Jake who I'd slept with the day before, first time; Jake who I could still feel all over me, mouths, fingers and cock, inside and out; Jake who'd knelt on my arms that morning, pumping in my mouth; who kissed me in the rain and might have been, at that moment, buying Tampax in the supermarket. It was obscene and so wrong, and yet Eddie's hard-on was angling up at me, flushed and lewd in that space of floral borders and sweet shabby homeliness.

He stepped back and I dropped to my knees. I shuffled closer, sex throbbing, juices slick. My mouth was open and I was about to swallow him when he put his hand on my forehead, stopping me.

'Manners, Katie,' he said. 'What happened to your manners?'

I pushed against his hand, eager to defy him and have him filling my cheeks, but his block was rigid.

'You don't get this for free,' he said, giving himself a little shake. 'I want you to ask. I want to know how much you want this dick.' He stepped back, fingers curled around his shaft, shunting with a slow tease.

I didn't move.

'Get up,' he said, and I did, not because he'd ordered me to but because I was angry and embarrassed, and I no longer wanted to be kneeling for cock.

He eased himself back into his jeans. 'Think about it,' he said, zipping up. 'Think about how much you want it and come tell me tomorrow.' His belt clinked, and he was all tucked away.

I left without another word. I had to walk through the pub to collect my coat and I imagined everyone knew my shame. I was furious: furious with him but more than that, furious with myself. I could see he was a nasty piece of work, a man to steer clear of. But I couldn't help the way I felt, and his cruelty had me wanting him all the more. Why? Because it did, and I couldn't reason with my groin.

Everyone's scared of the dark. You can pretend you're not; you can pretend you're an adult beyond such nonsense. But when you're alone at night, darkness is mortality, you're six years old and the wardrobe is a monster. Nothing can save you. Even love, the person lying next to you, can't help. Love can hold you tight and stroke your hair and make it seem OK but the darkness is still there, waiting for the next time.

Up here, I am very scared of the dark. And sometimes I'm scared of Jake holding me. But that night, later in the week, I was alone again. So much had happened since I'd last slept in the attic. Forget the granny flat; I'd virtually moved into Jake's bed. We put work on hold and hardly stopped fucking, both of us permanently horny, eager to explore and immerse ourselves in sex-charged, dreamlike days.

He had a way of picking up on stuff, intuiting what I wanted, even when I didn't know myself. I loved his instructions – lift up your skirt, show me your neck, suck my cock, make yourself come – and I loved them most when they were unexpected.

In the office one afternoon, when we finally made it into the annexe, he walked in from the workshop, dust-mask pushed up on his forehead. 'Bend over,' he said, and I did, over the desk. He pulled my knickers down, slipped the mask over my nose and mouth and fucked me. I gripped the desk, panting into the hot, humid mask, feeling I was breathing air that belonged to him.

In those early days, he was such a greedy man. And I was such a greedy woman. Sometimes, it seemed all we wanted of each other was more. But after a while, we needed a break. My flat-hunting was on hold. 'Stay here,' said Jake. 'If we find it's not working, we'll fix something else up. There's not much in Heddlestone, to be honest. I should've checked the Heskeths' flat. Sorry. I'd forgotten how bad it was.'

So I unpacked properly, asked Sally to send more of my stuff on, and stuck a few pieces about the attic, a couple of art postcards, trinkets, no photographs.

I was tired that night and went to bed in the attic. As I drifted off, my dream-fuzzed mind returned to the weird sense I'd had earlier of a presence outside my door. For a moment, I thought it was happening again then I realised it was just a memory returning as my brain sifted through recent events.

I had a twinge of apprehension, wondering if the sensation would return but it seemed unlikely. I was much more relaxed, a far cry from the tense, troubled woman who'd stumbled off the London train. All the same, the memory made me switch the light on, get up and turn the key. I've locked the door, I told myself, not to keep anyone out because there's no one here except Jake, and he's cool. I've locked it to give me peace of mind should I wake in a paranoid sweat at some godless hour. That, at any rate, was my rationale when I berated myself for being a superstitious ninny.

Eddie was in my thoughts before sleep overtook me but he wasn't in the dream I remember. You only remember dreams when you wake in the middle of them and when I was woken, I was swimming in the sea off a white-sand beach and a turtle was in the water.

And then I was wide awake in the pitch-black attic. I was perfectly still, brain on red-alert. Someone was sitting on my bed.

There was a pressure on the mattress edge. The only part of my body that moved was my eyes, looking left and right, straining to adjust. Nothing. Had he come in? Outside, the countryside was black and inside it was much the same. My heart rate was high, skin hot with a rush of sweat.

For God's sake, Kate, there's no one there, said one voice. It's just imagination.

Pretend to be asleep, said my other voice. Keep still and they'll go away.

I closed my eyes. I tried to breathe deeply like a person sleeping. I'd locked the door. There couldn't possibly be anyone here. Maybe Jake had a key. But I'd left mine in the door. No use. Couldn't be him. All I had to do was stretch my legs in the direction where I'd felt them sitting down and I'd know.

All I had to do . . .

All I had to do . . .

I was so hot. My armpits were wet, my skin damp against the bedsheets. I remembered being a child, terrified of what lurked at the bottom of the bed. Sometimes it was witches, sometimes tigers, never anything else. Back then, I was a kid whose feet didn't reach to the bottom. I was scared of the unknown. To defeat the fear, I'd sometimes thrust out my legs, relieved to find cool cotton not sharp teeth. At other times, I'd lie there, knees tucked tight, praying the witches and tigers wouldn't attack.

Move your legs, Kate. Kick at the place where they are. Or it is. Or he. She.

But I couldn't. I was paralysed, skin tingling as sweat began to cool. Then turn on the light. For God's sake, just do it. Now. Now.

Every time I said the word 'now' to myself, I failed. I'll do it on the next 'now', I thought but it was over in a heartbeat, another chance missed.

Now.

Now.

I lay there, immobile, blood pounding in my ears as I thought through my options. I would reach for the bedside lamp and simultaneously kick. Easy, all so easy. I would remove my hand from under the covers. I would put it into the dark room and I would reach for the switch, quiet as a mouse. And yet even as I imagined my hand reaching for the lamp, I imagined the clammy touch of another fastening on my wrist.

Now!

I gasped, thrashed and flailed for the light. 'Go away!' I cried. 'Go away!'

The room burst into brightness, a white slanted box packed with colour, shapes, depth and furniture. I glared at my bed, at the place where I'd felt the pressure, and there was nothing there. Absolutely nothing.

I couldn't believe it. I still had such a strong sense of a presence, of something being there, and I didn't trust my eyes. I backed away towards the bedhead. 'Fuck off,' I wailed, reaching for a pillow. I swung it at the air, back and forth, trying to keep focused on the place where the nothingness was. I banged at the mattress, swung the pillow past my shoulder, this way and that, hardly knowing what I was doing. I heard a voice sobbing, 'go away, go away' and saw wild curls of dark-blonde hair whip across my vision, the pillow slamming blocks of burgundy in front of me.

And then there was an almighty great crash and I was thrown into darkness again. I was no longer holding the pillow. I wiped my face and found it wet with tears. I was gasping for breath. I'd knocked off the table lamp.

Something had stopped. I'd stopped. It was OK.

I pushed back the covers and put my feet on the floor. The floor was wet. Would I have woken Jake? I found the lamp and righted it, switching it on. I'd knocked my water over. Excellent. Well done, Kate.

I was shaking and panting.

My bedside clock said 02.53.

It was a long time till dawn.

I made a cup of tea, got back under the covers and sat there. I didn't dare turn off the light. What was it about this place? What lurked here? Who else had slept in the attic?

I didn't dare lie down either. I felt too vulnerable, my head too low in the room. Instead, I just sat propped up against pillows, my duvet and blanket pulled high. I felt sure I wouldn't get any more sleep that night, or if I did it would be accidental.

I would be like Jake's paint-poisoned friend, Toxic Tony, sitting up asleep to avoid bad dreams, a puppet with snipped strings or a doll that gently breathes.

7

Jake tapped on the door. 'Can I come in?' he asked.

Sex! I thought. Sex, great! I was tired, having slept only fitfully, but his voice roused me in an instant. I was wearing a thin dressing gown, printed with little flowers, and I reckoned it would be off in no time.

'Sure,' I said, forgetting that the door was locked. Jake rattled at the door knob. 'Ah, hang on.'

I must have looked sheepish and Jake simply raised his brows.

'I like locked doors,' I said. 'Makes me feel secure.'

Unlike me he was set up for the day, dressed in black jeans and a charcoal-grey jumper that looked soft and expensive, despite having an unravelling cuff. In the space of one stressful, spooky night, I'd forgotten quite how stunning he was, dark curls spiralling around his face, those two moles printed on a cheekbone. The room was smudged with wintry light, above us the Velux windows showing oblongs of scudding cloud, my bedside lamp a small golden haze. Jake's skin looked creamily pale and he walked into the room, unashamedly shifty, turning to conceal something behind his back.

'I want to ask a favour,' he said, smiling coyly. I followed him and we made a brief play of circling each other as I tried to peer at what he was hiding. His eyes were chipped with silver, the skin etched with tiny lines. He had that gauche, hovering quality I'd seen at the train station, as if he were nervous of me yet determined to push past that. His social awkwardness, I'd come to realise, belied a fundamental self-assurance. It made me flush with lust. He was clearly up to no good.

'Go on then, ask,' I said.

He showed me what he was carrying: a length of thin coarse rope, looped several times around itself. He held it across his open palms, as if he were offering me not just the rope but some aspect of himself, something fragile and difficult. He stood there, looking hopeful, dirty and devious.

I smiled, taken aback because it had only just turned eight in the morning. Did he want to tie me up or did he want me to do the honours? I could see him watching to gauge my reaction, and his shyness was adorable. I pictured him spread-eagled on a bed, limbs roped to the corners, a sinewy star with a hard-on.

'What?' I teased. 'Did a sheep get stuck? Do I need to get dressed?'

And then, somewhat at odds with his boyish timidity, he took the end of the rope and, slow and menacing, wrapped it once around his fist. 'I want to tie you up,' he said, knuckles bone-white above the cord.

My groin flared and I tingled all over. I'd dabbled before – scarves and ties with certain boyfriends – but this looked major-league. He had a lot of rope there.

'Mmmm, kinky,' I replied, nervous but still game.

'Do you need the bathroom?' he asked. 'Because if you do, I suggest you go now.'

I took a quick pee, excited and edgy. I trusted Jake which, considering the short time I'd known him, could be viewed as a trifle incautious.

There was a ladder-back chair by the dressing table. Jake swung it into an open space, hooked the rope on the chair back, and beckoned me to him. I strolled over, feeling slinky in my pretty gown and glad, now, that my towelling bathrobe had been too bulky for my luggage. Jake kept the house warm for the dogs who, not having an ounce of fat on them, easily felt the cold. All the same, he plugged in the electric fan heater before freeing the ribboned belt around my waist. He opened my gown and eyed my flesh with cool scrutiny. Under his gaze, my nipples stiffened and heat crawled up my chest to my face. He released the gown without touching me.

'Sit down,' he said, and I did. He arranged the gown so I was mainly exposed, a broad stripe of folded, podgy nudity, with the garment a flimsy thing around my shoulders and arms. Then he took the rope from the chair back, shaking it out to its full length. It was several metres long and I guessed it to be hemp. I felt afraid when he looped the middle of it behind my neck. Carefully, he lifted my hair over it, allowing the two halves of rope to hang down the front of my body.

'What are you doing?' I asked.

'It's OK,' he said in a comforting voice.

I peered down at his hands as they tied some fancy knot just above my cleavage, pulling on enormous lengths of rope, friction rushing. With the knot complete, he left the rope hanging around my neck like a slack noose. Then he tied another knot a few inches further down, whisking the cord through itself, and then another until the rope dangled down the centre of my body, four knots and three loops.

'Leg,' he said. He lifted my right leg and slipped the rope beneath my thigh. 'And again,' he said, repeating the action on the left. He moved behind the chair, pulling the cords backwards until they lay beneath my arse, rucking up my dressing gown. He nudged my knees apart and reached between my legs, fingers tickling the fronds of my pubes as he arranged the ropes around my vulva. His touch was detached and meticulous rather than sexual but that didn't stop my juices stirring. The cord pressed either side of my lips, resting on the thin bones connecting thigh to pubis.

'Lean forwards,' he said, and I obliged, allowing him to pass both lengths of rope up by my spine then through the loose loop around my neck. The dressing gown prevented the ropes from pressing into the crack of my buttocks but that was their general position, lodged between my legs. Through the noose, the ropes then came down beneath my armpits and around to the front of me. This was some serious turkey-trussing, although I wasn't sure of the point. I could hear Jake's breath streaming in and out of his mouth, not quite heavy breathing but thicker and fluffier than usual. I sat quiet and still, moving only when he requested it, my hips becoming heavy with a need to fuck.

He threaded both rope ends through one of the loops between my breasts, lashed them back through the ropes down my spine and around again to another front loop. He worked with steady efficiency, and not once did he look me in the eye. His curls partially hid his face but I could see two patches of red on his cheeks as he focused on his task, threading, pulling and checking with a suppressed feverishness. A couple of times, he stepped back to inspect his handiwork, a glint of wildness in his eyes, his arousal making a mighty fine hump in his jeans.

To see him getting quietly steamed up turned me on hugely. But I still couldn't fathom the aim. My hands were free and I wasn't bound to the chair in any way. Several minutes later, the picture was growing clearer. Ropes lay across my stomach, above my breasts and below, dividing the upper half of my body into diamond-shaped segments, plump flesh spilling over coarse twine. And there was still plenty of length to play with.

'I'm going to tie you to the chair now,' said Jake, still struggling to meet my gaze. He pushed my knees wide, took an ankle and tethered it to the back leg of the chair. He did the same on the other side, strapping me so I was split wide open, knees, thighs and cunt, the latter all moisture. Finally, he clasped my hands behind the chair and bound my wrists with the rope that travelled up from my ankles. Hog-tied, I think the phrase is. And then some.

I could see the lift of his shoulders as he looked at me. I felt so explicitly open, arms pinned back, legs akimbo, breasts thrusting through their roped cells, scrunched up dressing gown poking out in tufts of flowery femininity.

'Japanese bondage,' said Jake. 'My version of. You're meant to feel still and serene. Do you?'

'Not exactly, no.'

'Good. Can you move?'

I knew he meant 'try'. I wriggled against my bondage, wondering about the dressing gown. Wouldn't this have been more effective naked? But then I realised some rudimentary clothing probably made it look as if I'd been taken against my will, a woman kidnapped or surprised by an intruder.

I began to feel a little creeped out. I tried to laugh, thinking, Now what? Jake didn't return the laugh. Instead, he made a couple of minor adjustments then stepped back again, apparently fascinated by what he saw.

'Try again,' he murmured, and, with a few grunts, I wriggled harder, partly because I could see he liked it and that made me like it too. And also because I genuinely did want to know how stuck I was. Pretty damn stuck, by the feel of things. I was powerless and vulnerable and while that got me hot, it worried me too. Jake was running the show, and I didn't know what the show was. Perhaps I should have asked before agreeing.

Too late, I guess.

After a while, he looked at my face and said, 'I've got a favour to ask.'

'What?' I said.

'I'll ask you later,' he said. 'But for now, I want you to stay like that and think about saying "yes".'

' "Yes" to what?'

'The favour.'

'But what?' I said. 'What favour?'

'I'll tell you later,' he said. 'For now, just think about saying "yes".'

Then he cast his eye over my parcelled-up body, clearly pleased at all the strange bulges he'd tied into my ample flesh. I made a little struggle, half-frustration, half for kicks. Jake shook his head and in a quiet, clenched voice said, 'Ah fuck, you look good.'

And then he switched off the radio and left the room.

'Hey!' I called. 'Jake! Don't go. Oi, come back!' I kicked against the ropes, futile but instinctive. I wanted to follow him but I couldn't even put my feet down. My ankles were strapped, my soles facing the walls. The chair and I were one. 'Jake!' I cried. But I had to sit there, jerking and squirming, making the ropes cut into me, as I listened to him pad down the stairs.

I struggled, calling after him even when he was long gone. The sod. He could have at least left the radio on.

The attic now was very, very empty. Quiet too. The weather was calmer than it had been. The electric heater whirred steadily, pumping out hot stuffy air that smelt of scorched dust. Intermittent bursts of wind whistled through one of the little ground-level windows. The radiators wheezed and groaned. In the en suite, the washbasin tap dripped occasionally.

Between my legs, I was soft and moist. If only he'd touched me, just a few easy rubs, some kisses or a couple of licks, anything to take the edge off my appetite. I strained to hear him but there was nothing. He'd left the door to the room open. The stairs led down to the floor where his bedroom was, the bathroom, his two puppet storage rooms and his defunct darkroom. He could be anywhere in the house, maybe having coffee in the kitchen or chiselling wood in the workshop. Heck, for all I knew, he might not even be inside. It could just be me, trussed up in an attic in an old orphanage on the Yorkshire moors, no one to hear me scream.

After a time, my lust began to fade. The dripping tap got annoying. I counted the interval between each drip and discovered it was irregular. I couldn't remember if Chinese water torture was based on regular or irregular drips. Perhaps it didn't matter. Perhaps it was the agony of water landing repeatedly on the victim's forehead, wearing away skull like stone. That, and the agony of waiting.

I began to feel weird. Every now and again, I wriggled against the ropes to remind me of my flesh, of the existence of my body. On the carpet were the prints of my feet, wet from my shower. My immobility transformed them into something luxurious and unattainable. Earlier, I'd walked around without giving a thought to it, an action so normal it was unnoticeable. I gazed at those footprints as if they belonged to another self, to a naive version of me who'd no idea what was in store for her. Through the open door of the bathroom, I could see the shower screen dappled with water, a blur of chrome behind it. I thought of Anthony Perkins in *Psycho* and in my head, the knife music played, wah-wah-wah.

Oh, Kate, stop tormenting yourself.

I said my name aloud. 'Kate. Kate Carter.'

At length, objects around me grew strange. I felt I was slipping away, becoming dreamy, almost disappearing into the physicality of my surroundings. I thought the strange feeling was starting again. I looked down at my body. My spread legs were slightly mottled, my pubes a springy fuzz with a few rogue hairs scattered on my thighs. I made a mental note to pluck them later. The urge to do so made my hands feel more bound than ever. My breasts, framed by the rope, looked peculiar, separated from the natural flow of my body. I began to feel disconnected and it occurred to me my flesh had been compartmentalised, reminiscent of a butcher's counter, of meat portioned into sections, beef tied up with string. Jesus, was that the point? To demean me in some way? Reduce me so I was less like Kate, and more like assembled pieces of meat.

Oh, dear God, I was an idiot.

Was I? Was I really incredibly stupid? Had I just allowed myself to be tied up by a man who had issues about women? I hadn't known him two minutes. It's the kind of idiot behaviour that, if you heard about someone else doing it, you'd smite your forehead and say, 'What was she thinking?'

I tugged against my ropes, a sob catching on my breath. I'd get a couple of inches in a newspaper, no more, because I was one of those oddballs into fringe sex, not a normal member of society, not a girl-next-door type the public could relate to.

But no.

This was just a bit of harmless fun, of course it was. I was fretting and overanalysing. If Jake had issues, it would have been apparent by now. The room swam and I squeezed back tears. Just a bit of fun. Yup, having an absolute blast here.

I tipped back my head, not wanting the tears to roll, then turned aside to focus on a different part of the room. There was my bed, rumpled and cruelly inviting. And there was a burgundy pillow strewn across the duvet, the pillow I'd used to try to beat up a ghost. How silly that seemed now, and yet even as the thought came to me, another thought followed: actually, not that silly because it had felt so real. Someone or something had sat on my bed. I'd felt it. I'd woken up with the sense of someone sitting down. And I'd gotten a tad hysterical, hadn't I?

I could see the patch on the carpet where I'd knocked the water over. I would be sensible and fill a bottle next time.

No one had sat on my bed. Of course they hadn't. It was probably just a spring releasing itself, an old mattress that hadn't been slept on for a while. I wondered who else had slept there, what kind of dreams they'd had. I wondered if they'd ever imagined someone else skulking outside or sitting on the bed. Perhaps they were saner folk, more used to rural isolation than I was.

I stared at the back of the open door. It looked like a murky, upright lake, its thick avocado gloss reflecting a liquidy patch of light. The Bakelite knob was solid and reassuring and I remembered gazing at it in fear, convinced it was going to turn of its own accord. I wondered if the dogs ever came this far up the house. They hadn't done yet. I hoped they didn't choose this moment to come sniffing around. Was Jake aware of me? Would he hear if I cried out?

The tap dripped, the heater whirred, the wind occasionally whistled. My feet were starting to get cold, and I wiggled my toes, wishing I could wiggle the whole of each foot or even put on a pair of socks. I wondered what time it was and whether, if Jake left me here all day, I'd get paid for it. I was, after all, due in work soon. Was I en route to being his whore? When he'd fucked me over the desk in work hours, was that immoral earnings?

And then I heard something beyond the door, a noise at the foot of the stairs. 'Jake?' I called.

No reply.

Most of the house is bare boards but the attic and stairs leading to it are carpeted.

Another noise.

'Jake, is that you?'

For a moment I thought it must be one of the dogs but no. That was the noise of firmer footsteps coming nearer.

'Jake!' I writhed against my bondage, uselessly and stupidly, the rope cutting where it rubbed.

I tried to laugh but it didn't feel that funny. There's going to be no one there, I thought. And yet, oh, Jesus, there will be. Like last night. I'm going to feel it again, that invisible presence. Sweat broke on my skin. I was going to feel it come into the room and there'd be nothing there. 'Jake!' I called 'Stop it! Speak to me!'

I would feel it on my skin, on the splayed dampness between my legs. I would feel it, as real as any touch, and I'd be rocking my chair, screaming for Jake as I tried to back away from the nothing that caressed me with cold, deathly hands.

The door moved.

'What's the matter?'

Jake.

It was Jake.

He came into the room, smiling wryly. His jeans looked fit to burst open with the strain of his erection.

'Why didn't you speak?' I snapped.

'Hey, it's OK,' he whispered, calm and comforting. I squirmed angrily, catching my breath. He walked over and pressed his fingers to my clitoris. 'It's OK,' he said. 'Ssshh, it's OK.'

He placed one hand on the chair-back, leaning over me, fingertips rolling the bead of my clit. 'Sshhh.'

'You sod,' I gasped. 'Why didn't you speak?'

'Shhhh,' he murmured. 'All OK.'

His touch was perfection, bringing me right down. I relaxed, my sobs easing. Within seconds my clit seemed to double in size as if all my terror had been transformed into lust. 'All OK,' Jake repeated, and my noises of panic faded to moans of pleasure. He ran a couple of fingers along my slippery crease then hooked them inside me, finding moisture.

'You're so wet,' he said. 'I knew you would be. You like this, don't you?'

At that moment, I liked it more than anything in the world. His fingers pressed on my wall, nudging my flesh in intense little rhythms while his thumb flicked. I felt so safe with him. It was too much for me even to speak. I mumbled incoherently as he masturbated me, nice and steady, building me to my peak.

'Have you thought about saying "yes"?' he asked.

'Huh?'

'To my favour?'

I hadn't given it a second thought.

'Have you?'

He obviously wanted words. 'No,' I mumbled. 'What is it?'

'If you say "yes" I'll tell you.'

'Tell me first,' I said. 'Tell me.'

'I can't yet,' he said. 'I want you agree to it first.'

He shifted his fingers a fraction, thumb on my sweet spot, upping the tempo and making me pant with nearness. Waves shivered along my legs, rising from ankles to thighs, lapping closer every time. 'Yes, OK,' I moaned. 'Yes.'

'I don't believe you,' he said. 'You'll go back on your word.'

My thoughts exactly.

'When you say yes, I want you to mean it,' he went on. 'Your tits look nice like that, all roped off.'

He withdrew his fingers then cupped the weights of my bound, jutting breasts.

'Jake, please,' I said. 'Don't torment me.'

'Wriggle,' he said, and I did as I was told.

I heard a noise snag in his throat and then he was backing away from me, unfastening his jeans. He freed his cock and it sprang out from his dark bush, glorious and potent, his tip so fat and ruddy.

'Oh,' I said, wanting it.

He gripped himself and began shuffling his fist, bright eyes pinned on my tied body. 'Fuck, I like you like this,' he said.

God, but I liked him too, loved that he was hot for me, standing there with his jeans around his thighs. He pumped hard and fast, head bowed, shoulders hunching as his hand became a blur. His face was loose and red, his thick brown curls shuddering as he wanked. I struggled and whimpered, knowing it turned him on to see my flesh shake. I was resentful too, jealous of his freedom to beat off.

'Uh, uh,' he grunted, and the sound of his pleasure was so acutely arousing I wondered if I might come simply from watching him.

'Uh,' he said, getting closer now, and he hobbled nearer,

awkward in lowered jeans. I protested, squirming extra forcefully and, with a hoarse cry and a twist of his face, he came, jetting hard across my stomach and thighs. His semen striped my skin in an echo of the ropes, leaving me criss-crossed and wet, dripping with his liquid and damp with my own.

He gazed at the sight, shoulders heaving as he caught his breath. Oh, but he was beautiful, gawping at me with his lips parted, the colour high in his face.

'Please,' I managed. 'I want to come too. So badly.' I leant out to him, the chair-back digging into the underside of my arms. 'Please.' I was excruciatingly close, I knew I'd be there in seconds. He could probably have blown on my clit and he'd have tipped me over the edge.

Jake looked at me as if I were an alien. Then he buttoned his flies. 'Back in a while,' he said and he walked out of the room.

'Jake!' I cried. 'Jake.' And then I wailed, 'Please don't go!'

My words hung in the silence: Please don't go.

I hate to beg. Through gritted teeth, I added, 'You bastard!' But as his footsteps retreated, I went back to begging. 'Please! Jake, please!'

He won't be long, I told myself. Don't get worked up. It's only sexual tension. It'll pass.

Oh, but when will it pass?

He was gone for around fifteen minutes and it felt like days. In his absence, I invested quite a lot in him, emotionally, psychologically and sexually. Every single thought was of him, memories of what he'd done to me, fantasies of what he might do next. In that storm of mad, perverted, obsessive desire, I had one heartstopping moment of awful detachment. I thought: I am a puppet. I am controlled by string. My body is in sections like the puppet-limbs he carves, all impotent and separate before he pieces them together, bringing them to life.

I promised myself I would find somewhere to live

within a week. I would ask around in the village. I would get away from Jake, regain some self-sufficiency and control.

And then I was back obsessing about him, his fingers, tongue and prick. Like hell I would leave. What was the favour? Something so kinky I needed to be tortured into agreeing? Or another thing entirely? Regular washing-up? I imagined a range of twisted scenarios he might want me to engage in, most involving me being tied to his bedframe, and by the time he returned I was nearly hallucinating with the need to come.

'Hey,' he said, rounding the door.

Astonishingly, he was aroused again, cheeks aflame, eyes all excitement. I wriggled for him, pushing my hips forward as best I could. 'Jake,' I breathed. It sounded like worship so I added, 'I really want to fuck you. This is driving me nuts.'

He gave a broad, satisfied smile. He stood there a few seconds as if savouring the moment or debating what to do. Then his smile fell away and he dropped to his knees, pressing his face deep into my thighs. He licked my folds, a flighty touch growing hotter and wetter till I felt immersed, a whirlpool of saliva and milkiness. His cheeks were warm against my thighs and I gazed at his mop of hair, wanting to grasp those wild corkscrews and hold him tight. His tongue tip spun around my clit, big light circles narrowing down to an intense focus, rocking just where I wanted him.

He drew away. 'What's your answer?'

I shook my head, fearing he might accuse me of not meaning it if I said 'yes'. I guessed my reward for saying yes would be my orgasm. And an easy, insincere 'yes' might threaten that.

'Give me a clue,' I said, thrusting my hips out again. 'And touch me.'

'No clues,' he said, and with a single finger he fretted my clit, driving me to distraction. Then he stopped and leant in to close his mouth over a nipple, his tongue twirling as his lips gently sucked. He swapped from one breast to the other, making me moan, and every now and then he would touch my clit or curl fingers in my hole. Pre-orgasmic stars kept rising in my brain but he wouldn't let them burst into fireworks.

Again and again, he took me to the edge. 'Please,' I begged.

'Tell me when you mean it,' he said. 'Say "yes" and if I believe you, I'll tell you the favour.'

I fought and fought against the word. It had to be good. When I said it, it had to be the truest 'yes' I've ever spoken because I had to climax. I was close to madness with need, tormented by the prospect of him leaving again.

Yes, I'll do it, I thought. Whatever it is, I'll do it, I'll do it.

Keep quiet, I thought. Hush. Don't tell him.

'I think you're going to come,' said Jake.

I love his flat Yorkshire vowels. 'Come' and 'slut' and 'succumb' are such rich words in his mouth. His touch was exquisite, so exact I knew I was gone. I was loose and whimpering, flesh straining against my web of ropes as he played with the split of my body. He tilted his head, his eyes a silver-grey sparkle, like a fish darting in crystal waters. He smiled, and his look said, I can do whatever I want with you.

'Yes?' he said, and before I replied, he knelt up to smother my mouth in a humid kiss. My orgasm swelled and I sobbed into his breath, tasting his saliva. He drew back a fraction and, with those sly, precise fingers, he kept me on the cusp. It felt like a long musical note of perfect pitch. I was strung out, adrift, terrified he might leave.

'Will you?' he asked.

'Yes,' I gasped. 'Yes. Anything. Please.'

And he released me, lifting me to my climax and I was tumbling fast and hard, coming over and over as every-thing around me dissolved. The walls went, the house too, and I was beyond the moors, lost in time and space, synapses firing, galaxies scattering, ego and sanity obliterated.

And through my ecstasy came the hard, dead cut of Jake's words: 'Fuck my brother.'

And my orgasm kept right on tumbling.

'Yes,' I said. 'Yes.' And I was freefalling in bliss, and right at that moment I wanted to fuck his brother more than anything in the world.

8

The puppet museum really creeps me out. It's worse now it's closed for the season and just knowing no one's visited, and won't do for some time, disturbs me. This house is so still. The dogs whimper in their throats and the fire crackles. Sometimes, I think if I listen hard enough I'll be able to hear the moon waxing and waning. We live in a world apart, and the museum is shut. But the puppets are still there, still smiling, frozen and unblinking, waiting for life. It's as if Jake and I have got this weird, inanimate family shut away in the annexe.

There are even more of them in the two spare rooms upstairs, a crush of heads, limbs and strings waiting to come out of storage. Jake's locked one of those rooms now. I'm supposed to be compiling an inventory of all his dolls but he's decided only one room needs doing. Apparently, I'm too nosy to be trusted.

Of course, I refused Jake's request to fuck Eddie. But prior to that, we had to have a 'talk'.

'Do you want this to be an open relationship?' I asked. 'Because personally, I prefer exclusivity.'

'That's cool. Me too,' he said. 'I'm not going to mess you about. I'm not seeing anyone else. Don't intend to. Christ, have you seen the people who live here? But Eddie's different. He's my brother, and I'd love you to –'

'No, I can't,' I said. 'I won't. I don't want to.'

'But I think you do. And anyway, you promised.'

'You conned me,' I said. 'I was so horny I was practically drugged. So I'm reneging, end of story.'

He didn't speak to me for a whole day. Can you believe that? I'm not playing this game, I thought. I'm not being manipulated by an overgrown child. But Jake's will is stronger than mine and after what seemed an eternity of stalemate, I said, 'Well, maybe I'll give it a go at some point. But not yet, OK?'

I think he was itching to talk because he accepted that and didn't pursue it further. I was unsettled by this new side he'd revealed. It was disturbing enough that he wanted me to sleep with his brother, but seeing him act like a petulant teen took the edge off my infatuation. But only briefly. When you're half in love, you're so eager to forgive you may as well have had your sanity removed.

For several days we were back on track, happy and horny in our own little world. Then it started to turn dark when Jake sent me to the puppet museum as part of my – can I say this? – my punishment. It embarrasses me to think I'll even accept his punishment. But I did, I do. I will.

'What the fuck do you think you're doing?' he said, standing at the door. His voice was ice. It terrified me. I felt like someone had grabbed my heart and upturned it like an egg timer. I really was caught out.

He must have moved as quiet as a mouse, and now I wonder how often he's done that: tiptoed to a door to spy on me and then retreated without my knowledge. He must be good at it, padding around in thick socks, avoiding all the creaky boards.

I was in that absurd, out-of-control living room, and I'd been watching the dinky, curtained TV set, surrounded by all the lurching madness of puppets, plants, train set, dark medieval art, a piano no one played and a dusty chandelier. Hanging from the stag antlers was Jake's Indiana Jones hat, the one he'd worn to collect me from the station. He told me once about abnormalities in antlers, how the growth of them is controlled by testosterone and how injuries cause deformities. A deer wounded in its right leg might develop a warped left antler, throwing the beauty of the other into freakish asymmetry. His head is full of fascinating trivia like this.

The vintage doll – Meredith, Laura or whatever her name is – was sat on the wicker trunk, staring at nothing, painted bootees poking out from under a froth of petti-coats. It has such an ugly face, small red mouth baring four tiny teeth, and a frizz of blonde nylon hair. Or perhaps it's just strange to see an adult doll face when we're used to seeing big-eyed baby faces. No. It's definitely ugly. I don't like that doll.

I hadn't forgotten Eddie telling Yelena it had a 'cloth cunt'. At first I'd thought little of it: he's just teasing her. But then I started to get curious because I remembered Jake saying the doll was a good luck charm. The TV was dull and I'd thought, Well, I wonder.

Jake was in the kitchen, listening to the radio. At least, I thought he was. Quick peek. There might be some truth in it. It could be a piece of rare Victorian erotica or an unusual medical object. I felt silly as I crept to the doll. Its body is rag, and its creamy-pale porcelain head and limbs are attached by strong thread. I held its feet so they wouldn't clack and rummaged under the tiered lace. The doll was wearing knickerbockers trimmed in satin ribbon and fastened with a tiny cloth-covered button. Imagine, I thought, someone actually sewed that button on. Atten-tion to detail pleases me, especially in areas you could get away with skimping.

I rubbed its soft crotch but couldn't be certain so began removing the bloomers, feeling silly and naughty. When the doll's mid-section was bared, I could see its crotch was no more than stuffed legs joining a torso, bland and smooth. Slightly disappointed, I was mainly thinking how foolish I was when Jake spoke.

'What the fuck do you think you're doing?'

I tried to make out I was just interested in the doll, curious about its layers of clothing.

'Is it valuable?' I asked. 'Sorry. Are you scared I'll break it?'

'Put it down,' he said calmly. 'And come here.'

I walked over to him, I'm not sure why, and there was such a look in his eyes. I hadn't intended to upset or hurt him, and whatever the problem was, my instinct was to try to resolve it. His eyes suggested a different mood. As I got nearer, I worried he might strike me. He was so coiled, his grey eyes narrow and thundery. But no, Jake wouldn't do that. Eddie maybe. His knuckles were closer to the ground. But not Jake. Well, not unless I wanted him to.

'Hey, sorry,' I said lightly. 'I didn't mean to –'

'Shut up,' he said.

I shut up, and we looked at each other. The way he spoke made me angry – how dare he? – but part of studying to be a librarian involves learning how to deal with difficult people. Let them speak. Don't antagonise them. Don't react with emotion.

'I have to punish you,' he said.

I gave a wary laugh. 'Like fuck you do.' My library skills were gone, and besides he wasn't a borrower. My role here wasn't to offer good service.

'Follow me,' he ordered.

'What?' I scoffed as he walked down the hallway. 'Are you serious?'

The trouble is, by that point I'd really fallen for him. I adore his mind and his body, and he makes me so hot. I wanted him then. I looked at his rangy gait, his arse snug in skinny-fit trousers, shoulders wide beneath his jumper, and I was dissolving. You've no idea how much it turned me on to have him gently order me to follow so I could receive my punishment. That soft command held so much understated confidence; he didn't need to bark or snap. He didn't need to assert himself. He knew I would follow, simple as that.

Initially, I didn't move. After all, I have my self-respect. I didn't want to go trotting after him, meek as one of the dogs.

Within seconds though, I started to fret I might lose him. He was heading for the kitchen and my curiosity was up. 'I have to punish you' meant, I was sure: you and I are going to have some new kind of sex that may disturb and excite you.

How could I resist? How could I defy his confidence? I might not get the chance again. 'I want to find you' he'd said with his hand between my thighs, and there were times when I wanted him to find me, times when I didn't. Anyway, I wasn't sure it was possible. I don't think I've found myself, to be honest, and don't imagine I ever will. It's not as if I'm behind the sofa, is it, nice and neat and whole?

But I think what Jake meant was he could find a part of me I'd always shied away from.

So I followed him, my heart all over the place, chest growing hot. I strode as purposefully as I could, calling, 'What? What's the big deal? It's only a doll. It's not as if I damaged it, is it?' And all the time I was wondering what he could do to me, how he might punish me and where he might take me.

In the kitchen, he unlocked the door to the workshop, saying, 'Come with me. I want to show you something.'

He seemed quietly determined rather than angry, perfectly in control. I followed him through the workshop where the night air was rich with the aroma of sawdust and pearl glue, a brown sticky substance he keeps heated during the day. It has nothing to do with pearls and everything to do with scraps of dead animal. It might have been the smell but as we passed through, the puppets swung from their hooks and, to me, they were little carcasses. I felt I was being taken into Jake's lair.

When we reached the museum, he turned on a few lights and switched off the security alarm.

'Come on,' he said, and we walked into one of the rooms where the walls were inset with wooden-framed glass cases, puppets posed and staring right through us. The lights are always low in there, but they were lower than ever that night, and the place had the faded decadence of an old and shabby theatre.

It was all so strange and faraway, and the cases seemed to emanate a faint glow, no glints or reflections. It was warm too because the temperature, I think, has to stay at a certain level. Or maybe Jake had planned this. I still don't know. I felt as if I were in a dark fairytale, lost and confused in a forest of strings, lacquered faces and eerie silent stares.

'Look at them,' said Jake. 'See this? My grandmother made the costumes. Look at the embroidery. Look at the frills, the ruff. And look at her face. My grandfather painted that expression.'

It was, without a doubt, a stunning puppet, a replica of Elizabeth I, virginal and haughty, looking as if she might prickle into life any moment. I almost wanted to curtsy.

'And look at these,' Jake went on. 'Made in Poland. They survived Hitler. And these. In Japan, this is Shakespeare. Puppets matter in Japan. It's a respected art form, takes years of training. They don't treat it as fodder for kids.'

I read the wording on the case he was referring to: *The Love Suicides at Sonezaki*. Well, it wasn't *Sesame Street*, that's for sure. Behind the glass were two beautiful dolls in rich brocade, blank white masks for faces, their eyes small and empty.

'You need to learn to respect them,' said Jake. 'They're antiques, not toys, every single one made with love and attention. You don't get this any more. You don't get such ... such precise beauty. Everything's mass-produced, factories turning out endless crap, hi-tech plastic. Stuff breaks. People get bored. Everyone's so restless, impatient. What's next? Entertain me, feed me. These puppets, they're made of wood and paper. They used to be trees. They were living things growing in a forest. Then they were carved into being, limb by limb. Do you understand?

Clothes were made for them, faces painted, joints made, strings attached. Over the years they've been repaired and restored. They can't be left to their own devices. They're almost human. They need to be cared for. Can you see that?'

He glared at me, dishevelled and flushed, his frown mark cutting a hard groove. I wondered how he could look so angry and pretty at once.

'They *are* lovely,' I said, aiming for tact.

'Don't move,' he said. 'I want you to see something.'

I obeyed, standing patiently while Jake went to fetch something from the reception area. He didn't, however, fetch something from reception. He shut the door and locked me in.

'Jake?' I said, addressing the emptiness. 'Jake?'

The lights dimmed even further. Hell, he really was locking me in. I hurried through the next room to the closed wooden door. I rattled it though I knew it wouldn't budge. But what else are you meant to do?

'Jake?' I was starting to panic a little.

A small window looked onto the reception area, a homely entrance with a heavy oak desk, puppet pictures, Jake's certificates and awards on the walls. I could see the main door, the clouded night beyond, and vague suggestions of the craggy moors. I couldn't see Jake.

'Jake!' I shouted, my voice ending on a little laugh because, although this was unnerving, it was also preposterous. 'Jake!'

No sign.

Punishment. A night locked in this hideous funhouse? Was that it? Surely he wouldn't. It wasn't sexy. It would get cold. I would want to pee and the toilets were on the other side of the door. Plus, it was incarceration and you can't do that to another person without good reason and authority. Well, that's how the world's meant to work. I could take him to court if he kept me locked up. I could

120

. . . I could wreck his collection, smash the cases, break the puppets into pieces, snap them like matchsticks.

But in truth, no matter how incensed I was, I didn't think I'd ever be capable of destroying such finely crafted beauty. Moments into my imprisonment, and it looked as if I was already learning respect.

On the inner window, a misty patch of my breath shrank to nothing. Either he was hiding in reception or he'd left, returning to the house via the main door. I stayed for a while, wondering if he might reveal himself. But there was no sign so I returned to the centre of the museum, wondering what to do next. There was a knot of annoyance in my stomach but more than anything, I was worried. Once again, I was reminded of how little I knew this man, and how isolated his house was. And yet I felt I knew him so well.

I trusted him not to hurt me. Or at least, I trusted him not to hurt me physically, except in a way I might enjoy. Emotionally, it was a different matter but I reckoned we were about evens on that score. Sometimes, I felt as if he were much more into me that I was into him. At other times, it was vice versa. Our relationship had started on such a wild intense level and we both had the power to hurt. I didn't think either of us would do it intentionally though; much as I never intended hurting you, much as I never want to hurt anyone. It's just a consequence of things going wrong between people. Life sucks.

Psychologically break me? I hadn't really thought about it at that stage.

In the museum, I stood and stared. What was I meant to do? Half of me wanted to slump in a corner and sulk. Another half wanted to kick out in frustration. But Jake was up to something, I knew that. It probably wasn't worth getting angry about. So I rose above it, and wandered around the room.

It was like moving through a gallery of stills, peering

at little faces as they gazed into another world. The purple curtain leading to the 'adult only' section was drawn back and I was about to wander in when a voice came from nowhere, filling the air like it was God Himself. I jumped at the sound. And God said, 'Show me your breasts' and He had a Yorkshire accent.

I spun around, scanning, and spotted a small high security camera trained on the room. Was he watching me? Where was he?

I laughed a little shyly.

I kept looking but could see no other cameras. I noticed small speakers fixed in a couple of corners and I remembered that sound of deep, soft breathing from my first visit. It had been so calming, a breath that seemed to wreathe itself around me, drawing me down to a bombed-out tranquillity. I hadn't made the connection originally but the state it had lulled me into was seriously sexy. It was similar to the way I feel when I'm melting towards orgasm, or the way I like it best: coming, not from fucking, but from when I'm flat on my back, legs spread, barely aware of my body because I'm half-lost, floating; and between my thighs someone's lapping at my folds, immersing me in warm, wet, slippery pleasure.

The strange moment I'd had on my walk out of Heddlestone was similar: sleepy and semi-erotic, with that added lucidity of vision, the acid-green moss, the frost-laced leaf, the wool on barbed wire like cream and iron candy floss. I could still see the images, stark in my mind's eye.

I could've done with some of that clarity then but instead I had Jake saying, 'Show me your breasts.'

I looked up at the camera, wanting to address him but I felt too belittled by the act. How could I possibly talk to a box of metal and plastic? Besides, he probably couldn't hear me. I'd be nothing but a fuzzy grey image on a monitor elsewhere, pleading up at him, mouth moving, face contorting. I felt like an insect in a box, a curious specimen under scrutiny. Unless the cameras were duds which was also possible.

Then the voice came through again. 'Show me,' he repeated. Then in a softer voice, he added, 'I want to see your breasts, Kate.' A pause before, in a cool, firm tone, he said, 'Please.'

He sounded like a parent reminding a child of its manners. Goosebumps rose on my skin because the dynamics had suddenly changed. This looked like it could be one hell of a sexy game. We were working in harmony, it seemed. He wasn't going to boss me about. He would be good to me and I'd be good to him, and together we'd make sweet music.

I wasn't sure how we would do that but the openness of this odd scenario intrigued and thrilled me. Well, we'll just see where this goes, I thought, and so I removed my chunky cardigan and flung it into a corner with a confident flourish. I sucked my cheeks into my teeth to try to stop myself grinning and stood confidently, hands on hips, head bowed in a pose of self-containment. I knew I'd look idiotic if I started eyeing up the camera for a response. I tried to imagine it was just me. Tricky, when I had an audience of vacuous, dead-eyed dolls who seemed, simultaneously, to see everything and nothing.

I unbuttoned my top in a nice slow tease. I thought of Jake in reception watching on the monitor, his long limbs arranged around the chair and desk, folded in here, extending there, my delectable daddy-long-legs. Was he gazing at the screen, half-dumbstruck, his cock rising in his jeans?

Oh, I love the way Jake looks when he's aroused. Some men I've been with seem to keep it in check but with Jake it's all there. He wants me. He's hot for me and I can see how true it is because it's all over his flushed face. It's in the coils and kinks of his conker-brown hair, an extra mussed-up quality, some wild energy romping among the follicles. He doesn't play up to a role. He doesn't faff about how he might appear. It's as if that self-conscious, slightly awkward aspect that's sometimes there, slides away in sex. He's bang in the moment, completely absorbed in me and in what we're doing together.

He's like that in the workshop too. He gets so lost in himself. I love to watch him working the wood, blowing dust off a new shape, smoothing his fingers over the grain. His touch is so measured and his concentration is absolute, for them and for me.

I pictured him in front of the monitor, rapt as I undid the final button and removed my shirt, back to the camera. I wasn't sure I could pull off a sexy striptease, especially without an audience, and so I did what felt like a natural move: I leant over to touch my toes, or near as damn it, and held myself in that loose stretch. I like doing this. I always do it in the mornings and after that, pretty much whenever I want throughout the day. I think it's good for my spine, and I feel the stretch in the back of my calves.

'I like that,' said the voice. 'I like the way your hair falls when your head's upside down. I can see your neck.' He paused for a moment. 'I love your neck. It's beautiful.'

He loved my neck! No one has ever loved my neck.

'Can you take your bra off?' he asked.

Holding the toe-touching pose as best I could, I unfastened my bra and let it slide down my arms to the floor. It was all so quiet in the room. The outside world had melted away. There were no windows, no people, no sounds. Just me trapped in a surreal box of puppetry, lost on the moors, and somewhere around me was Jake, a disembodied voice in the air. We could have been travelling through outer space.

Now what?

'Take your jeans off,' he said.

I was a lot less keen on this. What woman would want to have her big naked butt bared on a security monitor?

And then it occurred to me this was probably being recorded. No point having CCTV unless there's the evidence, is there? Would we watch it on video later? How was I doing?

I stayed still, feeling my head burn as blood filled it, my ears getting hotter. I reckoned the images would be suitably grainy, and my backside would be suitably blurred. So, glad of the chance to stand up, I removed my cords and footwear before bending over again in just my knickers, arms relaxed and floppy. My underwear was white and I'd nudged the leg elastic higher to expose my cheeks. I imagined Jake seeing me through the bird's eye view of the camera, a short, plump, near-naked woman almost touching her toes, perhaps looking intriguingly anonymous as criminals do on CCTV footage. What was she doing like that? What was she waiting for?

I felt exposed and vulnerable, my skin in contact with nothing. I drew slow steady breaths, and my entire body was tingling under his remote, mediated gaze. I didn't know which part of me he was looking at though I could hazard a guess.

Then through the speakers, his voice said, 'I want to spank you.'

His words detonated inside me and I was drenched in lust.

Oh, Jesus Christ, he wants to spank me.

I felt quivery everywhere: in my limbs, my veins, my head, in the breath that moved in my mouth, in the heart rate that seemed to have quadrupled.

I swallowed hard, keeping perfectly still. My face had flared with heat and, for some reason, the skin on the backs of my knees felt thinly stretched and delicate. He wants to spank me. All I could do was hold the pose. If my position didn't say 'yes,' then I didn't know what else would.

There was silence for what seemed like for ever. Yes, I

thought, I'm saying yes here. Look at me. Look at my buttocks, look at my posture, look at my eager, abject subservience.

And then the breathing started again, drifting from the speakers. It rose in the room like it had done the first time, barely audible, a slow lift and fall. It was as if the place was breathing all around me, and I could imagine the chocolate-brown walls swelling and shrinking like an alien lifeform. I heard the door unlock. I heard Jake's soft footsteps coming my way. He moved behind me and my head was booming with the rushing blood.

Looking backwards, I could see his black jeans, frayed and tatty by the heels of his big boots. He tucked my knickers a little higher, baring more of my cheeks, and ran a palm over the rounds of my arse. Feeling the grain of me, I thought. Carve with the grain, not against. I braced myself for the sting of his slap but he moved away to stand in front of me.

'Look up,' he said.

I craned my neck upwards. He was holding a paddle in two hands, displaying it for me. It was black and made of leather, and a section of lettering was cut out of it, a few inches long. It spelt 'slut'. That word again, the one he whispers to me with such dark, sexy charm. I laughed lightly, understanding at once. That would pattern my arse as my skin reddened under the impact of leather. Witty and modern, I thought, and so gorgeously horny, every spank repeating 'slut, slut, slut'.

But my biggest, wildest thought, the one that made something seize up inside me was: Where did he get that? Who's he used it on before? Who was she? Who the hell was she? And how did her arse look when she bared it to the paddle?

We'd never talked about other lovers. It was too early. Had someone lived here with him? The place seemed so much Jake's I couldn't imagine it. I was jealous; jealous of his past. A blank paddle wouldn't have affected me the same, but the wording personalised it. My arousal was tinged with an ugly emotion and, in that instant, I wanted him to hurt me and fuck me. I wanted him to inflict pain on my body and make me come. I wanted the pain inside to be overwhelmed by an easier, physical pain.

Who was she, the slut? That was our word.

Jake walked away, returning with a square stool cushioned in bottle-green velvet, a band of dark brass studs around the edges of its seat.

'Lean over that,' he said.

I did as told, my hands gripping two legs of the stool, head down, sex pulsing. Who? I tried convincing myself he'd bought it especially for me but there was a slight worn quality of the paddle and it didn't ring true. The room breathed around us.

'You must never touch that doll again,' he said. 'Do you understand?'

Then, briskly, he pulled my underwear to my knees, baring my arse completely.

'Slut,' he said, and I heard the catch of lust in his voice.

The paddle cracked onto my arse, right side. I felt it as a single, sharp blow and just as I was thinking, well, that hardly hurt at all, it blossomed to a rising heat, getting stronger and hotter.

'Ah, ah, ah,' I said.

'Oh, beautiful,' said Jake. 'It's coming, turning pink. I can see the word.'

I twisted round to look. 'Keep still,' he barked. 'Oh, nice. There in white. Branded a slut.'

A few seconds later, another burst of pain cut right through the first. I yelped and squeezed the stool-legs, drumming my feet on the carpet. 'Again,' said Jake, and a third leathery thwack scorched my flesh.

'And now I can't see what you are,' said Jake. 'It's getting blurred, ruined. But that's good, isn't it?'

'I ... I don't know,' I gasped. The paddle landed again, still stinging like hell although I seemed to be taking it better.

'Yes, it's good,' he said firmly. 'I bet you wish this was Eddie, don't you?' He paused, waiting for my answer and when I didn't offer one, he struck my other buttock. It felt like he'd set it alight. 'Don't you?'

'No,' I cried. 'I want you. You.'

The paddle landed again and again. 'Liar,' he said, and 'slut'. But then the words petered out and he worked in silence, swatting my cheeks and thighs, taking no notice of my pleas and shrieks.

It started to change at some point. I guess the endorphins were kicking in because the pain transformed itself into pleasure. And in a way, I was transformed too. Blurred. That was Jake's word and a good one. I was becoming blurred, losing my body yet feeling immersed in a wonderfully numbed hyperawareness. That hardly seems to make sense, does it? But that's how it felt.

When Jake stopped and cast the paddle to the floor, I stayed across the stool, sobbing and panting. The room breathed around us, and I didn't know what was inside and out. My buttocks were on fire, the heat falling into my body to surround the well of my cunt and meet the thundering beat below. I was poker-hot and throbbing, one mass of sensation. When Jake touched my wetness, I felt it everywhere, a slow explosion opening in my lower half. I couldn't isolate the feel of his fingers on a particular part of me. He was just bringing me pleasure and increasing the intensity, and I was turning into a flow of lava.

'Ahhh,' I groaned. I was vaguely aware of his fingers playing across the fat purse of my lips, and then I think he must have pushed them in deep because I was 'ahhing' even more, losing it, gone. I don't know what he did to me. It could have been that his arm was inside me to the elbow, fingers rippling like sea anemone fronds, and it was disolving in all the soft moltenness within me. And then I was coming undone, convulsing and coming. The moment seemed to go on and on, keeping me on that plateau of mindless bliss. And I sobbed freely, and for a while there was no more pleasure, no more pain. They were one and the same thing, and there were no words to describe it, nothing except 'me' which wasn't really me. A nothingness, a great glorious nothingness.

Transcendent. It's a big word, a big feeling. But that's what it was.

Occasionally, coming will make me cry. The release is so intense I can't help it, and that's what happened then. The slow sob of the previous few minutes gushed into something else. Usually, it's a few tears and I hide it well but this was a whole new level. I was racked and trembling. For several months, so many pressures had been building up – you, my deception and my guilty secrets, the move here, feeling so isolated and lonely, trying to resist Jake and failing and falling – and I couldn't keep it boxed in any more.

Amazingly, Jake didn't freak. He took over and let me weep. We moved onto the floor and he sat against the wall, legs outstretched. I lay with my head in his lap, my body curving into him, trembling, knees nudging his jeans, thighs slippery wet, buttocks still burning and no doubt patterned with a blur of indecipherable sluts. He stroked my hair, wiped tears from my face and rubbed my shoulder as I poured myself out.

'We're getting to understand each other, aren't we?' he said.

I didn't need to reply, and anyway I was too choked. It was a catharsis like I hadn't known for a long time, and I felt so secure, the room enveloping me like a slow-breathing womb.

When the tears started to ease, Jake sparked them up again by gently asking, 'Have you fucked my brother yet?'

'No!' I protested, and the tears surged again, this time in frustration.

'But I want you to,' he said. 'You said you would, didn't you?'

When I'd caught my breath, I murmured, 'No, I can't. Don't ask me.'

He twisted his fingers in my curls, winding them into a fist and pulling gently on my scalp. I love how he pulls my hair.

'Yes, you can,' he said kindly.

'No, Jake,' I cried. 'Why? Why do you want me –'

'Because I'm asking you to,' he said. 'And because I think you want to.'

His grip fastened tighter and I sniffed back the tears as his other hand reached to cup my breast. Lifting its weight, he massaged tenderly, squeezing and rolling my flesh. 'Have you sucked his cock yet?'

'No,' I said but my heart was thumping because I remembered being on my knees, desperately wanting to and Eddie's hand preventing me.

'Have you thought about it? Fantasised about him?'

'No' I whispered. 'I don't like him. I like you.' I sobbed out a little laugh. 'Usually.'

He ran his hand down my body, dipping into my waist, up over the flare of my hips and down the raw heat of my buttocks.

'I like you too,' he said. 'Usually.' He slid his fingers along the divide of my cheeks and found my wet swollen hole from that angle. His fingers dipped into my entrance and he stirred circles inside me. 'I think you're much dirtier than you know,' he said in a cajoling tone.

I moaned at his touch. He did have a point.

'Aren't you?' he said.

I whimpered as his fingers slid back to press the ring of my anus. He toyed with me there, sensitising the soft rim until I wanted him to touch me inside again. I slipped a hand between my legs and rolled my clit beneath my fingers, just the way I like it.

'You want to fuck Eddie, I can tell,' he said. 'It's in your eyes when I talk about him. I could see it in you that weekend after you met him. I don't know what you did together –'

'There was nothing,' I said. 'We didn't –'

'But you wanted it.'

He inserted a damp finger into my rear with a steady slide.

'No,' I breathed.

'You did,' said Jake.

'No,' I said, lying.

Jake drove another finger into me, and the stretch was so much tighter, the band of my muscle squeezing on him. I rubbed faster on my clit, panting and hot.

'It's OK, you can admit it,' said Jake. 'He has that effect on people, I know. He gets to them. Don't feel guilty about it. Ah, your arse feels gorgeous inside. You're so smooth and warm. Is it nice? Do you like this?'

'Yes,' I said. 'Yes.' And in a greedy surge, I shoved two fingers inside my other hole, using my thumb on my clit. I pressed against my inner walls. In my backside, Jake pressed forward. I gasped. I could feel him. I could feel his fingers. We were virtually touching inside me.

'Oh, God, I can feel you,' said Jake. 'That's so horny. I'm going to fuck you later. I might fuck your arse. Do you want that, babes?'

'I'm going to come,' I said. 'Keep there. Please, please.'

'What about Eddie?' said Jake. 'He could fuck you. Really fuck you. Do want that?'

'No,' I whimpered.

'I don't believe you,' he said softly. 'Tell me the truth. Let me in. Let go of it.'

I waggled my fingers back and forth and he pushed harder inside my back tunnel, finger slipping up and down against mine.

'He could fuck you. I could spank you, print slut on your arse then stand back and watch him fuck you.'

'Please,' I gasped. 'Ah, God.'

'Give me something,' said Jake. 'Give me something, Kate. Tell me a truth. Let go. Succumb to it. Tell me you want Eddie. My brother. My brother's cock inside you.'

I was lost, blissing out.

'My brother,' said Jake. 'He's almost me, Kate. Don't you want that?'

I panted, all fingers and thumbs.

In a sterner, angrier voice, Jake said, 'Do you want to fuck my brother? Tell me. I'm not asking if you like him. I'm asking if you want to fuck him. Tell me the truth. Now.'

I was right on the brink, ready to fall. I didn't trust myself to speak. Then when I did, it felt like such a deep truth, a late-night, alcohol-dazed truth I'd later regret. But the spanking and the sobbing had broken something in me and I felt I could trust Jake with my life. We were so close. We could share it all and erase the barriers. I could show him anything about me and it would all be OK.

'Do you want Eddie?'

'Yes,' I gasped. 'Yes, I want him.'

'Good girl,' said Jake, and he scissored his fingers apart inside me, and I fretted my clit until I came in great gulping breaths. All my nerve endings fizzed from top to toe. My calf muscles tensed with a sort of numbed electricity, face tingling as my orgasm shook.

'Yes, yes,' I said.

'Good girl,' Jake repeated, sounding sleepy and satisfied.

And when my orgasm faded, I was in tears again, gentler tears of relief this time.

We stayed sitting together for a while, Jake cradling my head in his lap, the room's slow hypnotic breath drifting over us. He stroked my hair again, and every now and then, he murmured abstractedly, 'Good girl. Good girl.'

9

The graveyard of Heddlestone's church is a romantic tumbledown affair of cracked, tilted tombstones, overhanging trees and creeping ivy. The light was fading, and the air was cold and damp, the ground uneven with coarse yellowing grasses. It's a place you could imagine sumpy earth giving way, leaving you knee-deep in a splintered coffin, an upthrust skeletal hand waving hello.

I'd brought the black dog with me, Noah, and he was merrily snuffling around the base of graves while I squinted at lettering that had worn away to a ghost's script. A mist hung over the moors and we were both wrapped up, me in hat, scarf and gloves, Noah in a dog jacket. I wasn't there for any particular reason. I'd been in the workshop all day and I just fancied a walk. It was a part of the village I hadn't yet explored. After seeing the graveyard, I reckoned I'd have 'done' Heddlestone. It's not very big, and there isn't much to see or do.

Jake's surname is Duxbury and I was probably hoping to see an historic Duxbury or two. There's a newer, tidier area beyond the drystone wall but in the original churchyard, none of the dates is recent. I wasn't having much luck with the Duxburys but it hardly mattered. It was fascinating and so sad. How young these people were when they died, adults in their twenties and thirties, and so many kids too.

I wondered if any of them were Betty's Bastards from the orphanage. It was strange to think that Jake's house was once home to all those children. What a life: no family, no roots, and you end up on the edge of this lost village, surrounded by miles and miles of moorland. But then it was probably better than being in the workhouse or getting sent up a chimney.

Through the trees, streetlamps in the village bloomed, hazy pockets of amber-peach warming the cold slate and heavy stone. The moors beyond Heddlestone had practically disappeared, their substance seeping into the fogged greying light.

I dawdled towards a yew tree, the ground in its deep green shade soft with dropped needles. Yew trees – graveyard trees – are said to have mythical properties but all I could think about then was how the roots were meant to poke their way through corpses. I remembered a news items from years ago of a yew tree being uprooted in a storm, its exposed roots decorated with bones and skulls and looking, in my mind, as if a grisly Christmas tree had emerged from the underworld.

Nonetheless, I still wanted to take a closer look. Yew bark is beautiful, thin outer layers peeling away to reveal salmon-pink wood. Sometimes the trunks are hollow and I was going to inspect it when I smelt a drift of cigarette smoke on the air. It was a strong smell from nearby and yet there was nothing nearby except graves and the tree. The surrounding drystone wall was still some distance from me so the smoke couldn't have come from beyond it. I turned, scanning the churchyard for the dog. In the gloom, all I could make out were haphazard gravestones and an old-fashioned lantern on the path to the unlit church. There was no dog, no movement.

I walked away from the tree, away from the cigarette smoke, away from whoever was there. My heart was pumping. I hoped I was walking away.

'Noah,' I called. I think I'd have called out for a dog whether I'd had one with me or not. My voice was light and quivery. 'Noah!'

A noise made me jump. I spun around as the tree burst into life. A blood-orange point of light whizzed through the air like a monstrous single eye, and a dark roaring figure hurled itself towards me. I screamed, stumbling backwards. Its hands were clawed high, arms raised like tree branches. It flung itself at me then clamped the upper half of my body in a hard hug.

'Ohmigod,' it laughed, rocking me from side to side. 'Ohmigod, I frighten you too much. It was meant to be little scare. I am sorry, really sorry.'

Little kisses pecked at my neck. Yelena, Eddie's wife.

She smelt of cigarettes and perfume, and her hat was in my face. Angry and shaken, I pushed her away. 'What the fuck – You nearly gave me a heart attack!'

Noah barked and came bounding over, tail wagging, light glinting on his name tag and reflecting in his eyes as a demonic yellow-green.

'Oh, I'm sorry,' she said, wrapping another hug around me. 'It was just joke.' Noah leapt up at us. 'Hey, doggie,' said Yelena, stroking his long head and patting his haunches. Fat lot of protection he was.

She stepped back, sucking hard on her cigarette. 'I'm Yelena,' she said. She flicked the end to the ground, blowing smoke sideways. 'And you are Kate. I am married to Eddie, Jake's brother. I saw you walking so I come to introduce. You know, I think they don't want us to meet because they know we will have too much fun together. You like it here? This place? Man, it is so fucking boring. I'm so happy you come. I want friend. I live above pub. Yes, we have pub! I can drink as much as I want! You can drink with me too! I am sorry to scare. Here, drink this. Wodka. Is good for shocks. Well, I don't know if it is true but I believe.'

She gave one of her bright, rattling laughs, unscrewing a silver hip flask. She was wearing a long duvet coat, pale Ugg boots and a big fur hat with ear flaps like a bloodhound's. If I'd been doubting whether she was the ballerina woman from the WMC, those boots confirmed she was. 'Here,' she said, thrusting the hip flask at me.

How could I refuse? 'Cheers,' I said laughing, then tipping the flask.

'Za zdorovie!' she replied, raising an invisible toast. She drank and asked, 'So why you here in this ... this place with dead people? You are very pretty. Are you having affair with Jake? Listen, did he tell to you about ghost? Ah God, I want to see this ghost. It is only exciting thing in this shithole. I am living here for year and half and it is making me crazy. There are two people in this village, good people, Paula and Ahmed, and sometimes we fuck them. You know? Like foursome? Wife swap?' Yelena shrugged. 'It is nothing to do here. Work, drink, fuck, make porn film, watch TV, eat big dinner. I am terrible cook but Eddie, Jake's brother, my husband, he loves to cook, eat, drink. Maybe next year I go university to study computers. I'm so happy you come here. Hey, one day we go to Leeds. We take a train and we have fun, get pissed, meet some men and fuck them. I don't tell to Jake, you don't tell to Eddie. I need fun. You want more wodka?'

I was dazzled and charmed. She didn't let up, interrupting her monologue only to laugh or fire a question. You like Russian wodka? Where you from? How long you stay? You like his puppets? Ugh, I hate them. You and Jake are girlfriend-boyfriend? Where is other dog?

Most of my replies were brief, partly because I loved hearing her talk but also because I wasn't sure of my answers. How long *was* I staying? *Were* we girlfriend and boyfriend? Sometimes it felt like we were husband and wife, at others as if I hardly knew him. And recently, after the spanking in the museum, there'd been more spankings, more bondage, more and more situations where I'd begged him to stop, begged him to make me come, begged him to hold me.

And, oh, when he holds me afterwards, I feel closer to him than I've ever felt to anyone. He breaks me down, strips me of inhibitions and when I've sobbed and climaxed until I don't know who I am, he wraps me in his arms, so soft and tender.

Do I sound like a masochist? I don't feel like one. The

point isn't the pain and I don't suffer. Or rather, I go beyond suffering and into a new space. If I could get there without it hurting, I would. I think that's why I like it when Jake calls me 'slut' and makes me feel bad. It takes me there, helps me lose myself.

Because that's the point. Jake makes me lose myself. I feel I'm submitting to my desires, not to his. In all other areas, I feel we're equal but in sex he becomes so huge and dominant, so in control, and I trust him absolutely. He pushes me until I'm gone, out of reach, and it's as if I'm in a nothing space, floating. I am so free there.

It's such a feeling to be free of yourself. I didn't understand it at first. I think it scared me but I'm getting to know and understand it. I'm coming to realise that I want this not because I'm worthless and I must suffer. It's because I'm human and life's tough. Letting go is so powerful. Surrender transforms me. I adore oblivion.

Once, Jake gagged and blindfolded me, turned me around, took me from one room to another until I was disorientated and dizzy. Then he fucked me, pulling my hair, being rough and cruel, calling me names because he knows I can't help liking it. He made me come twice, and I didn't know where I was, couldn't see, couldn't breathe properly, couldn't speak to him. I felt so far within myself, overtaken by my body, by touch and sound and ecstasy, and it was glorious.

Another time, he slipped a pillowcase over my head, bunching it at the nape of my neck as he fucked me like I was no one. It was hot and dark inside the hood, and I sucked cotton into my mouth when I came, loving the secrecy.

I love it too when he takes me over his lap and smacks my arse, his strong slender hand curving to my cheeks. It's best and it's worst when we're in the living room with the curtains open and I'm terrified of someone looking in. Once he pretended. He said, 'Eddie's at the window.' Outraged, I tried to wriggle free but he gripped my neck so hard it hurt. I couldn't look up and he kept smacking and smacking, saying, 'Look at her, look at my greedy slut, my dirty little lover.'

Purple bruises flower on my buttocks. Ligature marks flare on my skin. Welts stripe and slash me. Some days, I am like a thing he painted.

It's heaven here. When I'm lost to myself and I've put myself in his hands, I almost feel as if I *am* Jake, as if I'm floating on the air, intermingling with his voice because there are no words for me. I'm beyond speech. And he talks to me, tells me I'm beautiful, tells me he loves me, tells me it means so much to him that we can do this together and that I trust him as I do.

Because, yes, he tells me that he loves me. I don't know if he means it. It's usually after sex he says this, sometimes during. I haven't returned the compliment yet but, God, I've been close. Astonishingly, despite my many abandonments, some sane part of me manages to keep tight hold of those words. I'm besotted with Jake and I care deeply, but those words aren't for him.

But as I said, when he holds me close after sex, after extreme sex, the connection is like nothing I've ever known. It's as if we're both equally stunned and exhausted, the two of us cut off in this freaky house, united by the craziness of what we do, capable of transcendence, of meeting somewhere beyond ourselves.

I can only compare it to how a baby must feel when it's all sensation and need; a fluid creature with no sense of self, being scooped up by its mother who makes everything all right.

That's how I feel: scooped up, safe, without definition. And then it's as if Jake's building me up again, and the person I am becoming – the post-coital person, the person who is growing up in Heddlestone – owes more and more to him.

So when Yelena invited me to spend an evening with

her and Eddie – 'Hey, we watch porn and maybe fuck' – I thought it might be my chance to learn something for myself. Besides, Jake would be pleased and I knew I wanted Eddie, even though I didn't. Sharing him with Yelena might help resolve my contradictory lusts.

We were leaning against a large vault-style tombstone, darkness all around us. Yelena's nose looked raw and moist. The dog was all ribs and shivers, its tail hooked between its legs. Yelena's eyes were pinned on mine, awaiting an answer.

I must have looked surprised, an accurate enough expression, and she generously backtracked. 'Hey, come for anything. Come for dinner, drinks. We watch any film you want. I send Eddie away. Please come to my house.'

I said I'd love to.

'But not Jake,' she added. 'You only. Girl talk.'

'That's fine,' I said. 'I'm already looking forward to it.'

And I was. Although I didn't for one moment think we'd be watching *Casablanca* or that Eddie would be out.

Jake was painting my toenails when the doorbell rang for the second time that day. I eased my feet off his lap, toes splayed with balls of cotton wall, and said, 'Piccadilly Circus!'

We rarely have visitors. In fact, up until that point, the only people who'd called were Eddie and Yelena, a guy with a delivery of firewood and the milkman one evening to collect his money (because, yes, there's a milkman up here; they still exist). Our first caller that Saturday had been Odd Job Bob, a man I'd seen plenty of times in the village, wheeling around an old 50s-style pram heaped with tool boxes, rags, spare parts and whatnot.

We were in the living room and the big wheels came squeaking along the track. 'Odd Job Bob,' said Jake, as if sharing an amusing confidence, and moments later the bell went.

'Bob's come to fix your boiler,' Jake announced, returning to the room with a stooped fellow who looked as if he should have been put out to pasture some time ago.

'What boiler?' I said. 'I don't have a –' Jake was grinning and I realised Bob had got the wrong end of the stick. 'Oh, you must mean the Heskeths' boiler in the granny flat. Sorry, nothing to do with me. You'll have to ask them. But it doesn't need fixing on my behalf, not any more.'

Bob nodded patiently. 'There's something wrong in the attic though,' he said. 'Some problem with water.'

Jake, smiling to himself, thrust his hands in his jeans and said, 'Bob's got second sight.'

I smiled kindly, thinking, Shame he hasn't got first sight. 'There's no problem with the attic, it's fine, but thank you.'

'A leak, maybe?' suggested Bob.

I laughed. What was this? A repair man who intuits your repairs rather than you having to call him out? He could make a fortune. 'There's no leak, really.'

'Weren't you having problems with a dripping tap?' asked Jake, throwing me a mischievous glance.

Whose side was he on? 'Hardly,' I said. 'The bath tap drips if you don't turn it tightly enough. Probably needs a new washer but I don't –'

'I've got washers,' said Bob. 'In the pram.'

I looked to Jake for support but got none. I couldn't recall ever mentioning the dripping tap. After all, it was such a minor problem, and I'd got more than enough major ones to keep me occupied. 'It's fine, really,' I said. 'I'm sure Jake's got washers and if not we can –'

'Let him take a look,' said Jake, and I immediately realised what the deal was. It was some sort of rural job creation scheme, or a charitable handout in the guise of payment for services rendered.

'Oh, OK,' I said, and I hurried on ahead to give the place a cursory tidy and hide any stray underwear.

I was spending most nights with Jake and the attic was now more of an enormous wardrobe and a place to shower. That morning, I'd showered in the main bathroom with Jake. Any chance to see Jake naked and wet, and I'll jump at it. Water turns his hair to glossy black ink, and the loose hang of his curls makes me want to take sections into my mouth and suck water from the tips. I want to watch rivulets running over his pale muscles, shimmering on his back, his buttocks, his chest, spilling from his eyelashes and pouring from his elbows. I want to soap him and run slippery, sudsy hands over his lean torso, cradle his balls and glide my fist along his cock while we kiss in a tumble of tongues, smiles, saliva and water, our lips dissolving.

So yes, I'd showered with Jake, meaning I was surprised to find the attic carpet wet. A messy damp track started and stopped in the middle of nowhere. There were little patches spaced like footprints although nothing as defined as a foot or shoe. And there were bigger damp patches. Had Jake showered here? Spilt something? Had the dogs peed weirdly and excessively?

I knelt and patted the carpet. It was well and truly soaked, moisture seeping above the fibres when I pressed. I sniffed. Nothing to smell. Water.

The two men came into the room as I was looking up at the sloped ceiling. 'It's wet,' I said, and they followed my gaze. But there were no marks on the ceiling, nothing to indicate a leaking roof. I looked to Jake, expecting to find that amused smile but instead he looked worried, shocked even.

Bob, carrying a tool box, came to stand by the dampness. He nodded sagely and closed his eyes. Jake seemed rooted to the spot, gaze fixed on Bob. Bob's nostrils flared as he drew a deep breath. 'Thought so,' he said. 'It's Laura. She's back. She's not happy.'

Jake laughed falsely. I could hardly believe his face. It

was so full of lies it hurt to look at him. His smile was held in place by muscles alone, his skin had turned chalky and his eyes were so afraid they seemed almost to cower.

'Who's Laura?' I demanded.

'Laura's our –' began Bob then he cut himself short. 'You've not told her about Laura?'

The smile was still pinned to Jake's face and though he tried to stand casually with his hands in his pockets, his whole posture was tight as a bow.

'Not yet, no,' confessed Jake, and the colour returned to his face as two high patches on his cheeks.

'And the lass sleeps here?' said Bob.

'Well, no, she doesn't actually,' said Jake, increasingly embarrassed.

'Who's Laura?' I repeated, annoyed to hear them talking about me as if I weren't there.

A slow smile lifted Bob's expression as the import of Jake's words dawned on him. 'Ah, I see.' He grinned, looking at me in a way that made me feel as if he'd mentally stripped me naked. 'Well,' he said. 'Not to worry, then, eh? Show us this tap o' yours then I'll be out of your way.'

When we'd seen Bob out, I followed Jake downstairs. 'Who's Laura? Why is my carpet wet?'

'Take no notice of Bob,' Jake said.

'Come on,' I warned. 'Don't think you can fob me off that easily. What's going on?' He walked past me down the hallway to the kitchen. Laura was the name Eddie had give to Jake's toothy vintage doll but I didn't feel I could mention that. I didn't want to go into details of what I'd seen of Eddie and Yelena when Jake had bundled me into the wicker trunk.

'Noah went up to your room when you were out,' he said. 'Mucky feet. Think he was looking for you. Mud all over your carpet. The wet was me getting rid of them. Sorry. I should have mentioned it. Do you want tea?'

'And Laura?' I sat on the kitchen table while Jake

messed around in cupboards, keeping his back to me. His kitchen's a haphazard affair of Formica and granite, larder cupboards and white goods, overlooked by a grandfather clock and warmed by a Rayburn.

'Laura's a ghost,' he said. 'If you believe in that shit.'

'Well, no, I don't,' I said, and then I thought of the strange sensations I'd had in that room, the sense of a presence at the door and on my bed. 'Not really.'

Jake turned, smiling stiffly, hands in his pockets. 'No, me neither,' he said. 'But wherever Bob goes, ghosts are sure to follow. It's usually the Laura ghost, mind. Don't think he's got the imagination for many more. It's a local legend, some woman who supposedly haunts the village.'

I recalled Yelena mentioning a ghost when we were in the graveyard, but it had been neither here nor there, just another snippet in her non-stop chatter.

'Look, I'm sure I've got some leaflets about it somewhere,' said Jake. 'Tourist info. I'm not well up on local history. Sorry.'

'OK,' I said. 'One more question: how come Bob suddenly appears? First he says it's the boiler, second there's a problem with water in the attic. And there is. How did he know that?'

Jake tapped the side of his head, grinning. 'Smart man, our Bob. Psychic.'

'Tell me.'

Jake laughed. 'I don't know, honestly. He got confused. Coincidence. That's all. People get so freaked out by coincidences but they happen. They're bound to. They don't mean anything. Think of all the times coincidence doesn't happen. No one talks about that, do they?'

I let the subject drop. I made out it wasn't that interesting. I didn't mention any of the weird feelings I'd had since my arrival. Jake didn't say anything either. I knew he was hiding something. He must have known I was hiding something too, even if it was only my curiosity.

And so, with the random visit of a repair man, we

suddenly had secrets from each other, and we knew it. And we knew that we knew it, yet neither of us was going to spoil the charade of pretending nothing was going on. Something had shifted between us, and there was a barrier in place, a wariness and mistrust neither of us must reveal. We were playing roles like actors on set or kids in a world of make-believe. And the roles we were playing were Jake and Kate.

Him painting my toenails that evening was part of the pretence. It was intimate and domestic, and perhaps slightly too much. 'You've missed a bit,' I would say. Or, 'You're meant to be painting my nail, not my entire toe!' and 'I could do yours later if you want. Maybe your fingernails too, and a dab of eyeshadow.'

And all the while, an undercurrent of questions was running through my mind: What are you hiding? Should I ever have trusted you? What frightened you in the attic?

I did actually fancy giving him a mini makeover. I liked the idea of him looking androgynous and deviant. With his slim-hipped body, lush curls and those sly, girlish glances, he almost demanded an edge of twisted femininity. I got the impression he'd have been willing to let me, whether because he liked the idea or because he wanted to keep papering over the cracks, I don't know.

But when the police arrived, it all got put on hold. I guess we were lucky they turned up when they did. An hour later, and they might have found Jake in drag.

'Nothing to worry about,' said the policewoman. 'Just routine. Missing persons inquiry.' Draped around the tall fireplace mirror, the fairy lights made a cascade of hazy white stars, and in their fluorescent green jackets, the police looked garish and modern, intruders from the real world.

'Do you recognise this woman?'

Jake looked at the picture that was handed to him, shaking his head.

The policeman, who'd been glancing about the room,

said to me, 'Looks well lived in. Been here a while, have you?'

I wondered if it was a trick question. Was he making conversation or did he really want to know? 'It is a bit chaotic,' I admitted. 'Jake's the interior designer, not me.'

'You're quite certain?' the policewoman asked Jake. 'Her name's Chloë Lipsey. Went missing a few years ago. We've had a recent report of her mentioning Heddlestone before she vanished.'

Again, Jake shook his head, apologising.

'If you wouldn't mind, love,' said the woman, passing me the picture.

She was in her twenties, pretty and smiling. The smiles of missing people are so awful. I didn't recognise her although it struck me that, in some superficial way, she resembled me: fair skin, curly wheat-blonde hair. I'm not saying she looked like me, just that there were certain similarities.

It bothered me a little, and it seemed weird nobody else was pointing it out. But then I reasoned it was probably due to nothing other than me and the woman sharing a colouring that's fairly common in this country. One of Jake's coincidences that don't mean anything. And I was probably sympathising too keenly with her situation, being a runaway myself or, at least, being miles away from home.

Besides, it would be insensitive to make comparisons. This woman was missing. Somewhere in the world she had friends and family, heartbroken and desperate. Or maybe she didn't and that's why she was now just a routine inquiry.

I returned the picture. 'Sorry,' I said, and I meant it. I wanted to help and I felt useless.

I didn't want to sleep with Jake that night. I wanted to step back from him again, and now I didn't mind if he knew. There was something odd going on, and I couldn't carry on acting as if everything were normal.

I recalled Jake once telling me about shadow puppet theatre, how the women watch from the front, seeing only shadows, while the men watch from the back, seeing the mechanics, the operators and the puppets themselves. There was more than a hint of Plato's Cave in that tradition, and I felt like one of those watching women, presented with illusions and seeing only half the story, while those with power knew the reality, and having that knowledge gave them yet more power.

So no. I didn't want to sleep with Jake. I wanted time to think. But in the attic, the floor was still wet and it unsettled me. I was too scared to spend the night alone. So once again, I was back in Jake's bed, snuggling into the crook of his arm. And I didn't know if that was the safest place in the world for me or the most dangerous.

'*U tebya*,' I pronounced.

Yelena laughed. '*Ya xachu otsosat u tebya*,' she repeated. 'It means, "I want to suck your dick."'

I laughed. 'Hey, who knows? Could come in handy.'

'*Ya xachu lizat mejdu tvoimi nogami*,' said Yelena.

I couldn't make head nor tail of it, and we had to practise for several minutes, giggling and spluttering at my mistakes before I was even close.

'*Nogami*,' corrected Yelena.

'*Nogami*.'

Yelena laughed.

'OK, so what's it mean?' I asked.

Yelena looked me straight in the eye and said, 'It means, "I want to eat your pussy."'

I could feel myself reddening. This woman had designs on me, there were no two ways about it.

'Ah, you blushing,' she said gleefully, making me blush even more.

We were on the sofa in the flat above the pub, in a room like an inverted gift box, a floral border running around its middle, denim-blue walls beneath, lemon-yellow above.

For all its faded suburban conventionality, the room obviously wasn't lived in by a conventional couple. Not unless I've missed something and conventional couples have bookcases lined with porn videos and tanks of tropical fish where slivers of neon and iridescence swim among tiny castles and little shipwrecks.

The room looked ready to burst its seams. Magazines spilled from the rack, cushions bulged out of covers, wires snarled up behind equipment, and letters, junk mail, DVDs and unloved ornaments jostled for space on all available surfaces.

There's beauty and interest in the chaos of Jake's house and somehow, for all the dark eccentricity of his Aladdin's cave, there's no sense of stuff being on the verge of bursting out. Everything in Jake's house seemed to be there for a reason, namely he chose it. By contrast, much of the clutter in Yelena and Eddie's place was trash they hadn't got round to binning.

I'd been trying not to remember that I'd been there before, that Yelena's husband had pinned me to the wall and asked how Jake and I fucked. I'd seen him behind the bar on my way in. There's a separate entrance to their home but they don't seem to use it. Their domestic life is so blended with the pub that the bar is more like a porch entrance. I guess it's much the same at Jake's place: there is no work–life balance because they are one and the same thing. You come to understand this about Jake when, say, you open the freezer to take out some chicken breasts and find clay moulds of little puppet heads grinning up at you.

Eddie lifted the wooden counter flap. 'Go on up,' he said, gesturing me through. 'You know the way, don't you?'

'Thanks,' I said crisply, clutching my bottle of wine.

He smiled knowingly and with a hitch of his brows said, 'Catch you later, eh?'

I felt comfortable with Yelena, relaxed enough to kick

off my boots and tuck my feet beneath me as we chatted on the sofa. We were drinking wine from glasses etched with pub measures, Yelena going at twice my pace, her flesh bulging with such lovely carelessness from her dreadful clothes: a white leatherette mini skirt with metal stars studding the hem, a sluttily low V-neck sweater in schoolgirl bottle-green and a dreadful folk-peasant waistcoat ablaze with embroidery. It looked like a parrot had exploded on her back.

We were on our second bottle of wine when Yelena started teaching me how to talk dirty in Russian. I couldn't help but redden when I realised what I was saying.

'I like your blush,' she said. 'It's so pretty. I don't know how to blush. Maybe if I fall over I blush or maybe I just get black eye.' She laughed hard and leant closer to fluff up my hair. 'And your hair I love also. I think curls are not so often in this country. You are very lucky. You are like doll. My hair is so straight, so boring. I dye it because it is more exciting. When I was teenager I had the blue hair, now it is red. I am unreal, ha! I had boob job in Ukraine and botox.' She tapped her forehead. 'Cost me fiver!' She cackled with laughter. 'You want more wine?'

She was pouring before I could respond. From the pub below came the murmur of voices, low music, clattering glasses and laughter. The landing light shone into the dimly lit room and the aquarium hummed softly, fish shimmering like jewels. A lilac-blue lava lamp glowed on top of the TV, its lazy bubbles glooping up and down.

'Hey,' she began brightly but I interrupted. I'd been waiting for an appropriate moment but realised my only option was to shoehorn my question into the conversation.

'The police came to ours,' I said. 'To Jake's. Looking for a missing woman. Did they come here?'

'Oh my God, yes,' she said with dark glee. 'Chloë, Chloë somebody.'

'Chloë Lipsey,' I said because I couldn't forget the name.

'Yes, yes. They came to pub, ask people if they've seen her but everyone say no. I wonder where is she, who is her family. Family must miss her. I miss my momma. Moscow is far away. I was born Kiev but then we move to Moscow. Have you been in Moscow? Ah, man, I think you would love it. You are woman who like adventures . . .'

I let her babble on, giving up on my attempt to get some sense out of her. Missing persons inquiry. The police would be elsewhere now, asking other people. That's all it was.

I'd never met anyone quite like Yelena. She was so glorious and alive, the last sort of woman you'd expect to find in Heddlestone. But it seemed she was there because she genuinely loved Eddie, a man she'd met on holiday in Greece. 'He needed wife, I needed weesa,' she joked, but I could tell from the way she talked they were happy. She tottered around the living room, put on a CD, brought olives and gherkins from the kitchen, showed me photographs of her mum and told me about the fish.

'This one is betta,' she said, tapping the glass tank. 'It is fighting fish. Two men fishes are not good. One kills other. In nature, they don't do this. The fish don't kill. But in tank, a fish must die because is no place to hide. This is woman fish. There! Another! You see her? If you put mirror to glass, like here, fish go crazy, hitting his nose to tank, trying to fight with himself. You want to see?'

'No,' I said, half laughing. 'It's too cruel.'

Gradually, she started to wind down and the atmosphere grew less frenetic and more companionable. She asked why I'd moved to Heddlestone and I told her how life had stopped being good for me in London.

'Men,' she scoffed. 'Always men. Why they make it so complicated?'

'They probably say the same about us.'

She tucked her toes under my buttocks, smiled and reached out to wind a curl of my hair around a finger. 'You ever have girlfriend?'

She tipped her head against the sofa, giving me a dreamy gaze. My guess was she did this kind of thing a lot, or at least whenever she got the chance. 'You are lovely girl,' she said. She pulled on my hair, drawing me closer, smiling.

All I did was smile in return. She had such clear skin, such vibrant eyes, and our faces were inches away. Anxiety cut through my mellow, wine-soaked mood. If we'd been a man and woman, we'd have been seconds away from kissing. I'd never been with a woman, had never much wanted to but something shifted in me then. I could've turned my head away, could've made a light comment and changed the dynamics with no embarrassment for either of us. But I didn't because desire started to steal over me.

I'm still not sure what aroused me, whether it was Yelena for who she was, or whether it was the offer of something not quite standard. I'd been mentally prepared for her making a pass, and though the prospect had excited me, I wasn't sure how I'd feel when it came to the crunch.

I've become so much more open-minded through knowing Jake. I don't think I was closed or resistant before but I didn't actively seek unusual experiences. Jake's opened my eyes to new, darker pleasures and I'm often shocked by what we enjoy. Shocked too by how skilfully he brings me down, drawing me to that place I like, the nothing space where his loving violation all but disintegrates me. It's as if Jake knows me better than I know myself. I don't think this is a good thing.

With Yelena, I felt ready to be shocked again. My heart was thumping, and my hunger was strong and wet. The living-room door was open and all those people were drinking downstairs. It felt so teenage, the two of us on the brink of something illicit while the adults were nearby. It was deliciously risky.

'My God,' drawled Yelena with a gentleness I hadn't heard before. 'You are Jake's girl. He is lucky man.' Her lips were slightly open, her gaze steady with predatory lust.

I think I made the move. I'm sure I did. I don't recall how I felt – reckless? curious? eager? All I knew was I wanted to feel those lips on mine. I wanted to taste not-Jake, to breathe not-Jake, to be intimate with a person who was not Jake.

Our faces moved close then our lips fluttered together, moist and warm. We broke away, fluttered together again, and then again, lingering now, starting to search. We were tentative, polite, feeling the way with our mouths.

'Mmm,' she murmured and I felt the vibration on my lips. Her hand drifted across my neck and down the length of my arm. I was so aware of her touch, so excited and nervous. This was familiar territory to her but a whole new ball game to me. She played with my fingers. I shifted position, edging closer, and we kissed with increasing confidence. Her hand slid along my thigh, ruching my skirt higher. It was happening. Me and Yelena on the sofa in the grotty living room. It was happening.

'You been with woman before?' she asked kindly, eyes full of smiles. 'Tell me.'

I shook my head. 'Never.'

She made a noise in her throat, a deep sound like 'hurr'. It was so rich and chocolaty, and she was clearly pleased to be leading me astray. 'You are fucking sexy woman,' she breathed.

When she edged nearer her thighs parted under her faux-leather skirt, offering my eyes more flesh and teasing me with suggestions of what else might be parted. For the first time in my life, I understood miniskirts. They pulled you right in. She slipped a hand under my own demure, long-length skirt and ran a firm caress up my bare thigh. Without a pause, she pressed her fingertips to my gusset and began massaging with a strong steady action.

I caught my breath. Her speed and assurance shocked as much as it thrilled. I'd been pacing myself for tender explorations but she was as assertive and brazen as any man. No, probably more so. She paddled the fabric into my wet folds, her fingers sure and knowing. I moaned, and I moaned even more when she edged past the cotton to find me slippery and hot.

'Lie back,' she urged, and I gladly obliged, kicking off my underwear and dropping one foot to the floor. She whipped off her waistcoat and sweater, removed her bra and knelt half over me on the sofa, thighs bulging against white leatherette and stars. I could hardly believe she was there, inches away. I could hardly believe the nakedness of her breasts. They were full and high, her nipples dusky-beige discs, shrivelling to nubs as her hand rushed under my skirt again. I was fascinated by how ordinary her body seemed, by her pale skin, the faint freckles on her chest, the stubble in her armpits.

It stunned me that she was giving herself like this. She was a woman, sexual and horny, and for her to reveal herself to me, to another woman, made me heady with new lusts. Her appetite seemed vulgar and greedy, and it blew my mind. I loved it. I felt as if we were sharing some witchy intimacy, some mutual understanding in a secret world of our own.

I was all fired up to take a nipple in my mouth, my first female nipple, to test the feel of it with my tongue but before I could, Yelena lowered one breast to my face, almost smothering me in smooth, cushiony flesh. God, it was heaven. I'd never imagined it could feel so nice. I kissed and sucked, enjoying the slight deprivation of breath as my mouth and nostrils were filled with her weight. I was wriggling beneath her, my hips rocking into her masturbating hands, shameless and wet, wanting her fingers to fuck me to orgasm.

I caressed her big tits, sturdier than mine but that was obviously the boob job. I was thinking how gorgeous it would be if I could remove my own top and have her breasts squashed to mine, flesh on flesh, sweat on sweat, but I didn't want to break what we were doing. Later, I thought, later. Plenty of time.

And then a man's voice cut in. Yelena froze, fingers lodged deep.

'Well, well, that didn't take long.' It was Eddie, his voice coming from the open doorway.

Yelena gave a guilty little laugh.

My heart hammered.

Neither of us moved.

I heard the door shut and the room got darker as the landing light was blocked out. Had he come in or left? I could hear my own breath, quick and nervous, and blood roared in my ears. I tried to move but Yelena stilled me by hooking her fingers in a warning. The aquarium burbled gently, and the lava lamp glowed in the corner, casting patterns on the walls and making the gloom blue. Were we listening to see if he'd gone? I held my breath, waiting.

I tried to read Yelena's face. Was this going to be a problem? Her eyes were downcast, eyelashes dark with mascara. Her cheekbones glowed in the spectral light, her face taking on a waxy tinge. She reminded me of Jake's pallid Victorian doll.

And then I thought: You are like doll.

That's what she'd said to me: 'You are like doll.'

Her eyelashes flickered in a tiny blink. It seemed she was holding her breath as well.

A doll? Or *the* doll?

'Meredith' Jake had called it. But according to Eddie it was Laura. 'That's his Laura-doll,' he'd said when I'd seen them fucking on the sofa. 'It's got a cloth cunt.'

I could hear the faint whisper of Yelena's breath streaming in and out of her nose. Her big naked breasts dangled above my jumper and she had one arm on the sofa back, her underarm stubble glinting like iron filings. She was as still as a statue, her fingers fixed inside me. I could hear nothing of Eddie.

I had curly blonde hair and a pale, round face.

I looked like the Laura doll, Jake's precious porcelain-faced mascot who might also be a ghost.

I looked like Chloë Lipsey who was missing.

And Meredith? Who was she? Did I look like her as well or was that a name Jake had plucked from the air?

There've been times in my life when, head over heels in love but fearing it too good to be true, I've thought: What does he see in me? I'd never thought that with Jake. He made me feel so good, so in his league, and I never questioned his affections.

But I thought it then. And the thought was horribly literal: What does he see in me?

What? Or who? Who does he see in me?

Eddie spoke. 'Stand up, both of you,' he said. 'Stand up. I want to take a look at you.'

10

Yelena stood, tits ballooning heavily, her waist making a roll over the top of her white miniskirt.

'Stand up,' she urged quietly, so I did, figuring it was probably better than lying there, skirt crumpled around my spread thighs. I felt as shaky and scared as if I'd been called to the front of the class.

Eddie stood by the closed door, thickset and broad, his bald head gleaming in the violet-tinged dimness, eyes hollowed by shadow. He looked at us and, from the other side of the sofa, Yelena and I returned the gaze. We must have seemed an odd pair, Yelena with her red and brown hair in rumpled spikes, big breasts on display, and me next to her, five foot nothing, and apparently respectable in jumper and long skirt, quite the librarian except my knickers were on the floor.

'Come here, Yel,' said Eddie, and his voice was honeyed with soft menace.

I felt horribly alone as she walked away, the sofa forming a barrier between us, me on the rug, the marrieds on the other side. Had I walked into a trap? Was it those two versus me? Or me and Yelena versus him? Or was this not a battle?

'Stand there,' he said to Yelena.

In the bluish glow, they moved behind the sofa like strange ghosts, remote and theatrical; like glove puppets, actually, their legs hidden from view, making Yelena practically naked. Eddie directed her to stand against the back of the sofa, more or less opposite me. I looked to her for reassurance but she seemed not to register it. Her face sagged with horniness, and she had a dazed indifferent air. Anyone could do anything to that woman, I thought, and she'd take it.

Her expression didn't reassure but maybe she thought the same about my face. I was scared, yes, but I was also twisted up with a dark, grubby lust. I could almost taste it in my throat, that vast and dangerous hunger of Yelena's. I felt brave and reckless, more than ready to experience corruption. It was as if her kisses were spiked.

'Bend over,' Eddie instructed. His tattooed armband peeped as, with a hand on her neck, he pushed Yelena forwards so she was doubled over the sofa back, head to the cushions.

Now I couldn't see her face. She was a puppet, limp without her puppeteer's hand. It was just me and Eddie. He looked at me for a long time and, determined to the point of petulance, I didn't break the stare. I could hardly see his eyes but I knew their colour: stone-grey like Jake's, although when you look closer, Eddie has a colder crueller gaze, chips of flint where Jake has dove-grey softness.

Did Eddie see someone else in me as well? Is that what this was all about? Did they both have a thing for blondes and they liked to share? Did Jake console himself with antique dolls when he hadn't got a girlfriend?

Eddie's lips tilted in a small, mocking smile. 'And you,' he said.

He stepped away from Yelena, giving me space to move around the sofa back.

I stood there, undecided. I knew what I wanted to do: I wanted to obey him. I wanted him to take me over the way Jake did. I wanted to put myself in his mean, hard hands and have him fuck the very breath from me. I wanted to drop to my knees and suck his cock, have him clutch my hair as he pumped into my mouth. I wanted him to make me do defiling, hardcore acts I'd never even dreamt of. I wanted him to drag me right down.

But I didn't want him to know that, so I was rooted to the spot.

'I could always force you,' he warned, seeing my hesitation.

Part of me wanted that but a better part didn't. I didn't want to give him the pleasure. I wouldn't allow him to force me because he wouldn't understand it. So, shrugging as if it didn't matter, I walked around the sofa, knees weak with lust and dread. I stood where he directed me, a few inches to the side of Yelena's draped, rag-doll form.

In the sickly blue light, her shoulder blades and spine seemed unreal and futuristic. Her hands were on the sofa cushions, her hair falling in upside-down spikes of chestnut and deep red. For the first time, I realised there was a peculiar vulnerability to her. She was made of appetite – for life, for sex, for stuff to fuel her – and her urge for gratification seemed blithely, almost merrily, destructive. Someone who didn't have her best interests at heart could exploit that so easily. While she was clearly a connoisseur of kinky sex, there was a naivety there, a childlike enthusiasm which made me feel protective.

'Over we go,' said Eddie in a sing-song tone, and he tried to tip my upper half over the sofa back, just as he'd done with Yelena.

'Hey, hang on,' I said, stiffening against his pressure. 'Who do you think you –'

'Bend,' he said firmly, his hand firm on my neck. 'You're doing what I say now. You were about to fuck my wife, in *my* house . . .'

He made it seem as if that in itself were enough. And so what if I was? I thought. Does that give you a right? Do you think it's all the same? Me, Yelena, your house? Do you think we're all your property? And I might have said that. I might have challenged him. I might have elbowed him aside and said, 'Fuck you, mate. I'm outta here.'

But I didn't because for months I'd been unable to shake this man from my mind. Because I didn't want to desert Yelena. Because the hand curving to the back of my neck was massaging in a strong sensual rhythm, and then tracing ticklish circles behind my ears. Because I could smell him, and he smelt the way he had done when he'd pinned me to the wall: of pubs, men, warmth and a muted hint of deodorant.

Because I am weak.

'I could always give Jake a bell,' he said, exerting more pressure. 'I'm sure he'd love to see this. Love it.'

I flopped forward, roused even more by a fantasy of Jake being involved. I turned, head resting on the cushions, waves of my hair tumbling over the fabric. I glanced at Yelena, her face the only thing that was the right way up in an upside-down room. I averted my eyes, too embarrassed to make proper contact. Her fingers scrabbled for mine in a brief sisterly gesture. Although I was grateful, I knew Yelena's definition of OK was a long way from mine, so I wasn't quite comforted. Behind us, Eddie moved about. I heard a couple of drawers open. Then I heard a clink of metal and he stepped between our legs, shoving us apart.

'Here we go, ladies,' he said. He lifted Yelena's hand, snapped a handcuff on her wrist and just as I was protesting, he grabbed my wrist and locked the other cuff around it, the ratchets grating into place.

'Hey!' I complained, and instinctively tried to pull free.

'Ouch! Please, Kate!' cried Yelena as her hand jerked with mine. The cuffs were harsh and it had hurt me too, though perhaps not as much.

'Sorry,' I said, relenting.

'Relax,' she replied. 'It's OK. Just fun. He is pussy cat.'

I tried to accept, staying in position like Yelena, linked to her by a tiny chain. It was uncomfortable and I could feel pressure in my cheekbones, gravity doing odd things to my inverted face.

'My wife, Yelena,' announced Eddie, as if he had an audience. 'The village slut.'

I craned back, and saw that he was pushing up Yelena's

white skirt. It wrinkled around her waist and then I saw that he was tugging down her knickers, baring her white arse.

I sensed him step back, observing. Yelena was entirely passive, and my heart was thundering because I guessed I was next. I hadn't worked out what I would do but that was suddenly irrelevant because Eddie's hand was on my buttocks, and I didn't want to do anything except feel it. He rubbed circles on one cheek, stirring the fabric of my skirt. He must have realised I wasn't wearing underwear but he didn't pass comment. He just kept his big hand moving on my flesh, and heat was soon leaking onto my inner thighs.

'And Kate,' he said. 'Our new arrival.' Carefully, he raised my skirt then rolled and tucked the fabric into the waistband so it would stay high. My arse, like Yelena's, was on full view. 'And what's the betting,' he continued, 'she's our next village slut?'

He stepped back, presumably to take in the view of our bared arses, side by side over the sofa, our slits and pouches peeping below our cheeks. I felt so lewd and ashamed. But there was nothing within me, nothing at all, that might have prompted me to move. Only an incident on a par with fire or flood would have made me quit.

Eddie stepped between us, his jeans grazing my naked thigh, and reached to cup the backs of our heads. 'Kiss each other,' he ordered, pushing our faces together. Yelena was greedy now, her mouth moist, her tongue probing.

'Hot little bitches,' said Eddie.

His hand caressed my neck and I responded to Yelena's kisses, becoming as eager and wet as she was. God, it was good. Eddie was taking charge, turning us into his playthings. Strangely, the genuine connection I shared with Yelena seemed wayward and doubly thrilling, a negation of the power he'd assumed.

When he released us, we continued kissing. I guessed

there was symmetry in what he was doing, and when his hand roamed over my arse, I imagined his other hand doing the same on Yelena's cheeks.

'Now then,' he said in a mild, threatening coo. 'Let's see who's got the tightest little pussy, shall we?'

His fingers were there, spreading my lips then gliding inside me. Yelena and I moaned, abandoning our kiss as Eddie's broad fingers shunted in and out, making us click wetly.

'Does Jake do this to you, Katie?' he asked.

I wished I could conceal my pleasure but it was impossible. Groans were spilling from my lips as much as juices were spilling onto his fingers.

'Ah, man,' said Yelena. Her noises were more guttural than mine, and there was nothing there to suggest discomfort, shame or anger. I felt all three emotions, and God knows how many more.

Shame was the greatest, shame I wanted this man to treat me badly; shame I could let him do this. I knew I was being used but, to be honest, it was a relief, and I was probably using him too. Jake and I share so much emotional energy that this detached empty fingerfuck felt like a much-needed holiday from my heart. Even so, I couldn't fully love it. I still felt guilt and shame.

And I was ashamed of my shame. Aren't we meant to embrace our horniness these days? To take what we want from the twenty-first century's kinky candyshop of sex? But I don't want sweet indulgence. I prefer bad and debased over naughty but nice.

And yes, I'm ashamed of that but the strangest thing is, I've come to treasure that shame. It touches some dark corner of my psyche, a corner only Jake and Eddie can find. Jake's taken me to some shadowy places but he's intelligent and he cares. He can pull me apart then put me back together. Eddie is coarser. His limits, not mine, are the ones that count. I knew there'd be no soft words of love or arms to enfold me. He would pull me apart then leave me in pieces. He was dangerous. I feared he could demolish me and yet I couldn't turn away.

'Now then,' said Eddie, putting on a contemplative tone. 'Who shall I fuck first?'

'Me!' cried Yelena. 'Me!'

Eddie's fingers pumped us fast in an alternating rhythm as he murmured, 'Ip dip sky blue, Who is it? Not – Oh, dear. Lost my thread there. Start again. Ip dip –'

'Me,' begged Yelena. 'Oh, please, Eddie. Fuck me, fuck me.'

I did think it was a shade rude of her. I was their guest, after all. I was aching for him too, to have him opening me up till his cock was snug and deep. But I couldn't demean myself enough to beg for it so all I did was whimper while he continued fluffing his 'ip dip' song, and while Yelena continued demanding.

'Which one?' mused Eddie. 'Which hot little pussy gets the pleasure of my dick? Which hot little pussy gets none?' He was fingering us in harmony now, and I was so oily and pliant. 'Who's it to be? Who shall I fuck?'

I don't know how it happened but I lost control of a whimper. It morphed into something else and I heard a dry, cracked whisper: 'Me.'

Eddie leant closer. 'What's that, Kitty Kat?' he mocked. 'Did you say something?'

'Me,' I repeated, my voice still breath-light.

'Again?'

There seemed no point denying it. 'Me,' I snapped. 'Fuck me first, you ... you bastard.' Angry tears stung my eyes. I was angry at him but mostly I was angry with myself for wanting him so badly.

He leant back, withdrawing his fingers. 'Since you ask so nicely,' he began. I heard the clank of his belt and the hiss of leather running through the buckle. He stepped aside, nudging us together so our bare hips were touching. Without his fingers, I felt cavernous with need. I heard him move behind us, heard a drawer go again. Draped over the sofa back, I was so limp with lust I felt I'd been filleted.

Eddie stepped out of his jeans, coins jangling in his pockets. 'Since you ask so nicely,' he repeated, 'I'm going to do my lawful wedded wife first.'

'No,' I gasped.

I craned back to see him move behind Yelena, her groan of pleasure torment to my ears, the jolt I felt as he entered her as painful as a blow.

'No,' I repeated, as he began pounding away at her.

Her body banged against mine, knocking me in their rhythm. Whenever she moved her hand, my arm jerked with it, and her every breath and gasp was laced with bliss. It was agony, like being fucked but not feeling it. I was so wet and wide I was beyond horny. This was madness. It was a wanting more akin to possession.

'Please, please,' I said. 'It hurts.'

'What hurts?' Eddie asked gently.

'Nothing,' I cried. 'The nothing hurts. Please.'

'How's this then?' he said, and a cool hard object nudged at my entrance. 'A nice dildo for you. Don't say I never give you anything.'

He slid the length in fast and deep. My walls stretched to take the object, and the sudden fullness was so intense I was panting for breath.

'That suit you?' asked Eddie.

His arm drove back and forth, and he began fucking me with the fake cock while fucking Yelena with the real deal. His rhythm was erratic. Sometimes, he held her steady, his breath ragged as he worked me with the dildo, talking to me and watching as he twisted, pounded and wiggled the shaft. At other times, he concentrated on Yelena and I had to listen to the slap-slap of their flesh, feel the bump-bump of their grind and suffer the pain of his neglect.

'How's it feel, Katie?' he asked. 'You ready for a real cock yet?'

'Yes,' I croaked.

'Ah, no,' wailed Yelena. 'I'm going to come.'

'Yes, what?'

'Yes please,' I gasped.

'Tell me what you want,' said Eddie. 'Spell it out for me. I'd hate to get it wrong.'

'I want a real cock,' I said, not caring. 'A real cock, please.'

'One moment, sweetheart,' said Eddie, and Yelena complained as he withdrew.

He pulled the dildo from me and I spread my legs wider, pushing back, eager for him to slam it in deep. But then I was the one protesting as he returned to Yelena, her complaints turning to groans.

'Shut up, Yel,' said Eddie. 'I need to make a phone call.'

I heard his phone bleep then he was gyrating lazily into Yelena while she whimpered in compliance.

'Ammi!' Eddie said into the phone. 'You owe me a tenner!' He laughed at whoever had answered. 'Didn't believe me, did you? Swear to God, she's here, arse up, pussy spread. Aren't you, Katie?'

He ran a broad hand over one of my buttocks, a gesture almost fond and possessive. I loathed him. His fingers dipped down and he rocked my clit, and though it nearly killed me, I didn't make a single sound. I don't think I even breathed.

'Yeah, come on up, mate. She's all yours.' He ended the call with a chuckle then tossed the phone onto the sofa.

The noise from the pub below surged briefly as a door opened and shut. I heard footsteps on the stairs.

'It's Ahmed,' said Yelena, sounding pleased.

I knew at once who she meant. I'd seen him in the village, and I'd seen him look at me a little too long. A lot of people would do that when I was a new face but there was always something knowing about Ahmed's glances.

Perhaps I would look at him a little too long as well because Ahmed's is an Asian face, and a beautiful one at that. He's young, late twenties maybe, but his hair is already receding. It sweeps back from his face and hangs in lush Byronic curls, as black as night. His lips are full and have a damaged, chapped quality to them. No, they're more than full. It's as if they're so plump they won't close properly. His mouth is permanently parted, a fraction of a gap between upper and lower lip, so it looks as if he's forever gawping at a thing he wants. He has a slutty, fascinated air, and his brown-black eyes, set in dusky shadows, look soft enough to melt. Really, he ought to be in movies.

He's always stood out to me not just because he is beautiful but because he is Asian. There are big immigrant communities in the north-west but Heddlestone, being such an insular place, hasn't been much influenced by change and progress.

Behind us, the living-room door opened, light flaring briefly from the landing. And here it is, I thought. Here's progress. The door closed, plunging us into lilac-blue strangeness again, lava-lamp bubbles making shapes in a far corner. Veins of light from the aquarium shimmered on another wall and, in the water, jewels moved, flashes of sapphires, rubies, emeralds and amber with trailing fronds and fins, spines lit like tiny neon tubes.

'Oh, wow,' came Ahmed's voice, and I liked him for that. 'Where do I begin?'

'Here,' I growled. 'Here and now.'

'I don't think so,' said Eddie, slipping out of Yelena. 'Here, have the missus. Katie's mine. She's been begging for it all night.'

'Anyone,' I snarled. 'Anyone will do. Just ... anyone, please.'

I heard Eddie messing about with condoms then he stood behind me, clasping my hips, his boner resting in the valley of my buttocks.

'Say it again, Katie,' Eddie murmured. 'Say "please".'

He sawed back and forth, his cock's weight in the

groove of my cheeks. I was aching to have him inside me, aching to know what stalked my darker dreams.

'Please,' I echoed, my voice clogged and gravely. 'Please, please, please.'

I could hear Ahmed undressing a few feet away.

'And please, me too,' urged Yelena.

'I love it when women beg,' said Eddie. 'Especially cuffed ones. What do you want, Kitty Kat?'

'I want your cock,' I said quietly. 'Please.'

'Where do you want it?'

'Inside me. Please. I want it inside me.'

'Where inside you? In your arse?' He nudged his glans at the dip of my anus.

'No,' I breathed. 'Not there.'

'Tell me then, Miss High and Mighty,' he said, pressing where I was pinched and dry. 'Give us the words. Tell us where you want it.'

I gulped for breath. I'm bad with words and I loathe having to ask. That's why I like Jake, because I don't need to. That's why I like Eddie, because he makes me. Having three other people present made it worse than ever. 'I want it in my cunt,' I said softly.

'Where?' said Eddie loudly. 'Didn't quite catch that. Come again.'

I breathed steadily, trying to push past my discomfort. In the boldest voice I could manage, I said, 'In my cunt.' Nothing happened so, very clearly, I then added, 'Please. If you wouldn't mind.'

'In your cunt,' said Eddie as if mulling it over. 'Well, that's nice, isn't it? In Katie's cunt.'

Then his cock slipped down and he banged it in fast and deep. I wailed, dizzied by sudden pleasure.

'Like this?' he grunted, and he began rutting hard, gripping my hips and slamming me back onto him. His thrusts shook my body, making my cries weird and warbled. He felt so good, so incredibly good, and every part of me quivered with his force.

'How about a nice mouthful as well, eh, Kate?' gasped Eddie, his voice as jerky as my cries. 'Ahmed, do the honours. The wife can wait.'

'No, I can't,' protested Yelena. 'Don't be bastard. Give me vibe.'

'Stunning,' said Ahmed.

Eddie slowed and began to shake my buttocks with his hands, making the flesh wobble. It was bliss, little ripples of movement spreading to my groin. I touched my clit, sensation fluttering and rising. A vibe started buzzing next to me and Ahmed, naked and handsome, strode around to the front of the sofa as if he were wading through the ghostly blue gloom. His abdomen was flat and taut, skin with a sheen like caramel, and the hair on his body was a rich, sooty black.

Memories of Eddie, Yelena and a third man in the club came flooding back: Yelena with her hands bound high, dressed like some insane doll while two men prowled and poked before filling her at either end. That scene had been so dreamy and surreal, and I thought how this might look to an onlooker, debauchery and chaos in a subaqueous haze. In front of me, Ahmed's cock jutted from his black pubes, proud and thick.

With his looks and dark curls, he seemed a broader, shorter, more Asian version of Jake, and that made me very happy indeed. He surged towards me, planting one foot on the cushion, and Eddie grasped my hair like Jake does as I gaped for Ahmed. He was considerate in feeding his length to me, and I sucked and pulled, relishing the pinch in my scalp where Eddie held my curls. I was wedged tight between them, barely able to move, skewered on their sliding cocks.

Like some insane doll.

Yelena panted and gasped in climax.

'Oh, wow,' said Ahmed. Eddie rammed me with fast shallow strokes, and I cried around Ahmed's shaft, my peak hitting.

'She's coming,' said Eddie, and his fingers dug into my buttocks, giving my cheeks an extra jiggle.

'Ah, man,' said Yelena. 'I knew she was dirty.'

And I pictured her as she'd been all those months ago, dressed in a froth of white, a scarlet ribbon around her waist, on her head a wig of messy blonde hair, not unlike my own.

You are like doll.

Some insane doll.

We were both like dolls. It wasn't just me, it was Yelena in costume as well. And we were like one particular doll, the Laura doll. Were we also like the ghost Jake refused to talk about?

I came in a whirl of ecstasy and fear, cries muffled by Ahmed's cock. Voices seemed to reach me from a distance: She's good. I like her. She'd do another dozen, no probs.

I clung to a single thought: when I stop coming, this will all make sense. It'll all be OK, no need to be scared.

And then I did stop coming but it wasn't OK. It still isn't. I'll sleep on it, I told myself. There are too many bodies here, too much sex, lust and wine. My head can't process it. In the morning, it will all be so much better.

But I was wrong about that, very wrong. In the morning, everything was infinitely worse.

I had to sleep in the attic that night. I couldn't climb into Jake's bed when three other bodies had been on me, inside and out.

'I'll walk you home,' said Eddie when he'd closed the pub. I almost laughed: a man who'll demean you, fuck you, bully and torment, then politely offer to escort you home. I didn't think it was necessary. I was probably safer here at night than I was in Hackney. In the pitch-black countryside, imagination's the scariest thing.

Nonetheless, I accepted his offer. I wanted to know what would happen when it was just the two of us.

We'd been fucking for hours, all four of us in so many

permutations. I'd never known such pornography, never been close to such a riot of flesh, limbs and greed, of sweat and spattered come, of squelching and elbows. We were voracious, our inhibitions getting looser and looser until we were almost as one, doing what we wanted: demanding it, giving it, refusing it, taking it.

'No!' I said at some point because I wanted a cock not the dildo which was purple and non-human.

'Oh, yes,' countered Eddie. He was kneeling down and he grappled me so I was astride him, hooking me by the armpits, my back to his chest. Naked, he had more tattoos, a tribal Maori sprawl on one shoulder, and a crude Maltese cross on one breast that looked like it might have been a mistake. Yelena, doing as instructed, got behind him and grabbed my ankles. My back arched as Eddie leant back, offering me to Ahmed. Ahmed drove the dildo into me, Eddie laughing softly in my ear as I cried, 'No, no,' lying through my teeth and loving the word, loving how Eddie forced me.

It was bitterly cold outside, the market square quiet and dark, a few flecks of snow drifting softly. Our breath puffed out in vaporous blasts, our footsteps clicking and echoing on the flagstones. Even when you can't see the fells, you can sense them, smell their freshness in the wind, hear how sound vanishes in that lonely expanse. Sometimes, the moors are just the landscape you live in, stern, bluff and untouchable. Sometimes, they situate you right there, slap bang within your own mortality. You're a molecule in the universe, a dot in history that will one day be erased, not even another's memory to carry you forward.

That's how it felt then as Eddie and I left the village edge, turning onto the half mile track that leads to home and the museum. The night was thick with low cloud, and there was a small blur of moonlight. The snow gathered, flakes swelling in number but floating as gently as ever. They melted where they landed, and my face grew wet with soft, cold touches. I didn't care that I'd just been fucked silly by a bunch of people I hardly knew. I didn't care what Jake or you or anyone might think. I felt sore and stretched in every part of me, slutty with other people's fluids, my hair unkempt and knotty. It had been my choice. An opportunity had arisen and I'd taken it and loved it.

Eddie and I walked along the track in a silence that was close to perfect. The sky was feathered with snow, and I resisted the urge to mention the weather. It was difficult because it looked so beautiful, and I was wondering if we'd all wake up to a magical white world. The moors usually look fierce but that night they were starting to smudge, veiled by the fall of flakes. A few sugary crystals lodged in the tufted grass by the path and the distant slopes disappeared. Even the quality of the silence was different, muffled and gentler. The snow chilled my cheeks and lips, and I felt glorious and exultant.

For the first time in a long time, I felt I was at the centre of my own life, not running away from one thing, hurtling towards another. In the grand scheme of it all, I was tiny. But in the scheme of me, of my own life, I was fast becoming a giant. I hardly knew Eddie was beside me.

'Be good,' he said as we neared the house.

I looked at him, not knowing how to say goodnight, feeling the sudden need for a kiss and wishing Ahmed had walked me back because perhaps he and I could do that.

'Yeah, maybe,' I said. 'Thanks for seeing me home.'

'Any time,' he said. 'It's been emotional.' And with a roguish wink he turned on his heels, heading back for the village.

The outside light was on, snow spinning in its haze of pearl, but the house was in darkness. I tiptoed in, trying not to feel guilty. I didn't feel I'd technically betrayed Jake. After all, he'd been the first to suggest I sleep with Eddie for reasons unknown to me. But I did feel I'd betrayed him in that I'd gone further than that, and wanted to wallow in this new array of dark, disturbing pleasures. My wariness of Jake had cooled our relationship too, and I felt this was another slight against him, though that was never my intention.

Noah came trotting along as I locked the door but he didn't make a fuss. I was exhausted and bruised, and I added an extra blanket to my bed, kicking off my boots and crawling under the sheets, still in my clothes. I was freezing and the heating had been off for a while.

I tried to think about dolls, and how much to tell Jake about the evening because he was sure to ask. But my head was crammed with images of flesh, with snatched sentences and confusion. There was no room for thought, and I fell into a thick sleep the way you sometimes do when you're traumatised and your overstimulated self needs to shut right down.

When I woke, I felt as if I'd been asleep for years but it was less than a couple of hours. It was still dark, not long after 3 a.m., and something was wrong.

I lay there, listening. I was hot now, sweating inside my clothes, and the silence outside was that of heavy snow, a deadened silence. My clock radio cast a tiny light. I turned to lie on my back. I hadn't closed any blinds and the sloping windows were blank sheets of white, blocking out the sky. The small windows at floor level were tiny frames onto a world transformed into stillness, a secret snowscape holding its own soft moment, waiting for people to wake and discover it.

The roads across the tops were bound to be bad. I wondered if the village would get cut off. It was hard to tell how deep it was. But at that point, the snow wasn't the problem. No, the problem was downstairs on the floor where Jake and I usually sleep.

I'd heard a noise and, though I couldn't be certain, it had sounded like stifled female laughter. It had woken me and its echo still chimed in my brain. I didn't think it was part of a dream. It wasn't my imagination. I'd heard female laughter.

Jake wouldn't, I thought. He wouldn't. I knew I had no right to feel jealous, considering what I'd just been up to, but I felt its first nasty twist.

I lay there, straining for more sounds. Nothing at all. Maybe I'd misheard. Anyway, another woman seemed unlikely. Jake wasn't that sociable or casual, and hadn't he once said he'd no intention of seeing anyone else when we were together? I wondered for a moment if we were still together.

My head was jangling with images, fuzzy details of the night. Eddie, Ahmed, Yelena. Limbs, faces, mouths, genitals. Pale skin and dark butterscotch entangling in a blue haze. I ought not to do it again. If it made Jake feel jealous the way I felt jealous, then it was bad. I didn't want either of us to have such a poisonous little emotion.

I began drifting off again, craving sleep and a peaceful mind.

But I didn't reach that place because again I heard dulled shards of laughter. Female laughter, no doubt about it now.

I was ready to kill. I threw back the bedclothes, swung my feet to the ground then paused, blood burning. A few seconds later, hearing nothing, I stood. A mattress spring twanged. I didn't want to turn on the light so I walked cautiously towards the door, feeling around in the dark. I was steely and detached, anger making me bold.

I tiptoed into the bathroom and turned on the shaving light above the mirror. It added a muzzy glow to the main room, pools reflecting in the thick gloss of the pale green door. I was wearing my woollen socks and by the time I reached the door, my left foot was wet. The carpet again. I hadn't noticed any dampness when I'd come to bed but then I'd been drunk on flesh and fucking, unfit to notice anything. I was so clueless as to what might be going on in the house, in Heddlestone, that it occurred to me the liquid might be blood. I stood on one leg, pinched the sole of my sock and checked my fingers. No, no blood there.

Carefully, I opened the door. I looked out at the landing, a dark empty square, and released the breath I'd been holding. I inhaled, as slow and steady as yoga, although my heart was running a marathon. I stepped out and stood still, gazing downstairs to a section of Jake's floor, its darkness lifted by snow and moonlight from an unseen window.

It was an old house and I knew some of the stairs creaked. I wished I'd had the foresight to notice which ones. Not the top one, I thought, relieved. Or the next. Or the next. I paused to steady my breath again, my hand resting against the wall. I began to doubt myself. Everything was so quiet it seemed inconceivable someone else was in the house. I wondered what excuse I'd give if Jake discovered me now, creeping about in last night's clothes. I would say I was cold and I missed him, I thought.

I skipped a step when it creaked lightly at the touch of my foot, pausing again. Had anyone heard that? I took another step, gaining confidence. I was about to tread on the next step when, without a warning sound, a figure darted across the foot of the stairs. It was a woman in white. She was there and she was gone, muffled laughter following in her wake. The image stayed, a wild hurried figure, bare feet, a thin white gown, blonde hair streaming and a red ribbon trailing from her waist.

My blood pressure plunged. I felt woozy and sick. Two emotions seized me, both as pure and absolute as the other: sheer mind-blanking terror and the white-hot rage of jealousy.

Laura. The ghost.

The ghost I didn't believe in.

She had him. She was his. He was hers. They were together downstairs, in his cast-iron bed, forever making love.

I sank onto the step, reeling as if I'd been hit. Nausea rolled over me and my skin turned from fire to ice. And then my ears were full of screaming, a raw scorched voice splitting the night in two. 'Jake! Ja–ake! Jake!'

And it was only when he came stumbling up the stairs, naked and horrified, that I realised the screams were mine.

11

I bought a notebook from the post office. It's red with lined pages and a margin. More of an exercise book, I suppose. It's what I'm writing in now.

I felt a need to record events, partly to try to get it straight in my own head but also to show you this life I've lived here. I'd begun to realise I was in deeper than I thought. And I didn't know how I might explain it you when I was struggling to do that myself. I thought trying to unravel it and showing you the process of that, warts and all, was my best chance of being truthful. I feel I owe you an explanation. I've treated you appallingly.

I'm sorry, Ollie. I'm so fucking sorry. But I was stuck. I know you felt it too. I hope you can see it wasn't entirely my fault. We were dragging each other down, hurting each other in such quiet, awful ways. It's hard to fix a relationship when you don't know what's wrong. I couldn't identify a specific problem so I kept thinking maybe I was the problem.

I didn't know what needed to be changed: my perspective or our situation. I went for the most hopeful and tried to view it differently. I have a wonderful man, I told myself, so I've no right to ask for more. And I'd believe that for a while but it never lasted, so I was back to asking, 'Is this it? Is this as good as it gets?'

I was worn out with hoping and there were times I hated you. Making a clean break felt like my only option, my only way of discovering. Cowardly? Weak? I guess so. Easier for me to walk than to stay. We'd tried talking but it never got us far because we didn't know what we were talking about. And how are you meant to talk openly to the person you feel so distanced from? We'd become strangers to each other, and yet we were strangers we couldn't bear to hurt.

I wanted to breathe and I couldn't with you. I'm sorry, but I couldn't. And I knew you were gasping for air just as much because I'd seen the hate in your eyes too. How can people who love come to hate each other? It's unbearable.

I know it's inadequate but I'll say it again anyway: I'm sorry. I guess this journal is another way of saying that. I know it'll be painful but I want you to feel as if you've been here with me. This story's probably messy, angry, dirty, shocking and happy. But it's honest and passionate, and that's more than we've given each other for a long time.

I've been trying to remember how Heddlestone felt in the beginning and to understand how I've changed. It's hard to get a picture. I feel my head is closing in on me. I've been so scared recently, and setting it down helps me try to see events more objectively.

I feel caught and trapped here. When I started this notebook, I was convinced I was doomed. I thought I'd never be able to leave. I thought Jake, or some mysterious force, would imprison or destroy me. Now, I'm not so sure. If I do leave physically, there are other ways in which I'll never leave. Some part of me will always remain here and Heddlestone will always be part of me. I don't mean as a memory. It's somehow more than that. I'll never fully escape. I'm not even sure I want to.

That figure at the foot of the stairs had me imagining all sorts of horrors. You can fight flesh and blood, or you can try, but the supernatural is beyond reach.

I don't believe in ghosts. Or I didn't. And yet so many incidents were without explanation: the presence I some-times felt; the wet carpet and Jake's evasions; rumours of ghosts; connections with dolls; that creepy sexy indolence that sometimes washed over me; those moments of sensory clarity, sights and sounds becoming more than what they were. What were these things? Why had I travelled hundreds of miles to take a job in some backwater village?

I remembered that line from *Hamlet*: 'There are more things in heaven and earth, Horatio, than are dreamt of in your philosophy.' In Heddlestone, was I living among things undreamt of?

I'm pragmatic but I'm no cold rationalist. Science doesn't know everything, and there are many unexplained phenomena. Only shrivelled-up fools believe life is literal and quantifiable. We have music, art, beauty, nature, so much that can touch us in some miraculous way. And when we're touched like that, when we're moved or inspired, it feels to me as if there's another world behind this, behind ours, yet all around us. There's something half-glimpsed, a place of ghosts, ancestors and angels; a place where the play of sun on a silvery sea is something you might capture and keep.

I do feel, sometimes, that this is what life is: that we live on the borders, never quite knowing. Living here, on the hinterland of the moors, I guess I've felt it more keenly than ever.

Could ghosts exist? If there's something which splits off from us, a soul, a self or an essence, might that exist in the half-glimpsed world? Is that what Laura was?

Whoever or wherever she was, I didn't think she liked me much. I imagined her striving to bring about my downfall, sending my bus careening off the road and tumbling down a ragged moorland slope. She would haunt and taunt me, leave wet patches in the attic, laugh in the night, sit on my bed and drive me slowly insane. And all the while she'd be getting closer to Jake. Should I try to save him? Was he in danger? Could he and I ever have peace or was he already lost to her, locked in a tragic embrace?

'There's nothing here, babes,' said Jake. 'Your eyes are playing tricks. Your eyes and your ears. Just an owl or one of the dogs.'

He sat by me on the step, an arm around my shoulder as I wept and shook.

'I saw her,' I sobbed. 'I saw Laura.'

'Shhh,' he cooed. 'There's no Laura. It's just a story. It's nonsense. There's no one here except us. Me, you, Noah and Twiglet.'

He drew me closer. I felt revolting. I was still in yesterday's clothes, crumpled with sleep. My hair was brittle with dried come, Eddie's and Ahmed's, and my face was singed from the rasp of their stubble, especially Ahmed's because he liked to kiss. Jake nuzzled my head, rubbing my shoulder. After a while, in a soft cajoling tone, he said, 'You fucked Eddie, didn't you?'

I had no energy to do anything but sniff and nod.

Jake kept rubbing my shoulder. 'Good girl,' he said, printing a kiss to my hair.

Everything was quiet. A light was on downstairs, a shadow slanting across the staircase. There was no noise other than sniffles from me, and the deadened softness of the snow-cloaked outdoors.

'Did you enjoy it?' asked Jake.

Again, I just nodded. I was glad we couldn't see each other's eyes.

'Good girl,' he repeated.

We slept together in the attic room. Jake undressed me and held me tight until dawn. We didn't have sex. In the morning, he ran me a bath heaped with bubbles. He soaped me with a sponge, shampooed my hair then slathered it with conditioner.

'Don't come into the workshop today,' he said. 'You look exhausted.'

'I'm fine,' I murmured, although I wasn't.

'Hey,' he warned gently. 'I'm the boss. I'll phone and tell myself you're snowed in.'

I hardly go into the workshop these days. I've started to think there isn't much for me to do here. I'm not quite sure what this job's about any more. I think Jake wants me here, always has done, but I don't think it's to sort out his admin systems.

I spent most of that day watching old films, reading and gazing out at a chiaroscuro world, trees stamped like black lace on a plump snowscape, drystone walls making dark serrations. I went out in the morning to check for footprints but fresh snow had covered the postman's and milkman's tracks. Besides, I didn't believe she had footprints.

God, it was beautiful that day. If I'd had more energy I'd have wrapped up warm and gone running out to make snowballs like a kid. But I was shattered. So instead, I stood by the house and watched a crow, black and raffish, messing about on the lane to the village, the lane that was buried under snow.

In London when we saw crows, you'd always tell me how intelligent they were. It became one of our jokes because you'd say it too often, forgetting I knew. 'Oh, Ollie, look!' I'd tease. 'It's your mate, Albert Einstein.'

I've been thinking about you such a lot. It's like the line from that song: 'You don't know what you got till it's gone.' I'm sitting up in bed now, writing and thinking. The little lamp is on, and it's raining, drips sliding down the Velux window, glittering with light from my room. At night, I leave the curtains and blinds open, losing some warmth but gaining reassurance from being able to see beyond this house.

I considered typing up my story on the laptop but I don't want Jake to know what I'm doing. I'd worry he might be lurking outside the door, listening to the tiny tap-tap, hatching plans to access my files. This way, I can sit up in bed at night, perfectly silent, and he's none the wiser.

Besides, I prefer handwriting and I know you do too. I brought a few things here to remind me of you: a couple of birthday cards, a 'sorry' note you wrote after a fight, a strip of cut-out paper people, their hands linked, silly sweet nothings written on their bodies. Here, these items are treasure. Your words and handwriting feel so intimate, and yet it's as if the items belong to another era, historical artefacts. I almost didn't bring them – clean break, I thought – but breaks are never clean, and I'm glad I did.

I wonder how you've been feeling. I imagine you're still furious. I hope when this gets to you that you'll read it. I'll post it to you, recorded delivery perhaps. I'd like you to know these things before we meet. If we meet. Maybe there's a chance. And maybe you'll forgive me. I don't know. I don't know if you and I have a future. How can I consider that when I don't even know if *I* have a future.

I wish I was back in London, back in the flat we shared in Dalston years ago. We had so many happy times there. You know what I think our mistake was? Moving into separate places. I don't think our living arrangements were the problem, were they? We'd allowed ourselves to stagnate. Coming here has made me realise the importance of change. Even if the change doesn't go according to plan, it's movement. And without movement, you're dead.

I think about you such a lot. My memories of you are woven from the brightest strands. Odd moments. Lost in Venice, a shadowed alleyway and suddenly there was the water again, no one around except us, alone in the backstreets of that strange, sinking city. And we stopped to look, sunlight rippling on the canal, and from behind us came music. Someone was playing saxophone. A song drifted out from a window with shabby wooden shutters. It felt as if the music was just for us.

In the park one morning, you stopping to take a photograph of a shrub with yellow berries, me chatting to a man who had a beautiful red setter, its hair flowing like silky rust as it ran. I was so happy then, you doing your thing, me doing mine, separate yet together.

Cooking in the kitchen in Dalston, the little window that faced onto the brick wall of a building opposite, all our spices in mismatched jars and bags, a messy shelf of seeds and powders in saffron yellow, dun browns, fiery coppers. 'Here, taste.' A spoon held to lips. 'Mmmm.'

Small details, ordinary stuff, beautiful little fragments. I want to live where the moments are saturated with colour. I want a true palette, not this gaudy realm of puppetry, not this make-believe world where Jake holds sway.

Yelena's become a good friend. She clearly had no regrets – 'My God, that was hot night. We must do it again.' – whereas I was more circumspect. Initially, I struggled to meet her eye. We had lunch in the Punch and Judy cafe, and I was embarrassed to be sitting there with mugs of tea served by the six-fingered woman, having ordinary conversations while my mind teemed with memories of how we'd thrilled to Eddie's tattooed, numb-skull muscle.

'So tell me about this village ghost,' I said eventually.

'Ah, Lady Laura!' said Yelena. 'She haunt this place. She is Victorian woman in white dress. I don't see her. No one see her. It is very boring ghost.'

'And why does she haunt the village?' I asked as casually as I could.

Yelena frowned at me for several seconds, perplexed. Then her eyes popped wide and, in a tone implying I'd asked a really dumb question, said, 'Because she is dead?'

I didn't get far with her. I found one sentence on Google: 'The village is even said to be haunted by the ghost of a woman who drowned in Heddlestone Brook in Victorian days!'

Jake was still no help. 'Just a local legend, I told you. Yes, OK, so she's meant to wear white. But aren't all ghosts? You were just tired.'

'Did she drown?'

'Maybe. Rings a bell. I'll try and dig out those leaflets. But listen, that's not what you saw.'

I started to think he was right. Maybe I'd imagined it. I'd had a heavy night beforehand, so maybe my brain was jumbled and disturbed. I remembered seeing the brook in the woods on my first walk with Jake, before we'd even kissed. We've been back many times but that first view had been so exhilarating. It was worth leaving London for this, I'd thought, giddy simpleton that I was. It's such a fierce place, shining stones and noisy water tumbling through the trees. I could imagine someone going there to die, to vanish in the rich, riotous heart of this austere moorland.

I didn't want to imagine it though. That left me with two alternatives. One, I hadn't seen anything, just a trick of the light. Two, Jake was cheating on me. But if he was, wouldn't he be encouraging me to believe in ghosts?

I could have asked Eddie but we don't really have conversations. I'm sort of seeing him right now. If Jake and Eddie were two men in my London life I swear this wouldn't be happening. But here, everything revolves around the village and the people in it. Jake ties me up in knots. He's a puppet master to the bone. He wants to get inside my head, see the world as I do, and make me dance to his tune. My mind spins from the dark places he's shown me and my wrists chafe from the bonds.

Eddie's different. His dominance is physical and crude, and I can't resist. I don't know how I like it best or who I fear the most. But it hardly matters. I don't need to choose because I'm split between them, having it both ways. I'm very careful. I trust neither and am full of secrets. In one sense I feel I've got the upper hand but in all other senses, I haven't. There's something everyone's not telling me. Out here, I have no power at all.

I'll never fall in love with Eddie. I'm not sure if I'll ever even like him but with him I can be dirty, free and detached. I love fucking him and then walking away, no complications, both of us in tacit agreement that this is OK.

In London, I'd probably go to the cinema, meet friends, take up an evening class or embark on a project. There'd be a way for me to try to regain a balance if a man had taken over centre ground in a way that wasn't about love.

Although I suppose I do love Jake. He says he loves me too, and I believe he means it. I care about him. I love being with him. But he's too much and I think part of my love is that I pity him. He wants too much. He wants to get right inside my head and know me inside out. That's how he gets to feel secure.

Jake, for all his perversity, is an old romantic. He thinks love is about two people becoming one, a melding of head, heart and soul. In his ideal, I can't see where there's room for another to exist in their own right, an individual with a life beyond the pairing. Love, for Jake, is all consuming. He acts as if people can bond as happily and stupidly as dogs. It's just a matter of finding the right person. Love means so much to him and he lives in fear of losing it. I think that's why he feels the need to control.

Or maybe I'm just feeling bruised about love. Maybe I'm the one who's got the wrong idea.

Jake pretends he doesn't know about Eddie but he obviously does. I go to The Griffin some evenings, late at night near closing time. I'll have a drink then, when the pub's shut, Eddie and I will fuck over a table or on the carpet. Yelena is upstairs in the house. Eddie claims she knows and doesn't care. They have an open relationship. I don't ask questions. Afterwards, I go home and sleep in the attic. Once, Jake called to me from his bedroom as I was tiptoeing up to mine.

'Kate, come here,' he said. 'Come and fuck.' My heart skipped a beat. He knows, I thought. He knows I've been with Eddie.

I don't know what possessed me but I did as asked. He was wild for me that night, and I was for him. There was no kinky stuff, no bondage or spanking, just raw, hard, breathless fucking. Eddie was so much in my mind, his fingers and cock still lingering on my body, that it felt close to being in bed with both brothers. I felt so secretly filthy, such a quiet little slut, relishing how the Duxburys were sharing me as they must have once shared their toys. Jake, on top, clutched my hair, sweat on sweat, fucking relentlessly as I clung like a monkey, my fingernails raking his back so deeply he was marked the next day. 'Greedy little bitch,' he panted, and within seconds I was coming.

But Jake never asks questions. At first I claimed to be visiting Yelena, now I just say I'm going out. 'Take the torch,' he might remind me but that's about his only acknowledgement.

Things have become strange with me and Eddie. I don't like him, and I don't think he likes me; or at least, not in the way I might want a man to like me. But when we arrange to meet, I'm wet with wanting him, so wet.

About a week after our foursome, I wanted to see him again. I wanted to fuck. I wanted him alone with no one else to share the pleasure. Just me and Eddie. I wanted to have that slow menacing smile to myself, much as I'd had it when he'd pinned me to the wall and I'd fellated his coarse, malty fingers.

So, feeling brave and horny, I went to The Griffin. In the pub, I sat in the warmth of mahogany and crimson, a glass of whisky on the table, a book in my lap, brazenly observing Eddie behind the bar. Dark barley-twist legs of wood stretched from the counter to a high shelf where light sparkled on stacked, clean glasses. I watched Eddie pulling pints, his tattoo flexing as he eased down the pump. I saw him talking to customers, slicing lemons and moving in that confined space, his image reflected brokenly in the optics and engraved mirrors.

He kept glancing over, giving me those looks that get me right in the groin, cocky and dissolute, full of intent. Not to be outdone, I shot the looks right back. As last orders chimed and people began to leave, he brought a whisky to my table.

'You staying?' he asked.

'Yes,' I replied boldly.

He bent close to me and the smell of him made me soften. 'Good,' he said, leaning an arm on the table. 'Because I'd like to fuck you in the arse.'

He stayed there, fixing me with his cold, grey eyes.

My cheeks blazed and my heart thundered. I stared back, wishing I knew what to say. I couldn't think of a reply so instead I downed my whisky and said, 'I'd better have another then.'

It was nice to have him serving me, nice to sit there drinking while he chucked people out and tidied up. I wanted him so much. I wanted what he said. I wanted to feel his cock pushing into my narow hole. Doing it that way has always been a rare and special thing for me. It's something I start to crave when a session's getting heated, when I know someone well. Jake and I had engaged when sex needed to go further and darker; when we were striving to connect in the madness of pleasure and pain. Eddie's stark, clinical approach was new to me. The emptiness had a strange appeal, and I knew the madness would be mine to keep. Eddie and I could never connect. The emotional risk seemed greater.

He moved around the pub, putting chairs up on tables, and I was getting wetter by the minute. Nervous too. Eddie scared me, not because he was a bully – I thought I could handle that – but because he could make me lose my inhibitions. Without them, I didn't know where he'd take me. I trust Jake. He can measure me. Eddie, however, would have no qualms about exploiting my surrender.

'Night, John,' he called as the last customer left. He shot the bolts, turned the key and pocketed it. It didn't look as if I'd be leaving without his say-so.

'I don't want to talk,' I said.

'Bend over that table,' he said calmly.

I did as told. He lifted my skirt and pulled my underwear down to my ankles.

'I knew you'd be back,' he said.

I bit down on a gasp as he pressed lube into the crevice of my buttocks and cast a torn sachet to the ground. His cool slippery fingers oiled me up and down then, slow and careful, he eased a couple inside me. I whimpered, my circle of muscles tight around his big sliding knuckles, pain sparking.

'There we go,' he said, smooth and patronising. 'That nice?'

He rested one hand on the small of my back, his other twisting and pushing. When I felt his rubbered-up cock nudge into position, I gripped the table. He pushed forwards, his swollen bulb such a fierce, blunt pressure, and we seemed to be on the brink for ages, my body refusing to admit him.

'No, no,' I said, because at that moment I hated anal, wished I wasn't doing it, wished I didn't keep wanting it.

Then with a grunt and a rush, Eddie slithered past my barrier, and I was packed solid, panting with shocked pleasure because it seemed I loved anal after all.

'Stay there, stay there,' I gasped, glorying in his thickness, my rim burning around his girth. For a while, he did then he drew slowly back and began plunging in deep, over and over, his hand still firm on my back. I could hear his ragged breath and grunts. Unlike Jake who has no such hang-ups, Eddie doesn't like to reveal his pleasure so every groan was muted. Huffing and pounding, he kept speaking to disguise his grunts: 'You like that, don't you?' 'Tight little arse.' 'Ever get tired of dick?'

When I came, uttering shrill little breaths, he quickly followed suit. 'Jee – fuck, fuck,' he said in a low spittly voice, and I was so gratified and turned on to hear his capitulation that even now I masturbate to its echo. We stayed motionless, panting and silent as he shrank inside me. When he withdrew and tidied himself away, he said, 'Do you want me to walk you home?'

'No thanks,' I said. 'That was plenty.'

He no longer asks and I'm glad. I love that walk back,

going from one brother to the other, alone on the track, just me, the moors and the stars.

My arm hurts with writing. I steal every moment I can for this. I write and I write, hoping the words will make sense. Fear drives me: fear you won't listen, fear of this place, fear of being known and of not being known.

Sometimes, I'm so tired I can hardly see straight. It's a constant struggle to keep this journal on track. I keep wanting to stop the story and plunge you into the here and now, tell you about today and yesterday rather than what happened several weeks ago. I want to hear your voice too, have you right there in my ear. I can't count the times I've picked up my mobile and stared at your number, knowing the pointlessness of trying because you won't pick up my calls. I long for you and London. Even though I love these empty wilds, I yearn for London's hustle and bustle, for its tawdry lights, decent cinema, late-night bagels, beggars and thieves.

There's something draining about this place. Maybe it's because it's hard to keep your spirits up, or maybe it's too many late nights with Eddie and intense days with Jake. I'm so tired though, increasingly tired.

I kept thinking about the ghost, the doll, the missing woman. I didn't know what to do or where to begin. I knew I was being lied to somewhere down the line but I didn't know who was lying. I trusted Jake sexually but in other ways I was wary of him. I didn't trust Eddie on any level although I reckoned, if push came to shove, I'd be able to outmanoeuvre him. And Yelena? I trusted her peculiar innocence. She would never deliberately deceive me but I could imagine her accidentally letting me down because she was wayward and impulsive.

It seems silly I didn't think of it earlier but I woke one morning thinking, The doll, the Laura doll. Jake had got so angry when he'd caught me rummaging under its skirts.

I'd assumed he was angry because he was nuts and I'd molested his precious toy. And because he'd been looking for an excuse to punish me.

Jake's clever. The doll sits there in the living room, on a chair, a box, a chest. Sometimes it's in his bedroom, sometimes the kitchen or even the workroom. I saw it so often that I'd stopped seeing it. It was just Jake's lucky doll.

But that morning, it occurred to me the answer could be there, right under my nose just as it is in detective stories. I needed to get closer. I waited for several days until I was completely alone. Jake had gone into town. He'd had an idea to make chicken feet out of bent forks and was full of excitement, heading out to scour charity shops for whatever cutlery he could find. It was a relief to hear the door close and listen to the jeep crunch along the track.

The doll was on a loom chair in the top half of the living room where we eat and where Jake sews. I was feeling so jittery I actually scanned the room for cameras. The room is such a freaky peacock of foliage and fixed eyes, a camera could have been hidden anywhere. I saw nothing.

I stared at the doll, wondering if it had some unnatural power. It simply stared back like they all do, its blue glass eyes looking right through me. Its porcelain face was as cold and creamy as wax, its four tiny teeth peeping from cherry red lips. Just a doll, I told myself, picking it up. I gave its body a crude squeeze and felt it at once, a crackle, a stiffness, a body not entirely rag.

I slipped my fingers past its bloomers and felt a zipper. My hands began to tremble. I'd missed this the first time, presumably because I was too busy focusing between its legs. I didn't dare open it. I set the doll down and went to check the window. You can see all the moors and the track leading to the village. There was no one around, and yet even as I looked out of the window, I was half expecting to turn back to the room and see Jake standing there.

He wasn't. It was just me, Noah and Twiglet, and a crowd of puppets and dolls.

I had to untie the red sash to get to the zipper. I pushed the dress up, baring its soft white body, its lower legs like ceramic callipers. The zip was modern. The doll was made of antique china, head and lower limbs attached to a contemporary rag body.

I pulled the tag. The doll's back split open into a long zippered pocket. Inside was a red notebook, curled into a tube and secured with an elastic band. When I removed it, the doll went limp.

I got scared then. If Jake came back, I might hide the notebook but I'd never get the doll to sit up straight. I almost pushed the book back in but how could I? Heart hammering, I scoured the room for a new spine, took a paperback from a shelf and curled into the doll's back. It was a free book from a newspaper so I didn't think he'd miss it. I had no band to fasten it but the shape seemed to hold. I dressed the doll again, refastened the red ribbon. She looked OK: you wouldn't notice she'd been tampered with, apart from some crumpling around the bow. If Jake checked inside, I was done for but I had to hope he wouldn't.

When I pulled the elastic band, it snapped at once, its old, brittle remnants sticking to the curled cover. The notebook was the same as mine. Same size, same colour, same make, same everything.

I felt sick. Inside were pages and pages of plump, looped handwriting, the paper crinkled from the press of blue biro. On the cover was a name, Meredith Gibbons, and a date of birth: 17th October 1983.

I was shaking. I was too frightened to stay in the living room. I was alone in the house, but even so I hid the book under my jumper and hurried up to the attic. There, I locked the door and I began to read:

Women disappear from this place. Something happens to them. I don't think it's J or E. It's this village. Could be the moors. Something funny's going on. Something out there like a black hole, something that sucks people in. I don't know. I don't know.

I wonder if I'm cracking up. I have these thoughts, these dreams. I don't know where to turn. Nothing makes sense. I could love J if he'd let me but he keeps me at arm's length nowadays. All he wants is for me to be Laura. Laura, Laura, that's all that fucking matters here. That's all they fucking care about. No one cares about me.

I wish I could break free. Wish I had the strength. I don't know where I'd go though. I don't know where freedom is. And I'm so tired, like all the energy's leaking from me. E? Is E freedom? I think he's as bad as J. A while back, I thought I could love him. I know he'd look after me. Not like J. He's selfish and cruel, too in love with himself and his stupid puppets to love anyone else. I can't believe I fell for him. But then again, I can.

'What is it with you?' I said. 'Where are you? Where do the lies stop and start?'

'I care for you, Merry,' he said. 'Straight up, I do. But not the way you want me to.'

And what? I'm supposed to be fucking grateful, am I?

He's had me do some weird shit, really kinky. Some of it's rotten so I don't know if I should write it down. I wouldn't do it if I didn't like him. But then when he starts on me, I usually end up liking it. I like it when he spanks me too. I like it when he whacks my bum. I like it when he drips hot wax on my tummy and tits. I like it when he ignores me for days. I like it when he tests me because I'm not going to fail. I'm not going to give in and say stop, it hurts, I wanna go home. I'm going to meet him and match him, the fucker.

No one's ever treated me like this. I've never been like this. I'm an exhibitionist, the sort who'll flash her tits when she's trollied. J doesn't give me chance. He takes over. He pays me loads of attention, just like other blokes would if I took my top off. But it's all by his rules. I don't make him look at me. He looks for himself, all on his terms. Maybe I'm lazy but I don't mind that. I don't have to do anything except be me and he's interested. Piece of piss, really.

But I don't know about this Laura business. The story freaks me out. I really got off on it at first. Wow, she was some tough cookie, I thought. I still think that. No one'd believe she was Victorian. I used to think they were all prim and proper but she was in another league. A '4' 10" pocket of sex' who smoked Havana cigars, according to Jake.

Poor lass. She couldn't marry the bloke she wanted to. They wouldn't let you in those days. She was supposed to marry some nob who lived here at J's house. But she didn't want him. She was in love with his younger brother, probably having it away with him from the sounds of her. I can't remember the blokes' names. They were going to elope, her and him. God, it's all so romantic. Yeah, they were going to elope. Don't know where to though. But then the younger brother, the one she loved, he went off and got engaged to someone else. One of those marriages of convenience for money or something.

So Laura starts losing it then and I can't say I blame her. Can you imagine? Stuck in this arranged marriage and all the time she's in love with the brother. She'd have to see him all the time, be nice to him and his wife.

Well, it never got to that because she refused big-style. No, it's probably not right to say she refused. She made herself unmarriable. Is that a word? You were meant to be a virgin in those days, but I don't reckon she was. Well, she certainly wasn't after that night in the church. Yeah, in the fucking church. I guess because God's doors are always open. She got trashed and took a load of blokes into the church, blokes from the village who must have been lower class than she was. She lived a couple of miles away but that was nothing in those days. They walked everywhere.

And these men all fucked her in the church. They queued up, and one by one they fucked her. No one would marry her after that. Used goods. Or do I mean damaged? She must have known what she was doing, must have loved this younger brother so much. Probably thought if she couldn't have him, she didn't want anybody. And nobody got the chance because the next day they found her body in Heddlestone Brook. They say she did it herself, lay down in the water, and if you ask me I'd say she probably died of cold.

So that's Laura, a ghost story.

Except it's not. I wish it was. I wish it was all in the past. But it's not. It's still here. They can't let go of Laura. They worship her. They adore her. It's like she's their ideal woman – a slapper who won't cause any bother afterwards cos she tops herself.

That's what they want from me. They want me to be Laura. It's their Lady Laura day tomorrow. I've been chosen to play the part. I've been secretly fucking elected! J and E are making out like it's a big deal, an honour.

And you know what's really sick about it? It's

that I'm flattered. I'm fucking furious but I'm fucking flattered. It's probably because I have low self-esteem. It's like that nightmare at school when the smart kids are choosing their teams for netball or whatever, and you're stood there thinking, 'Pick me, pick me.' I was always the last to be picked, one of the humiliated kids.

And now I've been picked, I'm the first. The villagers like me enough to make me the centre of their celebration, want me to dress up in some white nightie and have that red ribbon around my waist. I lost it at first. 'No way!' I said. But then they talked about it some more, made it sound good, got me into the idea, got me horny. I suppose it's not much worse than some of the stuff I've done with J and E. So I've kind of agreed. But the main reason I'm agreeing is because I want to know what happens here, I want to know where the women disappear to. I think it'll give me a clue. If the worst comes to the worst, I might get more than a clue. I might be the one, and if that happens then these could be the last words I ever write.

Jake's just called up to see if I want a cup of tea. My head feels woolly. I'll be better after a cup of tea. In the morning, this'll probably sound like a right load of old bollocks.

There were no more entries after that.

12

I should have packed my bags that day. For my own safety, that's what I should've done. But how could I? How could I turn my back on Yelena when we were friends? How could I walk without knowing the truth about Jake and Eddie or this place or Laura? How could I quit?

I still don't know if staying was the correct decision. Can you ever know that? Probably not. I'm struggling to think straight right now. I'm sorry. I'm a little shaky. I'm exhausted. If my handwriting looks weird, it's because ... I hope you can read this. I hope it makes sense. I don't know if anything makes sense. I have to really concentrate. I'm in the attic. I'm sitting up in bed, writing. Hope I don't fall asleep.

I've locked the door. I've put the chest of drawers in front of it too. Maybe the lock's not enough. The floor's wet but I'm not going to let it scare me. I'm going to be OK. I don't want Jake to come in. I don't want Jake or Eddie. I'm going to be OK. She can't touch me. I won't let her.

Oh God, if you were here now. If you had your arms around me and I could lie on your chest. Still and calm. The two of us still and calm, clasped together. Safe. Sunday morning. Lazy, sexy, easy. And you could stroke my hair and it would all ebb away. That's what I want. More than anything, that's what I want right now.

I didn't quit when I found Meredith's book because that's what I'd done with you. I'd scarpered when life had got tough. I've grown up here. I've seen more of myself than I've ever done before and it hasn't always been pretty. I needed to see this one through, and knew I had to be careful. I felt I was finally getting close to the reason I'd come to Heddlestone. It was there from the start, that force that pulled me in, almost a physical tug, a compulsion I've never been able to explain. Meredith had felt it too. I wasn't going mad. I hadn't just followed a whim. Something beyond me had brought me here.

I'm so tired now, so drained.

I wanted to see Yelena. I trusted her more than the men. Or perhaps it was simply that I thought I stood a better chance of getting her to reveal something. The men I didn't trust, and they were too smart to let anything slip. So I tried to arrange to meet her but she didn't respond to my texts or my calls. Eddie kept fobbing me off: She's just popped out. She's in the bath. I'll get her to call you later.

But she never did.

'Where's Yelena?' I asked Jake.

He shrugged. 'Maybe she's away. She's got friends in Keighley. Sometimes stays with them. Probably had a row with Eddie.'

This went on for four days. Something was wrong. Jake wouldn't let me in the workshop. He actually told me not to go in and when I tried once, I found the door locked. He claimed he was starting to find me distracting. Nothing personal, he explained, it's just that he was used to working alone. Instead he had me sorting through paperwork in the reception area and working on the newsletter on his laptop. The museum would reopen for Easter and he needed to get that organised. I didn't mind. I didn't want to be close to him. He felt unsafe.

The atmosphere in the village disturbed me most. It was difficult to pinpoint. There was an odd air of expectancy as if we were leading up to Christmas but there was no impending event I could see, no decorations or chatter, no focus to the anticipation.

'Cold out, isn't it?' said Aileen in the cafe and she looked at me a fraction too long, a fraction too brightly.

'Those dogs of yours behaving?' said Badger, standing behind me in the post office queue.

'Missing London yet?' asked Janice in the baker's, twisting the corners of a bag of muffins.

People are friendly up here but this was different. Everyone seemed to have more time for each other, their smiles seemed more interested. And yet no one was saying why. It was as if we were all waiting for something or someone. I suspected it might have something to do with their Laura day, whatever or whenever it was. I thought it might even have happened. Was Yelena's disappearance connected to it or was she avoiding me? Or had something happened to her that they were all trying to cover up?

Yesterday was the worst. The village felt secretive and sly. Odd Job Bob was pushing his pram about, tapping on doors and cleaning shop windows with a squeegee. A bicycle was chained to a lamppost and it struck me as something I often see in London but rarely here. Two men were sawing a piece of MDF on a trestle in the street. The dogs were unsettled, whimpering occasionally and getting up from the hearth. The sky was the colour of pewter, and growing darker. I watched a kestrel hovering above the moors, suspended in a glinting thundery light before it plummeted for the kill. I'd seen kestrels do this plenty but yesterday it felt ominous.

Even the rain was strange. Usually, the heavens open and we get cold, sadistic rain that goes on for hours, slanting across the moors and putting the world out of action. We had a few spots of drizzle, light as a summer shower, and yet the sky glowered. It was as if everything were in limbo, even the weather.

'Have you seen Yelena?' I asked Aileen in the cafe.

'She were in 'ere this morning,' she replied. 'Poor lass looked done in.'

So again I phoned her but still no reply. In the evening, Jake kept taking calls, walking out of the living room or kitchen to go and mutter elsewhere. Eventually, I left him to it, coming up to the attic to continue writing. I had Meredith's notebook with me and I wrote out her words, praying Jake wouldn't notice its absence.

I was uneasy about the notebook being the same as mine. Meredith's was much thinner, as if pages had been torn out, but they were otherwise identical. I felt as if we shared a connection and, of course, we did or we had: we lived in a village where there weren't many shops from which to choose stationery.

Our greater connection was that we'd both felt drawn here and had got involved with the Duxbury brothers. Did they share all their girlfriends?

Whoever Meredith was, I felt I was walking in her footsteps. I wished I knew where those footsteps went, or where they stopped. I began to see links everywhere: she felt tired, I was exhausted. She needed to wash her hair. Wow. So did I. It was hard to separate ordinary coincidence from sinister similarities.

I wished I had more information. Unlike mine, Meredith's wasn't a journal or a story. There were a few entries about her day-to-day life but they revealed little. She mentioned a trip to look at some mills that had been turned into loft-style apartments. Another entry was gossip from home, a friend who'd borrowed money from another and now they'd fallen out. The pages were mainly taken up with snippets, shopping lists, doodles, notes to self, things to do: wash hair, shave legs, write to Aunty Sue, read magazines, listen to radio, do stomach crunches, avoid caffeine.

Her 'to do' lists were quirky and sweet: suggestions of how to pass the time rather than tasks that needed doing. But I could understand that. It can get quiet here and the nights are so long.

Yesterday evening when I copied out her diary entry, the words changed from her plump girlish handwriting to my own sloping scrawl. It looked strange. As soon as I get the chance, I thought, I'll replace the book inside the doll. But then I began to think that wasn't enough. I have to do something, I thought. I have to find out what's going on here. I have to find Yelena.

I kept looking at Meredith's words. 'Women disappear from this place.' I read it over and over. I didn't know what to do. I didn't want to arouse suspicion and I didn't know where to begin. I paced around the attic. I lay on the floor and peered out of those two-foot tall windows, the ones I once imagined were for puppets to stand in front of. The air near the glass chilled my face.

It's a weird room to live in, windows in the ceiling, windows on the floor. I see only skewed sections of life outdoors. It's started to feel like a den, my precious hide-out. I used to feel nervous here but not any more. It's the outside world that scares me. Here, I'm fine. I'm Kate Carter, madwoman in the attic. And I'm doing fine. Doing fine.

Last night through the little windows, I could see the moors under a cloudy, moonlit sky, vast and still. They looked as if they were waiting. They often do. I can't see the village from here but I wished I could. What were people doing? The day had been odd. Was the pub busier than usual? Or was this me being jumpy, letting my imagination run riot, making something out of nothing?

Eventually, I got so chewed up I crept downstairs. I had no real plan except to try to find Yelena or wheedle something out of Eddie, or maybe someone in the pub. The light was on in the workshop and I could hear Jake planing wood, radio in the background. I left quietly without letting him know, and it was only when I was walking along the track, the torch beam bouncing over chips of rubble and earth, that I thought: supposing that wasn't Jake? I'd heard the sound of his work but I didn't actually see him.

Of course it's him, I told myself. Get a grip.

The night was bitter, the pavements blotched with

dampness. There must have been another of those weird, fleeting drizzles. A scrawny grey street slopes down to the village, the road cobbled, and everything was quiet, curtains drawn, a couple of mumbling TVs. Under pools of amber streetlight, my shadow stretched and shattered on the cobbles, feet clicking on the flagstones. Do you remember that sound? Hard noises and cold echoes, iron and stone, clogs, drudgery and the ghosts of Northern industry.

There's only one shop on the first road, a rare concession to tourism: Paula's Parlour. It sells crafts, maps, fudge, teatowels and badges saying Brontë Country. I've never seen it open but it's the winter season and that's what you'd expect. But as I was passing something caught my eye, making me pull up sharp in front of the window.

Hanging there, among the cushions, billowing patchwork, ye olde biscuit tins and dried flowers, was a marionette, a blonde puppet staring into space, poised as if moving, hands and knees aloft. And she was wearing a white dress, a scarlet sash around her waist.

Laura.

Streetlight caught the acrylic-gleam of her face and gilded her frizz of synthetic hair. Her painted lips smiled at nothing and those awful puppet eyes stared out into for ever. Peeping from her sleeves were carved hands tipped with silver-white nails, and I knew at once Jake had chipped them into being, his big hands making tiny ones, bringing fingers out of lime wood.

A local legend, I told myself, hurrying on. No big deal. Perfectly appropriate for a local artist to sell his work in a gift shop. No need to panic.

But panic surged when I passed the baker's. Usually, the evening window is unlit, on display only empty white trays, paper doilies, a fake loaf of bread and a sheaf of dusty corn. But last night, though the window was in shadow, a puppet was sat on a shelf, gazing blankly, feet dangling. And, yes, she wore a white dress and red ribbon.

I scuttled past, as if not looking would make it not true. Yeah, I know. Story of my life. But it became true again in Marion's, the village shop whose window I find scary anyway. She arranges tins of soup and boxes of fruit jellies in pyramids as if we're still in the post-war years, celebrating anything that isn't dried egg. Another Laura puppet was half slumped against the greying lace backdrop, her smile rigid and ghastly. It was the same in the post office, the newsagent, the tiny hardware shop.

I walked around the village square, checked the roads leading off. There aren't many shops here. People drive out of the village to go to supermarkets, so we just have the basics. But every shop contained a marionette.

What did these people do here? What did they believe in? I felt I was walking through a sci-fi dreamscape being monitored by vacant-faced dolls. I wondered if their eyes moved when I couldn't see them.

Women disappear from this place.

Where was she? What had they done with Yelena?

No one else was around which isn't unusual and The Griffin looked as ordinary as ever, a pumpkin-orange haze emanating from small curtained windows. Was that to lure me in? Was I walking into a trap? I considered returning to the house, to the man in the workshop I'd assumed to be Jake. The devil and the deep blue sea. Who to trust? Who to turn to? The only person I believed in was myself. Oh, Yelena, please call.

Someone left the pub and the stone market square was lit with a flare of cheeriness and warmth. From a glimpse, everything looked OK, not to mention temptingly cosy. So I crossed the square, took a deep breath and entered. I was feeling fretful and confused by this point. It probably would have been best if I'd ambled in and casually ordered my usual. But, instead, I found myself addressing Eddie at the bar.

'I want to speak to Yelena,' I said. 'Why won't you let me speak to her?'

Eddie smiled. 'Whisky?'

'No,' I said. 'I want to speak to Yelena.'

He was full of false charm. 'Didn't she say? Had to nip off. Family trouble in Moscow. Mum's been taken ill.'

I glared at him, trying to work out if he was telling the truth. I could feel people watching me. It was the usual crowd: jovial groups of men, a few silent couples, blokes staring into their pints or reading the paper, Janet and Michelle with their halves of lager, smoking steadily even though it's banned.

'I don't believe you,' I said, keeping my voice low. 'I think she'd have phoned me or texted.'

Eddie raised his brows. 'She did have a fair bit on her mind,' he said, not even attempting to speak quietly. 'But tell you what, when I next have a word, I'll ask her to fetch you back a set of Russian dolls. Nice gift to make up for it.'

He turned to the optics, lifting a glass.

'What's wrong with her mother?' I asked.

'On the house,' he said loudly, placing a whisky in front of me.

I didn't even look at it. The words from Meredith's notebook churned in my mind: Women disappear from this place. 'What's wrong with her mum?' I repeated, speaking clearly now.

He shrugged. 'Might be a stroke. She's in hospital. They're running tests.'

One of the regulars, Adrian, was sat at the bar. 'Only fifty-six,' he added. 'Too young for a stroke if you ask me.'

I looked at Adrian, mid-thirties, a plumber whose van I sometimes see on the top road. Was he in on it as well? Whatever 'it' was.

'They don't know what's up,' said Eddie. 'Yel's in a right old state. You know what she's like.'

'Why didn't Jake mention it?'

Eddie shrugged. 'Probably because I haven't told him. I

don't tell him everything you know. Anyway, you know Jake. Shuts himself up, doesn't he? So I leave him to it.'

What could I do but accept what he was saying, at least for the meantime?

Besides, women don't simply disappear, do they? There are inquiries, murder investigations, families who care and newspapers to offer rewards. Maybe Meredith had meant something else. Perhaps I'd taken it too seriously because of the police asking about Chloë Lipsey, a woman who, after all, might not actually have anything to do with Heddlestone.

I took my whisky and headed for a table. I had so many questions but was wary of revealing what I knew. I didn't want to ask about the puppets outside. My best bet, I thought, would be to play innocent, to watch and wait. And all the time, I'd be on my guard, trusting no one.

'Kate,' called Eddie. I returned to the bar and he leant close, talking softly so no one else could hear. 'You staying for a nightcap later?'

'No, I don't think so,' I said. 'Not exactly fair on Yelena, is it?'

I was leaning over the bar, resting my glass there. With a small covert move, Eddie grasped my wrist, encircling it with his big clumsy fingers. I tried to tug free but his grip only tightened, making me aware of all the delicate bones he could crunch. Our faces were close. In the subdued light, he looked tired, shadows heavy beneath his eyes, stubble glinting like crystals of brown sugar. He looked rough and mean, especially when his eyes narrowed. He was really squeezing my wrist, hurting me and twisting the skin.

'Stay,' he said, and the word was a flat command. 'We have to talk.' I stared back, wishing he didn't look so hot and fucked up. 'Go upstairs if you want,' he continued. 'Wait there.'

'I'll wait here,' I said calmly, and when I sat down, I hid my hands beneath the table and rubbed my sore wrist.

Eddie ignored me for forty minutes or so until he rang the final-last-orders bell and people began leaving, a few casting curious glances at me. I wondered if they knew the reason I usually came here. Once I would have cared what they thought, but I didn't any more. Let them talk.

When the last person had left, Eddie slid the bolts.

I stayed sitting at my table. 'What is it?'

He went behind the bar and pulled himself a pint. He drank half of it in one go then switched off a light.

'Come here,' he said, setting down his glass on the counter. He sat on a bar stool, waiting for me.

I went to him, because I always do, wanting him and wishing I didn't. His knees were apart and I stood in the gap, meeting his eye. He chucked my breasts, nudging each one in a silly little lift.

'Here she is again,' he smiled. 'Chasing cock.'

'What do you want to talk about?' I asked.

'You.' He withdrew a bunched fist from his pocket and clasped my wrist in a worryingly quick gesture, then began winding something around it. It was a black stocking with a lace-top, presumably one of Yelena's which unnerved me. I struggled but only for the sake of appearances.

'Easy, lass,' he cooed, and I held still, eyes pinned on his, wondering whether to trust him. On my wrist, the fabric turned from a silky touch to a harsh, pinching bond, the nylon pulling tight as he fastened a double knot. Was he playing kinky or dangerous?

'We need to have a chat about you,' he said. Without getting off his stool, he leant to wrap the other end of the stocking around the brass bar that ran alongside the wooden top, tying it to one of the supports. The tattooed Celtic circlet stretched on his forearm, an inked echo of my nylon manacle.

Hey, it's only a bit of bondage, I thought. More Jake's style than Eddie's but maybe grey eyes and parents weren't the only things they had in common.

'Does Yelena know you've borrowed her stockings?' I asked, still standing between his broad knees.

'Yelena's in Moscow.'

'So you say,' I replied.

He arched his brows. 'What? You think I'm having you on, do you?'

I shrugged. 'I trust you as far as I can throw you.'

He gave me a sardonic smile and began stroking my breasts, his touch light and indifferent. It was as if the smile were the important thing, the caress secondary, an action he was doing to gauge my response. We were often like this after closing time, moving briskly into sexual territory, both of us up for it and dispensing with seduction.

'Do you trust Jake?' he asked.

'I don't think I should,' I said. I gave a small tug on my arm to test how tied I was. The skin twisted on my wrist. The answer was pretty damn tied.

'No,' said Eddie. 'I don't think you should either.'

He traced a thumb across my lower lip and I flinched from him.

'What is it with you two?' I asked. 'What's it about? What goes on between you?'

'What do you mean?' he asked, cool and condescending.

'Do you like each other? Hate each other? Love each other?'

He trailed a hand down the length of my body, stopping below my belly where he rubbed, stirring my underwear through my skirt.

'I love Jake,' he said. 'I love all the women he fucks. Love the way he sends them to me when he's bored.'

I didn't move. Anger coloured my cheeks and I could've spat. But I didn't move. I wasn't going to give him the satisfaction. He looked at me, gloating and awaiting my reaction, his hand still nudging above my pubis. All I did was get wetter.

'Jake gets bored easily,' he continued. 'You must have

clocked that.' He reached both hands into my top, straight into my bra to squeeze my nipples. He pulled hard on them, stretching my flesh back and forth, making circles with them and half lifting me out of my clothes. 'Why else are you here?'

'You bastard,' I breathed. 'It's my own choice.'

'Oh, come on, Katie,' he said. 'You must be able to see it. Are you trying to tell me he never suggested it? Never encouraged you to come over?'

'No,' I said. 'It's my own choice.'

'So you like me, do you?'

I shook my head. 'That's not what I said.'

'What is it then, Kitty Kat?' he said. 'Why do you come to me?'

'I don't know,' I said, a quiver in the voice I wanted to be firm. 'Does it matter why?'

'You come for my dick, don't you?' he said.

I scoffed. 'Well, it's not for the conversation, is it?'

He laughed at that and then hooked his arm hard around my back, jerking me to the stool. He clasped the back of my head and though I writhed and squealed, he held me fast, forcing a wet hard kiss onto my mouth, his tongue thrashing and intrusive.

When our mouths slid apart, I was panting for breath and he kept me in his grip. 'Tell me you come here for my dick,' he said. 'Tell me.'

I punched and pushed with my one free hand, trying to escape. 'Oh, fuck you!'

He jumped up. The bar stool fell, clanging against the brass foot rail and thumping to the floor.

'Ohhh, fighting, are we?' he said and he pushed me right around so my back was to the bar. The stocking twisted with me, and I wriggled and cursed but he held me there, trapped by his big, crashing, insolent masculinity.

'Get off me,' I said, trying to shove at his bulk.

'Truth hurts, does it?' he mocked. His grin flashed as he tried to grab my flailing hand. 'Jake's cast off, his hand-me-down. From big brother to little.'

'Liar,' I said.

He was aroused. His erection was a big knot in his body, and he ground himself deliberately against me, making me wetter than ever. Then he caught my wrist, and it was snared in his fist, and I was stuck.

'Who the hell do you think you are?' I panted.

He began winding another stocking around my wrist, a pink fishnet. Dear God, I thought, he didn't even select a matching pair. Poor Yelena, two sets ruined.

I jerked my arm but it was a feeble effort.

'Stop acting,' he said. 'You like this shit.' He tied the stocking beneath the brass rail again so both my arms were apart, tethered to the bar. 'Jake told me.'

I should have guessed. I sometimes wondered what Jake might have said. I was so baffled by their relationship that it could have been anything from discreet silence to 'Kate's a bit kinky' to a full-on revelation of all Jake's sweet, scary abuses.

I tugged at the stockings. 'Brotherly love,' I replied. 'How touching.'

I'd never been to Eddie with Jake's marks on my skin, except once. I think the pharmacy's sales of arnica must have doubled since my arrival but one particular night, a yellow-green vestige of bruises coloured my buttocks. Eddie had me over the table, cock sunk deep. He scraped his fingernails up my thighs and over my arse. 'Looks sore,' he had said fondly, and it got me hot because I knew he knew it was Jake.

I leant forwards to test the bonds of the stockings. I felt like a carved figurehead on the prow of a ship, surging ahead but static.

'I like you like that,' grinned Eddie. 'No trouble.'

'I can still kick,' I said.

'And I can still tie your feet to this rail.' He toed the brass foot rail and it chimed dully. 'But you'd probably like that, wouldn't you?'

We stood opposite each other, Eddie smirking, me as still as could be. Then he began unbuttoning my shirt, his gaze on my cleavage. He was calm and collected and I was an angry cat, taut and glowering.

'Let's have a look, then,' he said. He pushed the top back, baring my bra. For several seconds, he eyed my breasts, and though I tried to breathe normally, I simply couldn't. I was so furious and aroused all I could do was present him with flushed, heaving, clichéd bosoms.

'Ve-ery pretty,' he said.

He walked away behind the bar and returned with a pair of scissors. For a moment, I thought he was going to cut the stockings but instead he opened the tips at the little daisy linking the cups of my bra.

'No!' I complained.

'Keep still,' he said. With a snip my bra was in two pieces, ruined. My breasts dropped a fraction.

'I liked that bra,' I whined.

'So did I,' said Eddie. 'But I like it better in shreds.'

He moved my cups and straps aside, pushing the shirt off my shoulders. I was well and truly exposed, arms held wide, breasts and belly on show as if this were some debauched crucifixion. Using the scissor tips, he tapped each nipple, turning them into tight hard stubs that strained for more.

He grinned as he toyed with me, glancing from my nipples to my face, and in his grey eyes were slivers of steel, as cold and vicious as the scissor tips. God, I ached for him. He tip-tapped my nipples a while longer, eyeing me with mild curiosity as if this were a casual experiment.

When I finally released a tiny moan, he said, 'Oh, she liked that one.'

He pointed the scissors in the hollow of my collar bone then trailed a sinuous line down my body, swerving in S-shapes from left to right, the scratch light and metallic, almost a tickle. Then he set the scissors down on the bar and bent to take a nipple in his wet mouth. I moaned again and he drew back with his teeth, eyes rolled up at me, stretching my flesh until he held the very tip in a smiling bite.

I threw my head back, trying not to gasp, but when he bit down harder I couldn't help it. He released me, gave a leery smile, then collected his half pint and went to sit at a nearby table. He raised his glass and winked. 'To your good health,' he said.

I gazed at him, feeling half stoned, half furious.

'Please,' I said, though I hardly knew what I was asking for.

The lights were low, a few spots here and there, and our dark wood and crimson surrounds were rich and warm. His stubble glittered on jaw and head, and his tired eyes were so heavy and sexy.

Come to me, I thought. Touch me, force me, please.

For a couple of minutes, we stayed like that, saying little. Twice I struggled, an involuntary reaction against my entrapment. The first time, Eddie simply grinned. The second, he said, 'Mmm, struggle again. Looks cute.' A bit of bondage and he was Jake all over. I was motionless after that, fighting Eddie, not my tethers.

But before long, lust got the better of me and my resolve started to fail. 'Eddie,' I said. 'Please. What are we doing? Don't sit there. Please ... touch me.'

'Please,' he echoed. 'That's one of the things I like about you. So polite. Please, Eddie, please fuck me. Please, stop. Please, no, I can't.' He grinned and hitched his brows, glancing over my shoulder. 'And the funny thing is, she always can, can't she?'

At the sound of movement behind me, I swung around, twisting to see. I heard him before saw him, heard that one word of his I love and which I hadn't heard for a while: 'Slut.'

I whimpered, instantly humiliated. What an idiot! Of course, of course. How could I not have seen it coming? How could Jake not be involved in this? He emerged from the house doorway behind the bar. I caught his eye then turned away, dismayed to think how long he might have been there.

Eddie, sitting with his half pint, looked so smug. I heard Jake moving behind the bar, a clink of ice, a gush of liquid. He sauntered into the pub, glass in hand, and I felt sheer unadulterated lust.

In a faded narrow suit and his Indiana Jones hat, he was dressed for town, a gawky bohemian, displaced and out of time, moles like two devil-tears dotting his high cheekbone. He wore an expression I've grown to love, an intimate teasing smile, so faint it barely tilts his lips, and that low indirect gaze of his, that sly warmth.

He glanced at me, eyes flickering over my tits as he went to join Eddie. He perched on the table, a foot on a chair, other leg swaying, big boots patched in dry mud and wet.

'What's going on?' I asked.

They sat there, looking at me. I almost forgot to breathe. I'd never seen them both together, except marginally through the weave of the wicker trunk. Eddie hadn't been around on the rare occasions Jake and I had been to the pub. And now here they were, the brothers who'd practically rearranged me. Measured against Eddie's brawn, Jake looked so delicate as to be ethereal, and their grey eyes studied me, shackled and semi-naked.

'Together at last,' said Jake.

'How long have you been here?' I asked. 'Did you follow me?'

'Not really necessary, is it?' he replied. 'You're always coming here.'

Eddie gave a bawdy chuckle.

'Forgive the pun,' added Jake.

'But you know that,' I said. 'You know I ... I visit. You know that. And you just turn a blind –'

'Hey, easy,' cooed Jake. 'I'm not complaining. I'd have, um, come sooner if I'd known you looked this good.'

Bondage, ropes, strings. Jake's stuff, not Eddie's. I should have seen it as soon as Eddie had wrapped that stocking around my wrist.

Jake's power was oblique and slow, infinitely more powerful than his brother's. Eddie's was obvious, scarce more than a sneer and a swagger. I'd fallen for it all those months ago when I'd seen him in the clubhouse. It was so immediate, and it had gone straight to my groin. But he's a big, crass bonehead and he doesn't understand. Jake does. He sees me. He can fuck me like a slut, and respect me as an equal.

But he enjoys his control a little too much and he'd reeled me in, fucking with my mind while he'd fucked with my body. When he'd encouraged me to get together with Eddie, it had sometimes seemed he was letting me go but in truth he was just holding me all the tighter. Jake delights in messing with me and throughout he's cherished me, bringing what I crave. But I was starting to see his delight and compassion were held in a very fragile balance.

I don't think I fully grasped that till they were both sat there, side by side.

'What's going on?' I asked again. I looked from one man to the other. I wasn't sure who had the answers. 'Are you going to tell me?'

Jake's leg swung back and forth and he glanced down at Eddie.

'We want a favour from you,' said Eddie.

'Is this about Yelena?' I asked. 'Where is she?'

'Moscow,' Eddie said brightly.

I shook my head. 'What is this place? What goes on here? What do you want?'

For a long while, neither of them spoke then in a gentle tone, Jake asked, 'Are you horny?'

'What kind of question's that?' I asked.

'I want to know,' said Jake. 'Does my brother make you horny?'

This was too fucked up. Did they want a threesome? Because really, they only need ask.

'Does he?' repeated Jake. 'Do you want him? Do you want him in the way you used to want me?'

'Where's Yelena?' I asked, hurt by Jake's 'used to'.

'Moscow,' said Eddie, sounding ironically bored now.

'Who's Laura?' I continued.

'She's our village ghost,' Jake said smoothly. 'You know that. Why are you asking questions you know the answer to?'

I was trying to breathe calmly because I didn't want my bare breasts to keep moving. When you're under observation, half-naked with your arms splayed, any fragment of dignity seems worth the effort.

'Who's Chloë Lipsey?' I said.

For a small moment, Jake looked unnerved and Eddie less sure. If I hadn't been pinned like a butterfly with my heaving clichés on display, I might have felt a rise in power. I'd wrongfooted them and I was pleased but Jake was quick to recover.

'You know who she is,' he replied. 'She's a woman who once went missing. The police came asking.'

'Do you know anything about it?' I asked.

'Only what you know,' said Jake. 'Tell me, are you horny?'

I looked at them, at Jake with his slender wrist angling so faultlessly from his cuff, and Eddie with his thuggish muscle and very little else. I knew them both as individuals but together they were a new force: beauty, brains and tattooed brawn. I imagined all three of us were horny, me in particular, but only one was afraid.

I drew a deep breath. 'Who's Meredith?'

Jake faltered again. I saw a shift in his eyes, a tightening in his face, a shadow of anger. For several seconds, he looked at me suspiciously before saying, 'She's an ex-girlfriend. Is that from Yelena? Has she been gossiping?'

I swallowed hard. Just hearing the words 'ex-girlfriend' stung. 'When did you start to dislike me, Jake?' I asked.

He looked surprised, and I could see the tension fade from his face. 'I don't dislike you,' he said. 'I don't. You mean a lot to me.'

I gave a defensive sniff of laughter.

'I don't dislike you,' he repeated.

I waited for more words but none came. He just looked at me, confused, hurt, lustful. I couldn't work him out. Sitting there with his beer, Eddie watched on, his face clouding, his frown sharp. He drummed his fingers once against the side of his glass.

My heart was racing when I next spoke. Looking Jake dead in the eye, I said, 'Women disappear from this place.'

A slow smile curled Jake's lips, and he nodded as if comprehension had just dawned. My body prickled with sweat. I guessed I'd said a dangerous thing. It could be that already I knew too much.

Jake held my gaze. 'No, Kate,' he said smoothly. 'Women come to this place.'

I glanced from brother to brother. I understood at once. The draw. The pull. The reason I was here. They knew about it too.

They both stared back, two pairs of grey eyes in stone, slate, mist and rain; eyes that held all the grey glinting duplicity of this hunched little village.

'No,' I breathed. 'It's impossible.'

I felt sick to my stomach. All of a sudden, I was in the presence of strangers.

'*You* came,' said Jake. 'So obviously not that impossible.'

'You offered me a job,' I countered.

'Only because you wanted one,' he replied. 'I created that job for you.'

It made sense. Lately, there'd been days when I had nothing to do, and I'd been wondering if Jake felt he'd made a mistake. I'd thought I might have been facing redundancy if it weren't for our relationship, but it hadn't occurred to me I might have been duped from the off. But I'd got the post so easily, hadn't I? Not many applicants, I'd thought at the time. A weird, hotch-potch job in a remote village, so no wonder. I hadn't questioned it too deeply. I'd wanted out of London and a return to the North, not even caring about the drop in salary. When someone throws a lifeline, you don't stop to check the texture. You grab with both hands, don't you?

'How?' I managed to say. 'What do you mean? Why would you do that?'

'Because you wanted to come,' he said. 'Some people do. They feel it. It touches them. It's Heddlestone. It attracts certain people.'

In some way it let me off the hook. I hadn't been able to help myself, so perhaps I ought to have been relieved. But I felt sick and scared, furious for not being able to resist whatever others had fallen for.

'People or women?'

'Women,' he replied.

I laughed scornfully. 'How convenient.'

'You don't believe me?'

For a long time, I said nothing because I did believe him. 'How did you know?' I said. 'We never met. How did you know me? The museum? Was it then?'

Jake nodded. 'Remember how you felt in there?'

'Weird,' I said, remembering. 'Drowsy. Bombed out. Like I was going under. Losing it. But I wasn't frightened. What is it? Something's here, isn't it?'

'I saw you,' said Jake. 'Saw you on CCTV. I could see it had touched you.'

'Please tell me. What is it? What touched me?' I yanked at the stockings. 'Let me go. I'm getting scared. I want you to untie me. This isn't fair.'

The two men exchanged glances.

'Please, what's going on?' I said. 'What is this place? Why are there puppets in the windows? Tell me. Untie me, Jake!'

Jake removed his hat and his dark curls sprang up, soft light fuzzing the edges. He strolled towards me and hooked my hair behind one ear, his gesture so tender and intimate. God, how I love the smell of him, that earthy, musky, animal scent of Jake. He smells of sex and he makes me want it.

He lifted my wrist, nudging at the band of nylon. 'That's too tight, isn't it?' he said.

'Yes,' I said. 'It's starting to cut into me. Please, let me go.'

'In a minute,' said Jake. 'Be patient. And don't pull on them so much.' He fiddled with the knots, loosening them and bringing relief to my sore, twisted skin. 'Better?'

I nodded.

'See?' he said. 'I look after you, don't I? I always do. Hey, don't be scared. I'm not going to let anything bad happen.'

I scanned his face, not knowing how much I trusted him. I remembered a morning in bed once when I'd asked, 'If I kiss your two moles and make a wish, will it come true?'

'Try it,' he'd said.

So I printed two kisses on his cheekbone then said, 'I wish you'd get up and make a cup of tea.'

He'd flipped me over, making me squeal, and we'd laughed and grappled till he was fucking me from behind, and I no longer cared about tea. I wished we were there again.

'You'll look after me?' I said. 'Nothing bad? You promise?'

'Promise,' he replied. 'Trust me, you'll enjoy it.'

From his chair, Eddie called, 'Think of it as a minor gang rape.'

My heart flipped over, my groin rushed hotly.

Jake didn't take his eyes from mine but he raised his voice. 'Eddie, fuck off. She can think what she wants.'

'Very good of you,' I said dryly. 'Are you going to tell me what's going on now?'

Eddie muttered under his breath and walked away, behind the bar and into the house.

Jake sidled closer into the crook of my arm. He tilted my face up to his, stroking lightly along my jaw.

'You're thinking of leaving, aren't you?' he said. He was gentle, his fingertips stumbling over my lips, tracing my nose and cheeks the way he does sometimes, feeling his way towards a carved puppet, seeing with his clever fingers.

'I can't stay,' I said. 'You know I can't. I don't belong here.'

He closed his eyes tight, chin tipping back, nodding to the ceiling. His neck was stretched, peppered with stubble, and his Adam's apple was a strong but vulnerable bump that I longed to lick. If I were taller, I'd have done so like a shot. The jut shifted in his throat and when he spoke his voice was hoarse.

'I know,' he said, keeping his eyes pressed shut. At length, he opened them and looked down with a watery pink gaze. 'I wish you could stay.'

'You torment me,' I said.

He gave a quick laugh. 'I thought you liked it.'

I laughed in reply and then he was kissing me, his lips moving in sweet, flimsy pulses. Though I knew it was ludicrous, I started to wonder if I could stay, and I kept on wondering while his hand rubbed where Eddie's had rubbed earlier, stirring my underwear through my skirt and massaging my pubis. After our recent distance, it was heaven to have him with me again, kissing me, filling my head with his scent and making me disappear into lust.

You can close your eyes, you can plug your ears but smell is inescapable unless you stop breathing. I couldn't stop breathing him. I couldn't stop wanting him. I was breathing him, kissing him, and all the love and desire I had for him was sliding into my groin.

I should have seen through Eddie's claim that Jake, bored, had cast me aside. As usual, Eddie was trying to make me angry because he liked to play rough. So did I sometimes. I love the push of adrenalin but I love the push of risk even more, the push of Jake.

I opened my feet wider and Jake cupped my skirt between my legs, rubbing with his long sure fingers. I moaned into his mouth and even when I heard Eddie return, I didn't care. We carried on, lost in kisses, and my hunger surged higher when I felt Eddie at the other side of me, nudging into my arm. A broad hand closed over one of my breasts and squeezed. Eddie's hand. My legs felt as if they were air and water. I was half-naked, and they were fully clothed, kissing me, squashing, caressing and groping. I could do nothing in return. My hands were tied. I was aroused to near craziness. I needed to breathe, to groan and I drew back from Jake's mouth, panting excitedly.

Jake looked dazed, his eyes bright, mouth shiny with kisses. On my left, inches from my face was Eddie, wearing a cooler, more calculating expression. It broke the mood. This wasn't right. When I saw what Eddie had draped over his arm, I understood why.

'No,' I gasped. 'No!'

I don't know how I managed to speak. It was like a hand was gripping my vocal chords. 'No, you can't. I won't.'

Bondage or not, the brothers had me trapped, crushed by their bodies, bewildered by their minds. Hung over Eddie's arm was a white gown, cotton trimmed with lace, its skirt trailing. And over the gown lay a broad red ribbon, light glossing the satin like tiny pools of blood.

'We want you to be Laura,' said Jake.

'Tonight,' said Eddie.

'We want you to wear this.'

'No way,' I breathed.

Jake nodded as if I had no choice. 'People are waiting for us.'

'In the church.'

'You've been chosen, Kate,' said Jake. 'Chosen to play the part of Laura.'

I looked from brother to brother, grey eyes left, grey eyes right, my limbs going weak with fear and wanting.

'It's a real honour,' Jake continued. 'You should be pleased. I've arranged something special. I've thought about it a lot. I wanted it to be right for you.' He gave me one of sly, mischievous smiles. 'You'll love it, I promise.'

'Slut,' grinned Eddie, stealing Jake's word.

13

It was after midnight when we left The Griffin, making it March the thirteenth, the anniversary of Laura's death. It's still the thirteenth. I wish it would end. It's been a long day, so long, and it's not even dawn. I'm exhausted.

I'm not religious but even so, a church felt monstrously wrong.

I could see the set-up at once: me the sacrificial virgin being led to the altar, the congregation formed of men who planned to fuck me, one after the other. The thought of them waiting their turn, taking their place in a queue, made my groin throb with a thick, bloated beat. I was so wet I was spilling. And I was full of dread and shame, two emotions that had been wrapping themselves tighter since my arrival in Heddlestone. All I could do was trust in Jake, and that felt as if I were clinging to a very small hope.

I kept replaying Meredith's final notebook entry: *these could be the last words I ever write.*

There were twenty or so men. They sat in their pews, muttering and turning as I was taken down the aisle, a scared and sluttish bride in my white and red garb. My hands were tethered behind my back, a length of rope trailing like a huge mouse tail. Either side of me were Jake and Eddie, arms hooked in mine as if they were giving me away. But there was no wedding march, no pristine groom ahead with a carnation buttonhole.

Instead, on a low wooden stage fitted over steps leading to the altar was a small torture chamber crossed with a school gym. When I saw it I stalled, protesting and pulling back. This was way too hardcore for me. But Jake and Eddie simply squeezed their arms tighter, almost lifting me off my feet.

'It's fine,' said Jake. 'I promise. Say the word if you don't like it. But you will, you'll love it. It'll be the best thing you've ever done. The best.'

We have a safeword which has always been there for me if a situation gets too much. I say the word, or use a contingency action, and Jake stops. But nothing has ever been too much. Jake reads me, measures me, plays me, and I yield and yield, giving him my everything until I'm left only with my nothing. He has the perfect balance. Eddie, however, wouldn't know a safeword if it slapped him across the face.

We walked on. Candle flames flickered in the depths of polished oak, and the men's faces were carved with shadow.

I recognised a lot of them and graded them mentally: Ahmed, yes; Badger, no; Lee, Adrian, Phil, yes, yes, yes. Odd Job Bob? Dear God, no. Besides, he was surely past it. So maybe some were just here to watch. Ahmed. I liked Ahmed. After the session at Eddie and Yelena's, whenever we passed we'd politely nod, saying, 'hello,' as if we'd barely met. He turned to speak to someone, a smile breaking, his eyes on mine, those black Byronic curls sweeping from his dark handsome face.

Jake's music was playing, Stockhausen's strange noises, the whirring blades, dripping water and screaming winds. It filled the church with a sinister soundscape that made me conjure up images in the air, helicopters hovering by stained glass windows, droplets falling like magnified rain, a harsh wind whistling through stones, spinning the sacrament, riffling prayer books and making brocade robes dance like the devil. It was all around me, and the big pipes of the organ, gleaming brassily in the half light, were dusty dated objects that meant nothing to this new church.

This is what Lady Laura had done in the nineteenth

century. She'd offered her wrists to a villager, begging him to bind her. Then she'd burst into the church, followed by curious onlookers, declaring, 'Coercion is the only way he will have me.'

I couldn't help but like her. In the pub, Jake and Eddie explained the legend as they'd dressed me. I was so aroused I was nine-tenths delirious. They spun me this way and that, fastening buttons and tying bows, caressing me, teasing me, treating me like a flesh-doll, there for their sharing.

'She loved the younger brother but he betrayed her.'

'A cigar-smoking, four foot ten pocket of sex, according to one source.'

'Short woman, fair with blonde curls. You're the best Laura we've ever had.'

'Well, we'll see. Got to be better than Yelena.'

'Where's Yelena?'

'Moscow.'

'She was meant to marry the older brother but she loathed him. Lift up your arm.'

'She was having an affair with the younger, they planned to run away, live in poverty till he could inherit.'

'But he betrayed her.'

'Married a respectable woman instead. Her family had land. Older brother put him up to it, threatened to write him out of the will, leave it all to his favourite servant.'

'She was distraught. Turn around. Is that too tight? Are you wet?'

I tried to find parallels in Laura's story and mine but it wasn't that neat. She was a woman split between two brothers but in a very different way. I knew part of the legend already but there were new details.

When she'd ordered someone to tie her to the altar, she'd declared, 'Spoil me!' She meant 'ruin me, destroy my reputation and make me unfit for marriage' but I heard another echo in those words: indulge me. As I say, I liked the sound of her. We'd probably call her feisty today. She was a braver woman than me. She took whatever she wanted, and I imagine a crowd of stunned Victorian village folk, seeing the lady of the manor bound and begging for it, had quite a lot to offer.

Jake fluffed up my curls. 'Shall we have your hair loose or tied back?' He tucked strands behind one ear then brought them forward again. 'Loose, I think.'

I shook my head to make the curls my own again. Eddie looked on in satisfaction. Jake had made the gown. That's what he'd been up to in the workshop, cutting cloth, running seams, making his puppet-tailoring life size. It wasn't an elaborate dress: sham Victorian with long loose sleeves, low neck and soft waistline. The skirt hem was edged in deep broderie anglaise, and ruffles of lace decorated the bodice. The fit wasn't bad. Jake knew my body well.

'She drowned in Heddlestone Brook,' said Jake.

'I know,' I said.

'Tonight, in fact. This is her anniversary. Her ghost's said to walk the village, a woman in white, dripping wet. She drowned herself. Ran out of the church, couldn't take the shame of loving it so much.'

'I don't believe in ghosts,' I said, and there was a tremor in my voice.

'Well, that's good,' said Jake. 'Means you won't be scared, doesn't it?'

I don't know why they celebrate her. I asked and Eddie simply shrugged. 'Because we do. Why not?'

I guess that's the nature of traditions. They start from a small reason then grow into something else, gaining layers of meaning over time. I don't, for one second, imagine they honour her for being a nineteenth-century proto-feminist who defied convention for love and sex. More likely because she was a bit of a goer. And maybe they need this to help keep the community together as the rest of the world changes.

Yet I can't help feeling that they have no choice, that something here makes them do it. But I don't know what it is yet. I don't know if I want to know.

The night was drizzly, and we scurried past small shops where mini-me marionettes gazed into the distance. In the graveyard, the lamplight was speckled with fine rain, and I kept my eyes peeled for a drowned ghost skulking among crooked headstones, despite not believing in her. Jake held an umbrella above my head and Eddie carried the trailing rope. The cold took the edge off my appetite but in the dark wood vestibule, they warmed, dried and caressed me. A calor gas heater burned, the air above it a warped, gaseous sheet.

'Don't stand too close,' said Jake, worried about me going up in flames.

All the posters and flyers pinned in the entrance were years out of date. I realised this was no longer a church. It was a building in a village that had its own beliefs, its own unholy ghost.

And an unholy trinity, I thought, as the three of us paraded down the aisle. The torture gym ahead made my heart beat fast. All along, I'd worked with Jake, trusted him sexually, put myself in his hands. He'd never made me do anything I've come to regret. He seemed to intuit my desires, knowing how far to push me. I stared at the dais, appalled. I recognised the gymnast's vault from the clubhouse but everything else was new and ugly and frightening: a padded table-cum-stage, a rack that looked like a loading pallet set with leather cuffs, a metal frame with chains and, most terrifyingly of all, straggles of coarse lassoed rope hanging from an oak beam in the roof.

Jake had fucked up, big-style. This was a step too far for me, a huge step. They wanted to put me up there, subject me to God knows what and leave me at the mercy of these men?

I wriggled as we got closer, trying to freeze and dig my heels into the aisle carpet. 'No, Jake, no!'

'It's just the ropes,' he said. He urged me on with gentle firmness while Eddie kept pace. 'Don't worry. Everything else is just for show. Keeps the pervs happy. Nobody's going to make you do anything you don't want. You're mine. I own you. They know that and they –'

'You don't own me,' I said.

'Don't quibble, Kate,' he said stiffly. 'Tonight I own you. It'll be easier if you accept that. I own you and you're mine to give away. If you don't trust me on that score, then say the word and turn around now.'

My heart raced, my head spun but I said nothing and we kept on walking. His temporary ownership thrilled and appalled. It felt dangerous and safe all at once.

'We're doing ropes,' he continued. 'And I'm going to make you fly.'

His voice echoed over and over: going to make you fly, make you fly. It was happening again, the drowsiness that washed over me. I stumbled, feeling for a while as if I were on the brink of sleep, about to slide into a dream of hazy, erotic pleasure. All the faces looked at me from a remote, veiled world. I felt dislocated and serene, immersed in a sombre sensuality. The music had softened to an electronic Buddhist chant, water sprinklers hissing beneath, and then three notes of angelic glassy perfection dropped into the soundscape. I could see the notes, each one a crystal tear plinking into a surface of pure wide water, an image as big as the church, circles spreading and shimmering over the men's heads.

'Jake,' I breathed, and I hardly knew what my feet were doing as they led me onto the dais, planks creaking.

The glow of candles seemed to gather strength and the church was bathed in a yellow radiance, pale like the flesh of a golden pear. I knelt on the padded platform, side on to the audience, and the light dimmed to a darker richer honey.

All the men sat watching, some obedient in their pews, several sitting higher, perched on the back rest, feet on the seats. They made a sleazy congregation. Jake began doing something with the hanging ropes. Ahmed joined him while Eddie knelt opposite me on the vinyl-topped platform. Amber half-light sparkled on his sugary stubble, and he gave me one of his lascivious grins.

'Katie,' he rasped.

He held me above my waist and grazed his thumbs over the swell of my breasts. The sensation nearly knocked me for six. I wasn't wearing a bra – it was in bits – so my flesh was soft and free beneath the fabric. My nipples scrunched up under his touch.

'We're going to make you come and come,' he said. 'We're going to make you come so much you'll be begging us to stop. How are you feeling, Kitty Kat? Good?'

I nodded, breathing deeply through my mouth, feeling languorous and heady, gazing back at those hard, grey eyes.

'Excellent,' he breathed. Then he grasped the neckline of my gown, struggled with the first tear, and ripped it open to my waist.

I protested, not least because it seemed such a violence against Jake's handiwork. Eddie pushed back the cloth and my face blazed as my breasts spilled out. I could hear people muttering, and though I was mortified, at the same time it was OK. It was OK to be bared like this, hands tied, tits out, nipples erect. It was OK to be watched and feel hot and humiliated. It was all OK. It occurred to me I might be sedated but I couldn't hold on to that thought. It wouldn't stay fixed. It disappeared into the music.

Jake and Ahmed appeared, holding skeins of hemp rope. Jake untied my wrists and said, 'Arms up, babe. Through here.'

Obedient as ever, I let them slip thick hoops of rope down my body, keeping my eyes low and avoiding my audience. Jake and Ahmed threaded, pulled and knotted, and the rope was a rough caress on my skin, ticklish touches turning fierce and tight. When they stopped, my trunk was held in a web of bondage, ropes above and below my breasts, more belted around my hips. I feel so secure when Jake encases me in rope. It's as if the bonds will keep my body intact while I let the rest of myself go. Without the ropes, I might disintegrate entirely.

They had me lie face forward on the padded platform while they made adjustments down my spine. I was entirely passive, letting it all happen. I didn't even protest when, a man at either side, they drew my arms back and began tying my wrists to my ankles, making my body arc backwards.

As they worked, Sean approached the stage, the guy with the Elizabethan beard from the clubhouse. I knew him only slightly. He muttered something to Eddie, laughing and undoing his flies. Then he knelt up against the platform edge, clutched a handful of my hair, and shoved his cock in my mouth. I was shocked but I loved that I suddenly couldn't speak.

'What do you reckon?' asked Eddie.

The guy held my head firm as he slipped in and out. 'Yeah, she'll do,' he said. 'As long as she can last.'

'She can last,' came Jake's level voice.

I sucked him – I hadn't much choice – and I'm sure my eyes were popping in outrage. My shock wasn't so much that I was fellating a stranger but, given the grand entrance and cod-Victorian gown, his lack of ceremony seemed insulting. He was using me like a hole and I adored it. I was without speech, my intellect stoppered. I was becoming nothing again, so intoxicatingly absent.

Then the world lurched. The ropes dug into my flesh. My body jerked unevenly. A hundred and one candle flames danced. There was nothing beneath me. The platform was receding and so were the stage's scuffed planks. I swayed. Sean rose with me, holding me under my shoulders, giving me only shallow lengths of his cock. My gown hung down, bunched around my thighs. I was airborne, inches above the platform.

224

'You OK there?' asked Ahmed, stepping into view.

I managed to nod with my eyeballs. I wanted to pant with fear and excitement. I was in a cradle of rope, suspended from an oak beam. Would it hold me? Or would I bring the church crashing down on our heathen heads? Someone removed the padded platform. Sean stepped back, pumping his cock in my direction.

If I fell, it would be a three-foot drop before I hit the deck, arms tied to my ankles, so nothing to protect me. I shook the thought away. Jake had rigged this up. And when it comes to rope and weighting, there's no one I trust more. He's spent a lifetime studying this, albeit in miniature.

From behind me came the tear of fabric, and I felt new breezes on my skin as my gown was ripped from hem to hip. Unseen hands tugged and tore until the skirt was flung aside, leaving me in nothing but shreds of white bodice, the red sash around my waist, and loop after loop of coarse fuzzy rope. My arse was bare, my thighs splayed with my ankles trapped by my wrists. I hung there for all to see, suspended in Jake's ropes.

I remembered a small incident from my early days of Jake teaching me to walk the gangster marionette. His guiding hands had threaded and encircled me as he'd tried to demonstrate the right moves. I'd thought then of him spinning me in an invisible web or a cocoon, a creature to be devoured, or a creature to be transformed. I didn't know which. I still don't.

'Give it to her,' came Jake's voice and an astonishing sensation surged between my thighs. I heard it, felt it, a vibe pulsing at such a rate it seemed as if a current were running through me. Someone held it to my clitoris and moments later, I was bent and bucking in my rope web, coming with a force that wrenched me.

'Oh, yeah,' said Sean. 'Orgasm one for the lady.' Seconds later, he shot his load somewhere on my back, somewhere in my hair. I heaved for breath, stunned by my orgasm. I was horny, yes, but that was something else, a convulsive climax that peaked and stopped before I knew what was happening. It was extraordinary.

As the pulses ebbed away, I swayed alone. Everything seemed unreal. Nothing touched me. Someone gave me a little push, and I swung heavily back and forth, wondering how astronauts feel in zero gravity, wondering who was behind, peering into my parted thighs.

My suspension had an odd quality of sensory deprivation. Even though my ears were full of music, my eyes full of sights and my groin full of lust, I felt groundless and detached, removed from what was happening and yet so very present. It was the strangeness I'd felt before but on a whole new scale. It didn't feel how it looked. It didn't feel hardcore. It felt heavenly, insubstantial, and I was drifting into a trance.

Eddie strode into view, naked save for a pair of black work boots, his cock towering in front of me. I craned up. He was all muscle and threat, his tattooed skin gleaming, the fuzzed hair of his belly and chest catching gossamer glints of candlelight. In his hand was something akin to an over-sized microphone.

'Magic wand,' he said. He set the vibe going and held it to my lips, the speed so fast it made my face feel blurred. 'It'll make you come and come.'

I jerked away. It made my teeth vibrate, made my fillings feel weird.

Jake came to join his brother, almost as naked. He wore his big boots and a black leather jerkin reaching down to his arse. His erection angled high, its head a blood-violet flush I wanted butting at my throat. Carefully, he moved strands of hair from my face, pulling stuck wisps from my mouth and getting rid of all the irritating fluff I couldn't remove for myself.

Then, fisting his cock, he smiled down, that crafty glint in his eye. 'Slut,' he mouthed.

It was an exchange for me and him alone, and I whimpered, still adoring how he said it.

'Make her come again,' he said, calling to someone behind me. Eddie tossed the wand in that direction and Jake crouched on his haunches, stroking my forehead.

'I want to take you to that nothing space you like,' he said. 'The one where you're all pleasure and pain and coming. The one where I strip you down and make you small, where you lose yourself, all gone.'

Then he walked away. Other people on the dais stepped back too, giving the ragged congregation a clear view of me strung up there, naked and open. My clit was still sensitive from coming, and it hurt to have the wand buzzing on me. The vibrations seeming to flay me. I wailed in protest until the pain pushed past itself, unleashing a rush of pleasure. A short, hard orgasm squeezed my core, making me squirm and thrash in my basket of rope.

I panted for breath, swaying, letting my head dip.

'Oh, Jeez, I need to fuck you,' said Jake, and the planks bounced noisily as he walked away. 'Someone hold her,' he said.

Like a shot, Eddie was in front of me, candlelight gilding the toes of his boots. When I looked up, his cock was waiting for me, a drop of pre-come hanging on its tip. For one heightened moment that clear bead seemed a tiny globe reflecting all of the church, the faces, the candles, the coloured glass and the racked body of Christ. I tongued it away and suckled as Eddie tucked his hands in my armpits, steadying me at his height.

I gulped on Eddie's length as behind me, Jake moved between my thighs, his fingers plunging into my wetness. I'd been aching for a touch inside ever since Eddie had grabbed my wrist at the bar. I recalled him saying, 'Here she is again, chasing cock.' I wanted penetration so badly it was agony. I was wide open, so needy I felt excavated.

'Is she OK?' asked Jake.

'Yep,' called Eddie. 'She's safe. Go.'

Jake's cock nudged at my entrance, and then he was filling me up, driving deep and hard. I groaned on Eddie and squeezed tight for Jake, wanting to feel every nuance of his swollen cock. My inner walls clung to him, gripping as he slid back, resisting as he thrust. He slammed frantically, fingers digging into my hips. I could hear him huffing and gasping, could picture his curls bouncing, his face mad and rosy with excitement.

And then he gasped, 'Give it to her again. Give it . . .'

My clit was red-raw and pain flared as the vibe hit. I gagged on Eddie's cock, struggling to cry out, and not knowing if I wanted to howl from pain or pleasure. It hardly mattered because soon they were one and the same thing, and I was coming strong and fast, my body snapping with spasms.

'Beautiful,' breathed Jake, slowing himself as my climax rippled around his cock. 'Just beautiful.' Then he said, 'Again.'

I didn't think I could take it any more, I really didn't. If my mouth hadn't been stuffed with flesh, I'd have been begging them to stop. But my mouth *was* stuffed with flesh and I probably wouldn't have meant it. The wand buzzed, and through the pain, the pleasure kept building, swelling, trying to push itself forwards. My inner thighs trembled, taking me closer to that pitch, and my entire stomach area started to gently clench as the convulsions approached.

'Come on,' hissed Jake. 'Come on, babes.' He gave me several hard, deep shafts, every thump of him urging me closer. 'Come for us. Show us how you come. Show the people. Show us all.'

Eddie withdrew from my mouth. I came. I swear my cries must have carried to the rafters. My whole body was in that orgasm, jerking and thrashing, and I was practically obliterated. Anything might have happened, anything might have been done to me. I wouldn't have known, I wouldn't have cared. I was nothing but coming and coming.

And then it stopped and I was gasping for breath. All around me was activity, voices, urgency. I was pretty much in a stupor by this point, limp as a rag. The external world was swilling past me, men coming closer, the light such a rich old gold, the music billowing in a cacophony of weird sounds and beautiful notes. The music was so affecting, so lovely. I was being lowered, the padded platform was back, they were untying me, releasing my wrists and ankles. My limbs tingled as blood rushed into them. I shook my arms. I thought it was over. I sagged against the rope-cradle, kneeing on the vinyl surface, heaving for breath. Voices came to me.

'She's too good.'

'Too dirty.'

'Sod the ropes.'

'Both of you do her. Do her together. We'll wait.'

'Then hand her to me. I'll fuck her to kingdom come.'

'Pussy and arse. Not a spit-roast. A DP.'

'Oh, man. Double dick her. Go on, Jake.'

'Look at her, she's gagging for it.'

'Eddie?' asked Jake.

Eddie stood in front of me and gave himself a little wank, tipping his eyebrows at me as if to say, You want some of this?

And, oh God, I did, I did. I wanted what they were suggesting. I wanted it like nothing I've ever wanted. I wanted both of them, deep and dark and thick inside me. I'd had so many dreams about the three of us, Jake and Eddie greedy for my flesh, eager to fill me, but I'd never imagined anything at this pitch. I was melting at the thought of them having to get so close, at their thighs, balls and cocks nudging to possess me as they rammed both my holes. The entire world could have been watching and I'd still want them.

I looked over my shoulder to Jake who was already warming lube on his fingers.

'Do it,' I breathed. 'Hard.'

He grinned, eyeing me from under lowered lashes, my owner. God, he looked good, flushed and high, curls stuck to his face, his leather jerkin and the teardrop moles giving him the air of an eighteenth-century rakehell.

I felt so bonded to him, as if only he and I understood the impact it was having on me. Jake knew when I whispered, 'Do it,' he'd succeeded in taking me to that place. Here, I had no cares, no self, no limits. I was all his, and yet at the same time I was all mine. I hardly existed and it was beautiful. I was pleasured to the point of disappearance, and all I wanted was cock.

'Do it,' I repeated.

Eddie was there for me, lying back on the platform, and I crawled onto his bulk, straddling his sheathed length. He filled the vacancy left by Jake, and I rocked in a heavy, languid rhythm, incapable of anything more. Jake's hand pressed into my buttocks and he slathered gel there before easing two fingers into my rear. I couldn't imagine this working. There wasn't enough room inside me and yet I longed for it to work.

'Lean over,' said Jake, and he tipped me forwards so I was angled above Eddie's chest, rooted deep. I stared at the Celtic bangle inked on Eddie's forearm, needing a focus but not wanting to meet his eye or the eyes of anyone else. People were crowded around us and I didn't want to identify faces. I just wanted them as a mass of eager, randy men, jostling for a view of me.

Eddie reached up to fondle my breasts. 'Look at me, Kitty Kat,' he said. 'Don't be shy.'

In my back entrance, Jake's fingers pushed and spun, his knuckles threatening to burst my rim. Reluctantly, I met Eddie's twinkling grey eyes, gasping and whimpering as Jake widened me even further. Eddie was flushed, a sheen of sweat on his smooth head, mouth twisting in a grimace of seedy encouragement. 'How's this?' he said, and he pinched my swollen clitoris.

'Ah, ah,' I said as soreness sparked there.

'Someone gag her,' said Eddie.

As if in agreement, Jake grabbed my hair, tipping my head back and making me wince in pain, mouth stretching wide. I wanted it. I wanted to be silenced and overtaken so when Ahmed offered a thick red dildo, I clamped my mouth on it. I sucked breaths through my nose, fearing that without the stopper, I'd be hyperventilating.

Ahmed watched me with keen dark eyes as I bounced harder on Eddie, hips congested with pleasure. 'Stunning,' he said, twisting the stick into my stifled gasps.

Jake was kneeling on the platform, his cock pushing at the bud of my arse, stout and rounded. He drove harder and I cried around the dildo, yielding to him.

'Oh, sweet,' said Eddie.

With a grunt, Jake surged in, jamming my tightest hole with his fierce swollen flesh. He felt immense, so solid and strong it brought tears to my eyes.

'Jeez,' said Jake and he tipped me further forwards, shunting deep in my rear while Eddie held a slower rhythm. My body was so stretched and full. I felt floppy, fucked to the point of feebleness. When Jake pushed past my sphincter, all my strength had seemed to ebb away. I felt boneless, pronged on their cocks, those two powerful rods my only support.

'Ease her back a bit,' Eddie said.

And from Jake, 'Shift your leg a bit, Ed.'

It felt as if my body was breaking, split between the two brothers, bisected by lust as their hands held me, moved me, groped me, worked me.

Then Jake said, 'Make her come again. Make her.'

I shook my head, mumbling into my dildo, terrified of being made to come again. I didn't think my body could handle such convulsions and yet I knew I'd never make this stop. A man I didn't recognise approached, aiming the wand at my clit. His manner was so cool and on target he might have been watering the garden.

'Fuck,' said Eddie, blinking hard and clearly feeling the vibes.

I ground down, and I could feel it coming, a climax to annihilate me. Someone was wanking, someone in the audience, just a prick poking from pair of flies, a fist blurring. People were gathering around me saying stupid things – fuck her, hot little bitch, and you go, girl. It was like being at Jake's house, eyes and faces everywhere. But these were real eyes, real faces, and it seemed as if our regular audience of puppets had been transformed into flesh and blood.

Eddie's face was contorting, agonised by bliss. The scent of his sweat wafted up to me, his broad hairy chest inches from my face, hair tufting from his armpits. Jake's hands gripped my arse as he fucked me, his gasps and curses turning me on so much.

I'd lost count of my orgasms but with the next one, I was on the threshold for so long I thought I might never come. Tiny tremors held my body, shivering under my skin, tightening my breath and threatening to cramp my thighs. Eddie was thick and deep in one hole while Jake was thicker still in my other, my passage snug and slick around his big shunting cock. I could hardly keep upright. I was made of nothing but orifices to be filled. And then I came hard, clenching and twisting, scattering in freefall through Magellanic debris and streaming stars. Flying.

And that's when I saw what no one else did. I wailed in horror but no one noticed. She was crawling down the aisle. All eyes were on me and though I thrashed and cried and tried to warn with my eyes, no one took a scrap of notice. They thought I was enjoying myself.

She was soaking wet, moving slowly on her hands and knees. Her blonde hair hung in matted straggles, her white gown stuck to her back, a red sash dangling from her waist.

I screamed, stoppered by the dildo, and still they thought it was pleasure. Water dripped from her hair, and her gown dragged, its heavy sweep trailing wetness along the carpet. She clambered onto the dais, nudging through the crowd. People jostled and moved for each other, urging Jake and Eddie on, oblivious to the creature on all fours, bedraggled and sodden.

Maybe they can't see her, I thought. Maybe it's just me. Maybe this is it. My end.

And then she was there at my side. I could feel the chill emanating from her as a slimy hand reached out. Fingers pawed at my waist, a touch that was ice cold but real, flesh on flesh, wet on sweat. And she threw back her head, her throat bared as she cried, 'I wanna be Laura! I wanna be ghost. I wanna be fucking ghost.'

Yelena.

For a moment, I thought I might die.

I have to sleep now. It's dawn. I can't see the horizon but the sunrise is seeping into my room, staining it with an orange toffee colour. It's like I'm seeing the attic through a filter. It's so lovely.

This place was never an orphanage. It belonged to the man Laura was meant to marry, the older brother. They brought her drowned body up to the attic, trying to hide the scandal. I'm not sure who they wanted to hide it from when half the village had probably fucked her. The carpet's wet. That might have been me. I don't know. I was shivering and soaked when I got in. Or maybe it's ghost water.

Jake came running through the rain, begging me to stop, to let him carry me. I can't talk to him right now. I've been writing for hours. This matters, this moment of me telling you my story. Jake can wait. The central heating's been on all night. I was so cold when I got back, wrapped in Ahmed's coat. Tired as well but too scared to sleep, knowing they had brought her body here and then seeing wet patches on the carpet.

The cockerel just crowed. Used to love that sound. Now I think, 'Bloody bird.' More than anything, that tells me it's time to leave.

I'm going to sleep now. So tired. Sorry. Kate has to sleep. Easier now the dark's gone. She needs to lie down. The room is the colour of amber resin, all the tilted walls touched by a new sun.

Kate Carter, nestled in the cell of a honeycomb. Yes, it's lovely, so lovely.

Yelena's just visited. I had to move the chest of drawers from the door.

'Jake's not here,' she called. 'He said he will leave you.'

She meant he'll leave me alone. The drawers were so heavy. It took such a long time, inch by inch. I'm limp and exhausted, even though I've slept. I feel I'm fighting something. It's as if my dreams are trying to pull me under, draining me. Yelena had some biscuits and two mugs of tea. The drinks were lukewarm by the time she got in. 'Kate, Kate, are you OK? Shall I push?'

We moved the drawers back in place, blocking the locked door. No one's coming in unless I let them. It's late morning, still the thirteenth. I feel it should be the fourteenth because I've slept but it isn't. This could be the longest day of my life. Barricading the door might have been a mistake. I can hardly hold this pen. My words are a trail of ink, black crawling into white, trying to write on the lines. Can you read this? I'm running out of pages here. My notebook's nearly full. I wonder if I'll have the strength to move those drawers again. Did I just seal my fate? Am I entombed, buried alive in the attic, turning into a ghost?

But no. Not a ghost. This is what Yelena came to say. Not a ghost, not Laura, just a jealous threatened woman trying to scare me from the village.

'I'm sorry, I'm sorry,' she sobbed. 'Please stay. Don't leave me.'

She looked terrible, her eyes bloodshot, skin sallow, her auburn-striped hair sticking in mad directions. I guess she hadn't slept much either.

My head spun. 'The water on the floor?'

'Me. I have key to this place. I make it to frighten.'

She'd been in my room countless times.

'And the night I saw Laura?' I'd already asked the question and I already knew the answer but I needed to keep asking. 'At the bottom of the stairs?'

'I'm sorry,' she said. 'I was in Laura costume. There is legend of ghost but I make it real to frighten. I am sorry.'

A new thought occurred to me then, more dreadful than ghosts, drownings and desecrated churches. 'Jake? Were you ... Are you fucking Jake?'

She glanced down. 'Only little bit.'

I felt I'd been punched in the stomach. 'No,' I managed to whisper.

'I'm sorry. Please, Kate. I'm sorry, sorry, sorry. Don't leave me.'

'While I was here?' I breathed. 'You and him? Downstairs?'

Her face was streaked with tears, snot bubbling from a nostril.

'In his bed?' I continued. 'You laughing? He was in on it all as well?'

'He would send text,' she said, and her voice was so clogged and nasal she barely made sense. 'But he don't know I make ghost for you. I don't tell to him.'

I passed her the box of tissues. 'Blow,' I said, and even to my own ears the word was full of poison. I may as well have said 'bitch'.

I hated her. I wanted to forgive her, to pity her greed and naivety, but all I could do was hate. I hated her more than I hated Jake. She could have stayed away. She could have refused him and left us alone. A weak man, I thought. So weak. I felt sick to my stomach to think of them fucking: Jake, achingly beautiful, so sensitive and clever; Yelena slovenly, loud and crude. How could he? How could he do that to me? How?

And yet hadn't I gone to Eddie, night after night, hankering after loud and crude? But that was different. Jake knew about it, he'd wanted it to happen. Or perhaps he'd only wanted it because he understood that I did. 'I want to find you,' he'd said, and in trying to do that, had he seen how I'd longed for a bitter taste of his brother? Had that hurt him the way this was nearly killing me now?

'They are brothers,' Yelena went on. 'They make Laura day. They share woman. They are kinky, you know?' She laughed. 'Ha, you know this fact. Eddie say me what he do with you.'

I burned with embarrassment. 'I'm sorry,' I said, aware of the irony. 'It never meant anything. Eddie just –'

'Hey, I don't care,' she cut in. 'Me and Eddie ... we not you and Jake.' She put a fist to her heart. 'We strong here and we have sex with other people. It's not problem for us. I think it's problem for you though. I think you have too much feelings for Jake so you don't like to make Laura. They have stupid club and all men decide who is best Laura. This year is me or you. No one want me and so they shut me away because I want to say to you the truth. Did you like? In church? You like what they do?'

I closed my eyes. 'Where did they shut you away?'

'With Ahmed and Paula. At their house.'

'Then I didn't like it,' I replied. 'I did at the time but now I don't because that's wrong. They shouldn't have done that to you.'

'Hey, it's OK, it's not problem,' said Yelena. 'I fuck Ahmed and Paula for week. It's like holiday for me. It's good.'

I laughed, opening my eyes. 'Then, yeah, I liked it,' I said. 'As long as you were OK.'

She told me about her stay and how, when I was in the church, she and Paula had been making their own Laura entertainment. After one vodka too many, Yelena had stormed out into the wet night, angry and jealous, determined to have her say. We laughed at what a wreck she'd looked, crawling up the aisle. And we laughed till it hurt at the commotion she'd caused. The men had scattered at the sight of her, wailing, shouting, roaring. Eddie had screamed in a rough falsetto – 'like I pull his balls off,' Yelena said. And I'd hugged her, zonked from coming, so relieved to see her safe and well.

'Ahmed is good man,' she said. 'And Paula. You must meet with Paula. We can be three friends.'

We talked in a confused, rambling fashion. I had so many questions but my brain was half asleep. I told her about the strange sensations I'd had, the feeling of a presence, the dazed states I slipped into. She shook her head. 'Your mind,' she said, tapping her temple. 'Just imagination. It's strange place. Big and empty. The moor. I think it open doors in people's head. Just imagination.'

I remembered Jake driving me from the station when I'd arrived. 'It can get lonely out here,' he'd said. 'The moors play with your mind.'

I lay back on the bed, gazing up at the white sloping walls and an oblong of sky above a Velux window. It was a thin watercolour blue, early spring. I replayed what had happened, rewriting my past with new information. It made sense. It's the way I would have thought of things before I came here. A rational explanation for everything.

'Do you forgive?' she asked.

After a long pause, I said, 'I don't know. Who are the other women?'

'The Lauras? I am not sure. Last year it was me. They say to me I am not good Laura and I can't be Laura twice. But I wanted it. I wanted to be it again. I like it. In the church they all fuck me. I wanted it.'

'I saw you once,' I said. 'In the clubhouse. You, Eddie and another man. You were dressed up like a ballerina.'

'Ha, I remember this,' she said. 'You see us? You like?'

'What were you doing?'

'Just playing. I like to play Laura game, to wear colours, white, red. I make ghost face. They like to fuck me. Every year is a different Laura but I want always to be Laura. I am always practising.'

'So what happens to the Lauras?' I sat up, cross-legged on the bed.

Yelena shrugged. 'They leave.'

She pronounces 'live' and 'leave' as if they were the same word.

'Leave?' I checked. 'Go away?'

'I think, yes. I am here only two years. Eighteen month. Last year I am Laura. I love it but they say too much, too easy. Is, ah, Meredith before me.'

'I found her notebook,' I said. 'There were some diary entries then it just stopped in mid-air. She was going to be Laura then she never wrote again. I thought something terrible must have happened to her. She spoke about a pull, a force. I felt it too.'

Yelena shrugged then tapped her head again. 'It mess with your mind here, believe me. I think she leave, maybe forget to take her book. I don't know. Everyone want to leave. Stay with me, don't go. I want friend, not these crazies.'

'Then come with me,' I said.

I have a plan, you see. I'm coming back, getting away from here. I need to sleep before I leave. I'm so tired, so drained. I'll never make it to the station like this. I could fall asleep sitting up. There's something else I should have asked Yelena. My notebook's nearly full. I'm on my last page. Something's not right. Something missing. I don't know. My mind's dizzy, trying to separate truth from lies. This pen's like lead. Maybe tomorrow, the fourteenth.

You'll know my plan soon. I'm going to post this book. I'm coming back to you. Not straight away. I want you to read this first. I hope you're reading it. I'll stop in a B and

B, somewhere by the coast perhaps. Sea not land. Then I'll come back. Give me a week or so and I'll be there.

Please be waiting, Ollie. Please. I do love you. If you never read these words, then I guess it went wrong.

Yelena won't join me. 'We can be like Thelma and Louise,' I said. 'We'll take your car, drive north, south, anywhere we want. We'll just get away and see where we end up. You could come to London.'

'I can't,' she said. 'I want to but I can't. I hate it here. I'm dying. It's too small. But I can't leave.'

'You can,' I urged. 'You can do anything you want in life.'

She shook her head. I remembered Jake saying how impossible it was to leave Heddlestone. At the time, I'd thought he was referring to something uncanny about the village or the moors, some force that held, keeping you like quicksand, pulling you deeper. Now I saw it for what it was, small town inertia.

'Come with me,' I said. 'Everyone's so stuck here. You're too bright for this place.'

I meant it. She's luminous. I adore her.

'No,' she said, soft and sad. 'You don't understand. I can't leave.'

So I let the subject drop. She has a husband, a home, a pub to run. And I shouldn't be encouraging people to walk out on relationships.

Let's try, Ollie. I've only a few lines left here. Let's talk. Let's try and work it out. Remember those memories of mine woven from the brightest strands? I want more of those, more of you and of us. A future. Oh God, I hope this helps. I'm running out of space. I want you to read this and know what turns me on, deep inside my mind. I don't want Jake to find me. I want you to be the one, the one who finds me, the one who knows me. And to understand me when I say I don't want that either. But I'm offering what I can. Forgive me, please.

I'm writing in the margin now. No space left. I love you, Ol. I'm coming back. Please be there. I want us to live again, be happy, explore, breathe freely. I don't know what else to say. I'm just going to fill up the margin with all I can say, all that matters. I love you, I love you. Can you hear me, Ol? I can't say it any louder that this. I love you, I love you, I love you love you love you love love love

Jake stopped reading. He closed the notebook. He felt sorry for Yelena. She'd ended up wanting Kate to stay almost as much he did. But no, she'd never been near his bed, she had no keys to the attic. He wished Kate had never had to think that.

He curled the notebook into a tube, tears prickling. There'd been some lies, yes, but he'd only ever done it to protect Kate. He checked himself. No, he'd done it to keep her, hadn't he? But he meant no harm. He hated Heddle-stone. If he could leave he would but this place wouldn't let you. Laura wouldn't let you. If you tried, she'd take you for herself, take you elsewhere. She'd draw you down like a drowning, pull you into her void, her nothing space.

He snapped an elastic band around the cover, securing it to make a spine. That's all he could do. He would put it inside a doll and name it Kate, tie a scarlet sash around her waist, and she'd take pride of place in the house, another lucky mascot. He would move her from room to room and she would watch over him, keeping him safe.

And Meredith could join the others in storage, the family of fair-haired dolls who gazed into a world beyond, dolls named Rachel, Louise, Isabel and Chloë, dolls he'd loved and lost.

Visit the Black Lace website at
www.black-lace-books.com

LOOK OUT FOR THE ALL-NEW BLACK LACE BOOKS – AVAILABLE NOW!

All books priced £7.99 in the UK. Please note publication dates apply to the UK only. For other territories, please contact your retailer.

WILD KINGDOM
Deanna Ashford
ISBN 978 0 352 33549 4

Salacious cruelties abound as war rages in the mythical kingdom of Kabra. Prince Tarn is struggling to drive out the invading army while his betrothed – the beautiful Rianna – has fled the fighting with the mysterious Baroness Crissana.

But the baroness is a fearsome and depraved woman, and once they're out of the danger zone she takes Rianna prisoner. Her plan is to present her as a plaything to her warlord half-brother, Ragnor. In order to rescue his sweetheart, Prince Tarn needs to join forces with his old enemy, Sarin, whose capacity for perverse delights knows no civilised bounds.

Coming in December 2007

THE SILVER CROWN
Mathilde Madden
ISBN 978 0 352 34157 0

Every full moon, Iris kills werewolves. It's what she's good at. What she's trained for. She's never imagined doing anything else . . . until she falls in love with one. And being a professional werewolf hunter and dating a werewolf poses a serious conflict of interests. To add to her problems, a group of witches decides she is the chosen one - destined to save humanity from the wolves at the door - while her new boss, Blake, who just happens to be her ex-husband, is hell-bent on sabotaging her new reltionship. All Iris wants is to snuggle up with her alpha wolf and be left alone. He might turn into a monster once a month, but in a lot of ways Iris does too.

MINX
Megan Blythe
ISBN 978 0 352 33638 5

Miss Amy Pringle is pert, spoilt and spirited when she arrives at Lancaster Hall to pursue her engagement to Lord Fitzroy, eldest son of the Earl and heir to a fortune. The Earl is not impressed with this young upstart and sets out to break her spirit through a series of painful and humiliating ordeals.

The trouble for him is that she enjoys every one of his 'punishments' and creates havoc at the Hall, provoking and infuriating the stuffy Earl at every opportunity while indulging in all manner of naughtiness below the stairs. The young Lord remains aloof, however, and, in order to win his affections, Amy sets about seducing his well-endowed but dim brother, Bubb. When she is discovered in bed with Bubb and one of the servant girls, how will father and son react?

Coming in January 2008

ONE BREATH AT A TIME
Gwen Masters
ISBN 978 0 352 34163 1

Kelley is a woman with a broken heart. She doesn't need another complication in her life, and certainly not another man. But when she stumbles across Tom, the things she thought she didn't want are exactly what she needs. As they fall for each other and engage on a compelling journey through dominance and submission, both lovers strive to shake away their dark pasts. But is blinding passion enough to prevent them being ripped apart?

LURED BY LUST
Tania Picarda
ISBN 978 0 352 33533 3

Not long after Clara Fox receives an email from a stranger who calls himself Mr X, her curiosity and daring involves her in a world of sensual experimentation and adventure. But juggling her kinky liaison with Mr X with her other intense relationships soon becomes complicated. And what will her former boyfriend Paul do, as he tries to win her back, when he finds that Clara has gone beyond the pale?

Black Lace Booklist

Information is correct at time of printing. To avoid disappointment, check availability before ordering. Go to www.black-lace-books.com. All books are priced £7.99 unless another price is given.

BLACK LACE BOOKS WITH A CONTEMPORARY SETTING

- ALWAYS THE BRIDEGROOM Tesni Morgan — ISBN 978 0 352 33855 6 £6.99
- THE ANGELS' SHARE Maya Hess — ISBN 978 0 352 34043 6
- ASKING FOR TROUBLE Kristina Lloyd — ISBN 978 0 352 33362 9
- BLACK LIPSTICK KISSES Monica Belle — ISBN 978 0 352 33885 3 £6.99
- THE BLUE GUIDE Carrie Williams — ISBN 978 0 352 34131 0
- THE BOSS Monica Belle — ISBN 978 0 352 34088 7
- BOUND IN BLUE Monica Belle — ISBN 978 0 352 34012 2
- CAMPAIGN HEAT Gabrielle Marcola — ISBN 978 0 352 33941 6
- CAT SCRATCH FEVER Sophie Mouette — ISBN 978 0 352 34021 4
- CIRCUS EXCITE Nikki Magennis — ISBN 978 0 352 34033 7
- CLUB CRÈME Primula Bond — ISBN 978 0 352 33907 2 £6.99
- COMING ROUND THE MOUNTAIN Tabitha Flyte — ISBN 978 0 352 33873 0 £6.99
- CONFESSIONAL Judith Roycroft — ISBN 978 0 352 33421 3
- CONTINUUM Portia Da Costa — ISBN 978 0 352 33120 5
- COOKING UP A STORM Emma Holly — ISBN 978 0 352 34114 3
- DANGEROUS CONSEQUENCES Pamela Rochford — ISBN 978 0 352 33185 4
- DARK DESIGNS Madelynne Ellis — ISBN 978 0 352 34075 7
- THE DEVIL INSIDE Portia Da Costa — ISBN 978 0 352 32993 6
- EDEN'S FLESH Robyn Russell — ISBN 978 0 352 33923 2 £6.99
- EQUAL OPPORTUNITIES Mathilde Madden — ISBN 978 0 352 34070 2
- FIRE AND ICE Laura Hamilton — ISBN 978 0 352 33486 2
- GOING DEEP Kimberly Dean — ISBN 978 0 352 33876 1 £6.99
- GONE WILD Maria Eppie — ISBN 978 0 352 33670 5
- IN PURSUIT OF ANNA Natasha Rostova — ISBN 978 0 352 34060 3
- IN THE FLESH Emma Holly — ISBN 978 0 352 34117 4
- LEARNING TO LOVE IT Alison Tyler — ISBN 978 0 352 33535 7

BLACK LACE BOOKS WITH AN HISTORICAL SETTING

☐ THE CAPTIVATION Natasha Rostova ISBN 978 0 352 33234 9

☐ DARKER THAN LOVE Kristina Lloyd ISBN 978 0 352 33279 0

☐ ELENA'S DESTINY Lisette Allen ISBN 978 0 352 33218 9

☐ FRENCH MANNERS Olivia Christie ISBN 978 0 352 33214 1

☐ LORD WRAXALL'S FANCY Anna Lieff Saxby ISBN 978 0 352 33080 2

☐ NICOLE'S REVENGE Lisette Allen ISBN 978 0 352 32984 4

☐ THE SENSES BEJEWELLED Cleo Cordell ISBN 978 0 352 32904 2 £6.99

☐ THE SOCIETY OF SIN Sian Lacey Taylder ISBN 978 0 352 34080 1

☐ TEMPLAR PRIZE Deanna Ashford ISBN 978 0 352 34137 2

☐ UNDRESSING THE DEVIL Angel Strand ISBN 978 0 352 33938 6

BLACK LACE BOOKS WITH A PARANORMAL THEME

☐ BRIGHT FIRE Maya Hess ISBN 978 0 352 34104 4

☐ BURNING BRIGHT Janine Ashbless ISBN 978 0 352 34085 6

☐ CRUEL ENCHANTMENT Janine Ashbless ISBN 978 0 352 33483 1

☐ DIVINE TORMENT Janine Ashbless ISBN 978 0 352 33719 1

☐ FLOOD Anna Clare ISBN 978 0 352 34094 8

☐ GOTHIC BLUE Portia Da Costa ISBN 978 0 352 33075 8

☐ THE PRIDE Edie Bingham ISBN 978 0 352 33997 3

☐ THE SILVER COLLAR Mathilde Madden ISBN 978 0 352 34141 9

☐ THE TEN VISIONS Olivia Knight ISBN 978 0 352 34119 8

BLACK LACE ANTHOLOGIES

☐ BLACK LACE QUICKIES 1 Various ISBN 978 0 352 34126 6 £2.99

☐ BLACK LACE QUICKIES 2 Various ISBN 978 0 352 34127 3 £2.99

☐ BLACK LACE QUICKIES 3 Various ISBN 978 0 352 34128 0 £2.99

☐ BLACK LACE QUICKIES 4 Various ISBN 978 0 352 34129 7 £2.99

☐ BLACK LACE QUICKIES 5 Various ISBN 978 0 352 34130 3 £2.99

☐ BLACK LACE QUICKIES 6 Various ISBN 978 0 352 34133 4 £2.99

☐ BLACK LACE QUICKIES 7 Various ISBN 978 0 352 34146 4 £2.99

☐ BLACK LACE QUICKIES 8 Various ISBN 978 0 352 34147 1 £2.99

☐ MORE WICKED WORDS Various ISBN 978 0 352 33487 9 £6.99

☐ WICKED WORDS 3 Various ISBN 978 0 352 33522 7 £6.99

☐ WICKED WORDS 4 Various ISBN 978 0 352 33603 3 £6.99

☐ WICKED WORDS 5 Various ISBN 978 0 352 33642 2 £6.99

☐ WICKED WORDS 6 Various ISBN 978 0 352 33690 3 £6.99

To find out the latest information about Black Lace titles, check out the website: www.black-lace-books.com or send for a booklist with complete synopses by writing to:

Black Lace Booklist, Virgin Books Ltd
Thames Wharf Studios
Rainville Road
London W6 9HA

Please include an SAE of decent size. Please note only British stamps are valid.

Our privacy policy
We will not disclose information you supply us to any other parties. We will not disclose any information which identifies you personally to any person without your express consent.

From time to time we may send out information about Black Lace books and special offers. Please tick here if you do <u>not</u> wish to receive Black Lace information. ❏

Please send me the books I have ticked above.

Name ....

Address ....

....

....

....

Post Code ....

Send to: Virgin Books Cash Sales, Thames Wharf Studios, Rainville Road, London W6 9HA.

US customers: for prices and details of how to order books for delivery by mail, call 888-330-8477.

Please enclose a cheque or postal order, made payable to Virgin Books Ltd, to the value of the books you have ordered plus postage and packing costs as follows:

UK and BFPO – £1.00 for the first book, 50p for each subsequent book.

Overseas (including Republic of Ireland) – £2.00 for the first book, £1.00 for each subsequent book.

If you would prefer to pay by VISA, ACCESS/MASTERCARD, DINERS CLUB, AMEX or SWITCH, please write your card number and expiry date here:

....

Signature ....

Please allow up to 28 days for delivery.